JOHN A.'s CRUSADE

ALSO BY RICHARD ROHMER

FICTION

Ultimatum (1973)
Exxoneration (1974)
Exodus/UK (1975)
Separation (1976)
Balls! (1976)
Periscope Red (1980)
Separation II (1981)
Triad (1981)
Starmageddon (1985)
Rommel & Patton (1986)
Red Arctic (1989)

NON-FICTION

The Green North: Mid-Canada (1970)
The Arctic Imperative (1973)
E.P. Taylor (1978)
Patton's Gap (1981)
How to Write a Best Seller (1984)
Massacre 747 (1984)

JOHN A.'s CRUSADE

A NOVEL

RICHARD ROHMER

Stoddart

Published in 1995 by
Stoddart Publishing Co. Limited
34 Lesmill Road, Toronto, Canada
M3B 2T6
Tel. (416) 445-3333
Fax (416) 445-5967

Canadian Cataloguing in Publication Data

Rohmer, Richard, 1924–
John A.'s crusade

ISBN 0-7737-2884-8

1. Macdonald, John A. (John Alexander), Sir, 1815-1891 - Fiction. 2. Canada - History - Confederation, 1867 - Fiction. 3. London Conference (1866-1867) - Fiction. I. Title.

PS8585.03934J6 1995 C813'.54 C95-930657-9
PR9199.3.R6J6 1995

Cover Design: James Ireland Design Inc.
Printed and bound in Canada

Stoddart Publishing gratefully acknowledges the support of the Canada Council, the Ontario Ministry of Culture, Tourism, and Recreation, Ontario Arts Council, and Ontario Publishing Centre in the development of writing and publishing in Canada.

To Sir John A. Macdonald,
and to Scott McCann and William Hanna
without whose input this book would not exist

JOHN A.'s CRUSADE

1

December 1–3, 1866
London, England

LATE ON SATURDAY, DECEMBER 1, 1866, THE FAST NEW CLIPPER ship docked in Liverpool. A tall, thin passenger stood on the deck, impatient to disembark. John A. Macdonald, having suffered through a long, frigid, stormy crossing of the Atlantic, hurried down the gangplank to collect his trunk and valises. He couldn't wait to get his chilled-to-the-bone body on the next train for London and his usual haven there, the elegant Westminster Palace Hotel, a long, narrow, pie-shaped structure at the junction of Tothill and Victoria streets near Westminster Abbey and the Houses of Parliament.

From the letters and messages that he had received in Ottawa, Macdonald suspected that his extremely late arrival would bring both joy and anger to the some twenty-odd Maritime and Canadian political colleagues who were waiting for him at the hotel. Joy because he had finally arrived and the long-awaited London Conference on Confederation could finally get under way. Anger because Macdonald had delayed his departure from Ottawa for such a great length of time. The conference had been scheduled to begin in September, and some of the Maritime delegates had arrived in London as early as the end of July. John A. was sure they had twiddled their thumbs and spent a small fortune of government money waiting for him to turn up.

Yes, Charles Tupper and his negotiating team of four from Nova Scotia — Jonathan McCully, William Ritchie, William Henry, and A.G. Archibald — were upset. As were Samuel Tilley and his New Brunswick crew of Peter Mitchell, Charles Fisher, J.M. Johnson, and Robert Wilmot. John A. told himself it would be a wonder if they even spoke to him.

But the Attorney General and Minister of Militia Affairs for Canada had good reasons to delay the trip. His explanation would satisfy not only the Maritimers but his own Canadian delegates as well — Cartier, McDougall, Howland, Galt, and Langevin.

Macdonald had learned that there was no possibility that the British North America legislation would be dealt with at that time — that summer or fall — because the Imperial Parliament was to be prorogued on August 10 with the earliest prospect for its reconvening being late January or early February. Macdonald had made the decision to postpone his departure to London for another reason. The summer had been filled with attacks by the Fenians, and he wanted to wait until winter conditions made it impossible for them to launch their assaults across the Niagara, the Detroit, or the St. Lawrence rivers. It was only on November 14 that Macdonald sailed from New York to join his colleagues.

Macdonald's fears about anger from his frustrated colleagues were unfounded. Instead, when he arrived at the Westminster Palace Hotel on Sunday morning, he discovered that a celebratory luncheon had been prepared to welcome him properly and happily.

"Mind you, John A.," his close friend Alexander Galt warned him before they left their spacious second-floor rooms to go down to the luncheon, "there's been a lot of unpleasant muttering about your not being here."

"I'm not surprised."

"Wilmot's been the loudest, griping and bitching every day. 'Who the hell does that Macdonald think he is?' — that sort of thing."

John A. shrugged. "Really, Alex, I can't blame Wilmot. He's been sitting over here for weeks . . ."

Galt nodded. "Try months. Watch out for him, John A. Right now if the old boy had a knife he'd stick it to you somewhere. He won't say anything to your face, but he'll make it difficult for you during the negotiations, mark you. He won't let on though."

John A. smiled down at the squat, square-faced Galt. "I hear you, Alex. Now let's go down and have that welcoming luncheon. It'll be good to see everyone again, even though I'm the skunk at the garden party. Ah yes, and Hewitt. You said he'd be here for the luncheon?"

"I sent a message to him as soon as you arrived."

Lieutenant Colonel Hewitt Bernard, barrister and solicitor, was Macdonald's private secretary. Originally from Jamaica of a Huguenot family who had been plantation owners there for generations, Bernard, already a qualified lawyer, had emigrated to Canada in 1851. He settled in Barrie, where he had secured a position in a law firm.

In addition to his successful legal practice Bernard was a writer, an activity that had caught the attention of John A. Macdonald, who in 1857 had decided that he must have a private secretary to help him deal with his massive amount of paperwork and organize his life.

By 1857 John A. the lawyer had already been in the political arena for thirteen years and during that period had steadily climbed the beckoning steps of power and recognition. In 1844, after serving as an alderman in his beloved Kingston, he had been elected a member of the Parliament of Upper and Lower Canada, a parliament that had difficulty even in deciding where its capital should be as it moved back and forth between Montreal, Toronto, and Quebec City.

By 1854, after many monumental battles with his political antagonist, Reformer George Brown, Macdonald of the Liberal-Conservative party had been named Attorney General for Upper Canada. By 1857 at the age of forty-two he was elected leader of his party, which had as its distinguished Quebec head his friend and colleague, George Etienne Cartier. The team of Macdonald and Cartier had striven mightily to make confederation a reality.

The invitation to Hewitt Bernard to be John A. Macdonald's private secretary was accepted without hesitation. In February 1858, accompanied by his mother Theodora and his sister Susan Agnes who had earlier joined him from England, Hewitt moved to Toronto where the private secretary took up his demanding new responsibilities.

Shortly after the family settled into their new lodgings in that impressive city of forty thousand souls with its modern gas street lighting, fine brick or stone homes, huge churches, and impressive edifices, Susan Agnes Bernard, aged twenty-one, first set eyes upon John Alexander Macdonald.

Hewitt had taken her to a concert at Shaftesbury Hall. As they took their seats before the program began, he saw his chief — as Hewitt called him — sitting in the front gallery with some ladies. There was no opportunity for an introduction but Hewitt was able to point out John A. to an impressed Agnes. Many years later she wrote how he appeared to her on that first occasion as he leaned on his elbows and looked down at the audience: a forceful yet changeable face, showing a mixture of strength and vivacity, topped by bushy, dark, peculiar hair.

When the Parliament of the Province of Canada had begun its sittings in the newly completed buildings in Ottawa in 1865, Hewitt, accompanied by the Bernard women, had moved with his chief to that remote town.

There the Bernards had shared quarters with John A. Macdonald in a residence known as the Quadrangle.

So it was that the widower Macdonald, who had lost his beloved, ever-sickly Isabella in 1857, had become familiar with the Bernards and they with him, including his attributes and idiosyncrasies. Not the least of those latter was his tendency to take refuge from pressure by imbibing whisky to the point of becoming "ill," as the Canadian press sometimes generously described his alcoholic condition of the moment.

But Theodora could not tolerate the grubby, shanty-town atmosphere of primitive Ottawa. In late 1865 she and Agnes crossed the Atlantic to the centre of British culture and society, the great city of London, England, where they could lead a civilized existence.

As Macdonald was aware, Hewitt had preceded him across the Atlantic, and was staying at the flat of Theodora and Agnes on Grosvenor Street.

Now Macdonald and Galt, loyal friends devoted to the cause of a united British confederation in North America, went down the stairs into the vast lobby of the Westminster Palace Hotel, elegant with its many columns and trees and plants. As they walked down the high ceilinged corridor toward the entrance to the Prince Albert Room where the luncheon party was gathering, Galt gave his friend some last words of advice. "Remember, John A., they're all relieved and happy that you're here, except for Wilmot. They're all your friends, lad, even Wilmot, bless his pointed Maritime head."

John A. entered the Prince Albert Room to tumultuous applause from all the delegates — except the dour-faced, heavily bearded Wilmot.

John A.'s quick eyes spotted him immediately. Wilmot was standing with hands clasped behind the tails of his black frock coat, greying black brows furrowed, heavy-lidded squinting eyes fixed on the man he, Robert Wilmot, hated most in the world at that moment.

John A., the master conciliator and politician with years of parliamentary experience behind him, began to, as he called it, "work the room." He shook the hand and looked without wavering into the eyes of each delegate, smilingly apologizing in few words for his tardiness.

Finally there was but one man left to greet. Confront is a better word, Macdonald thought as he stepped toward the Honourable Robert Wilmot.

Macdonald held out his hand, saying, "I hope you will forgive me for not being able to be here sooner, Robert. I do apologize to you. It was not meant to be a slight to you or our colleagues."

John A. thought for a moment that Wilmot might not accept his offered hand. Such a refusal would have been an unacceptable, irreversible loss of mutual political face. The ultimate public insult by Wilmot.

Two, perhaps three, lengthy seconds passed. Wilmot did not move. John A.'s eyes stared into those of his challenger. Then Wilmot's lids blinked and his gaze briefly shifted from Macdonald's face to some unseen object over John A.'s right shoulder. Then the Maritimer's slitted eyes went back to Macdonald's as he reached out to limply accept the offered hand.

Wilmot spoke through gritted teeth. "Your arrogant refusal to join us when you were supposed to has cost me a fortune, Macdonald, a goddam fortune. Three months in lost fees and my marriage. D'you understand that — my marriage!"

The man's bitterness was visceral. Macdonald was momentarily at a loss for words. He dropped Wilmot's lifeless hand and responded in hard tones: "Robert, I had no choice, none whatever. I'll explain to you and everyone here what happened. The Fenians raids —"

"Bullshit!"

Macdonald didn't flinch. "No more bullshit than your caterwauling about being stuck here at government expense in the lap of imperial bloody luxury with all your expenses looked after, including your wife's if she'd chosen to join you."

"She didn't."

"Believe me, Mr. Wilmot, I can understand why she wouldn't want to be with you. These past three months have probably been the best of her life as your wife."

With that thrust firmly skewered in place, John A. turned on his heel and took the glass of scotch whisky that George Cartier had at the ready for him. Lifting it high, he shouted, "Gentlemen!" And when he had their attention, "Gentlemen, I am delighted to be with you. My abject apologies for the delay, but if I may speak a few words to you after lunch . . ."

There were jovial cries of "No, no. God save us," and the like.

"If I may speak a few words I will explain the threat this summer, the threat and the attacks of the Fenians which prevented me from being with you earlier."

There were shouts of "We believe you, John A." and "Give the lad another whisky."

John A., his long face lit by a broad smile, exclaimed, "I'll drink to that and to the opening of our historic conference which George and Alex have informed me is to start in this very room the day after tomorrow."

The next day, Monday, December 3, had been left open for John A. to recuperate from his long journey and to meet with Hewitt Bernard. During the Sunday luncheon he had arranged to have Bernard come to the hotel at two o'clock the next day to discuss with him, Cartier, Tilley, and Tupper the proposed agenda for the opening of the conference. The first item would quite properly be the selection of the conference chairman.

Monday morning John A. had reserved for himself. He would take a long, after-breakfast, come-rain-or-shine walk through his favourite city in the world. He needed that promenade in order to reaffirm his values, traditions, and strong loyalist emotions for his still-young

Queen. Victoria Regina was the sovereign of the world's most far-flung and powerful empire, of which the British American colonies were a large, but relatively unimportant, portion.

Thus it was that on a crisp, cold morning overseen by a cloudless sky, rare in winter or other months in imperial London, John Alexander Macdonald set out on an invigorating promenade from the Westminster Palace Hotel. It was a walk that was destined to alter forever his nearly full life.

At six feet four inches, Macdonald was an imposing figure as he strode forth, the beaver collar of his black greatcoat snug against his freshly laundered, stiff wing-collar and four-in-hand cravat that encircled his neck like a tight but not uncomfortable vise. His tall grey stovepipe hat sat almost squarely on the mounds of bushy reddish-brown hair that almost covered his ears. Pearl-grey gloves covered the fingers that were, like his body, long, thin, and knobby. His right hand encircled the loop of his stylish wooden walking stick, which he occasionally tapped against his polished boot or held against his narrow-legged striped-grey trousers.

Stimulated by the cold air filling his lungs, his mind and body were feeling well and content after his hearty breakfast of kippers and toast. Macdonald walked a brisk pace, his eyes first gazing on the spires of Westminster Abbey, the majestic resting place of countless British heroes. He went north along Prince's Street to Birdcage Walk, then west along it toward what was for him the true centre of the British Empire, Buckingham Palace, the residence of the reigning monarch, the beloved widow Queen, Victoria. Standing across from the Palace at the entrance to the broad, tree-lined Mall, Macdonald watched the company of red-coated, busby-capped soldiers of Her Majesty's Grenadier Guards as they completed the intricate manoeuvres of the elaborate ceremony of the Changing of the Guard. As he stood mesmerized by the royal scene, John A. wondered if he would ever have the privilege of entering those magnificent iron gates to be presented to Her Imperial Majesty. Ah, he thought, that would be a grand experience, but not likely to come to pass.

Then he was off again, moving smartly north across Green Park toward Piccadilly Street, his cane tapping out a quick rhythm on the gravel path. When he reached that famous thoroughfare he found it teeming with horse-drawn carriages, wagons, and trams. The broad sidewalks were filled with pedestrians bundled up against the frigid air. White plumes of breath flowed from their reddened faces like vanishing ribbons as they walked. Turning east on Piccadilly, John A. headed for his favourite shops in the Burlington Arcade.

Slowly he worked his way northerly through the Arcade gazing intently into the shop windows, which presented a treasure trove of objects he could never find in Kingston or Toronto, let alone Ottawa — gold and diamond jewellery, china, vases and artifacts from the exotic Far East, amazing clocks, timepieces in all manner of exquisite designs.

He paused in front of Beauchamps, the shop that stocked shirts that actually fitted his slender torso and gangling arms. He went in and bought four shirts and eight winged collars. He could wear the collars with a cravat or with his lawyer's tabs when he appeared gowned in court as the Attorney General.

Well pleased and feeling extravagantly expansive, he left Beauchamps to retrace his steps toward Piccadilly. Something had caught his eye in a jewellery shop window. Yes, there it was. In he went, priced his find, purchased it, and immediately placed his first diamond stickpin high on his carefully tied cravat. He admired the diamond, preening himself ever so slightly in front of the jeweller's mirror. He wouldn't do up his fur collar now, at least not until the freezing air forced him to.

Leaving the jewellery shop, he went north again through the Arcade and turned left on Burlington Gardens to walk a few steps to Bond Street. His intent was to take a leisurely stroll down Bond to Piccadilly, inspecting the shop windows on the way. Then he'd go down St. James Street past St. James Palace, across The Mall, and make his way back to the hotel in time for luncheon before his meeting with Hewitt at two.

Holding his package of shirts and collars in his left hand and swinging his walking stick with the other, he turned the corner onto Bond Street. As he did so he almost ran into two elegantly dressed women, both of whom stopped in their tracks, eyes wide open in surprise.

"John A.! Of all people."

"Theodora Bernard, as I live and breathe!" Macdonald, too, was surprised, pleasantly so. "And Agnes. How wonderful to see you both."

Agnes Bernard laughed. Looking at her mother, then back at the smiling John A., she said, "Hewitt told us you'd just arrived, but we never expected to see you here on Bond Street. How delightful!"

Theodora added: "You look wonderful, John A., so handsome. And obviously you're well. How long has it been since we've seen you?"

As Macdonald answered Theodora, his eyes were fixed on Agnes's face. It was a different look that Agnes caught immediately. "It's nigh on two years, I expect. Yes, two years. All of us change in that length of time and you two certainly have changed."

Gallantly he turned to the mother, saying, "You have grown even more beautiful, dear Theodora. Your time in London has touched you lightly."

She smiled. "John A., you haven't changed, you flatterer."

"And as for you, dear Agnes, I scarcely recognized you. You've blossomed most attractively. Most attractively, I must say."

Agnes could feel the blush rising in her face.

John A. thought it was a face that showed strong character, an angular face with a shapely nose, sparkling mischievous eyes, pearl-like teeth, a wide, perfectly lipped mouth, dark hair coiffed neatly back under her round muskrat fur hat. Macdonald felt that he had never seen Agnes before, even though he had laid eyes on her many times in Canada.

Agnes was made apprehensive by John A.'s scrutiny, but his attention did not displease her. Not by any means. In fact she decided to let him know that his overt interest was discreetly welcome.

"You must come and have tea with us soon," she said, smiling warmly.

"I'd love to, but I'm afraid . . ." He hesitated.

Theodora said, "I know what it is. Your conference starts tomorrow, so tea will be out of the question. You meet through teatime, do you not?"

"Exactly."

"Then why not come to dinner?"

"Tonight?" Agnes added. "We're just two blocks or so from here. Hewitt told us he's meeting with you this afternoon — he can bring you afterward."

John A.'s ruddy face was shining with pleasure. "Wonderful. I was going to dine with some of my colleagues — Cartier and Galt. You know them. But I'd much rather be with the ladies Bernard. Much."

With that said, they parted and went their separate ways. As the ladies Bernard walked on arm in arm toward their Grosvenor Street flat, Theodora said, "I saw the way John A. was looking at you, my dear."

Agnes merely nodded.

"And you did not give any sign of discouragement, did you?"

Eyes down slightly and deep in thought, Agnes shook her head. "No, Mother."

Theodora pressed on. "You know, my dear, he's so much older than you are — twenty-two years. And we both know he gets . . . ill with too much drinking."

"Yes, Mother, I know all that! For heaven's sake, we've only just met the poor man again and all he's done is make some flirting eyes with me. He hasn't asked me to go to bed with him, let alone marry him."

"He'll do both, mark my words!" Theodora was certain she knew what was going on in John A.'s widower's mind.

"And if he did, Mother, I'm not at all sure I could cope with that illness of his." Agnes was silent for a moment. "But he is a splendid man, is he not? The finest man in Canada — the ablest, I should say."

Theodora chuckled, then wrinkled her nose as the wind of a passing, prancing, ebony young horse caught both of them full on. "God, what a stench! Yes, undoubtedly the finest and ablest man in Canada — except for our own dear Hewitt."

"Yes, Mother."

It was not so reported in the London *Times*, but the mass of polar air that engulfed the British Isles on December 3, 1866, remained unmoving for six icy, clear days. Then it moved slowly northeastward across the Baltic, where it sat in crystal-blue splendour over St.

Petersburg and the regal Winter Palace of His Imperial Majesty Alexander the Second, the Tsar of All the Russias.

2

December 10, 1866
St. Petersburg

THE EVEN GAIT OF THE PAIR OF SINEWY YOUNG HORSES GAVE the sleigh that familiar gentle back-and-forth motion, a movement that had always comforted Edouard de Stoeckl, especially when he was in the incredibly beautiful St. Petersburg. And doubly so on this crisp, frigid, morning as the Imperial sleigh carried him over a blanket of yielding fresh snow toward the massive building that housed his master, the Tsar's powerful Foreign Minister, Prince Gorchakov.

De Stoeckl's ship had docked in the bustling ice-rimmed harbour at high noon the day before. Now he was on his way from his hotel, the Grand, to the Winter Palace to pay his respects and make a preliminary report to Prince Gorchakov. He expected that the Prince would provide him with an itinerary and the time of the meeting he hoped to have with the Tsar to discuss a most pressing topic.

The Tsar's Washington plenipotentiary sat huddled under a bulky blanket, the high collar of his ankle-length sable coat turned up to cover his neck and face, the flaps of his matching fur hat pulled down to protect his ears from the crackling cold. For the moment, de Stoeckl was thoroughly content.

The pleasurable sights that his squinting eyes took in had driven from his fretting mind — at least for the moment — his nagging concerns about the meeting with Tsar Alexander and his pompous brother, the Grand Duke Constantine, to discuss the Empire's most questionable possession, the remote, and because none of the dignitaries who would be at the conference with the Tsar had ever been there, the almost fictitious, lands and waters thousands of miles to the east and across the North Pacific known as Russian America.

De Stoeckl could hear the soft, snow-muffled clopping of the horses' hooves mixed with the tinkling of myriad bells on the polished leather harnesses strapped over purple blankets emblazoned with the Imperial double-headed eagle. Beyond the swaying, high back of the sleigh driver, he could see the massive rumps of the ebony horses, tails twitching, swaying in unison like a pair of locked pendulums. De Stoeckl could see their alert, pointed ears and the billowing white clouds of breath that came back from their snorting, puffing heads. Above was a crystal-clear blue sky unblemished by even the hint of a cloud, the horizon broken only by the towers and roofs of the massive buildings that fronted the broad approaches to the looming gates that opened into the high-walled courtyard of the Winter Palace.

This was a sublime moment for de Stoeckl, short minutes that captured his heart's desire, a yearning that had developed during his seemingly interminable posting in that power-mad, politically corrupt bastion of new republican democracy — Washington. Oh, to be back in St. Petersburg or, if not that magnificent capital of the Russias, then Paris or London or some other cultured, sophisticated principal European city. Anything to get out of Washington. But de Stoeckl knew that he would never have a posting in St. Petersburg.

He had long since decided that when he retired — perhaps in two years' time when he was sixty — he would take his young American wife to live in Paris. She could accept the "City of Light" but could not abide the prospect of living in a place such as St. Petersburg, which was so different from her beloved America. She had long since learned from the difficult experiences of past visits to St. Petersburg that apart and away from the glittering, sumptuous façade of the Tsar's court and the palaces that contained it, the real Russia, the world she would have to live in if her Edouard had to return to a post or retirement in the capital, would be intolerable. She would be thrust into a totally different culture and language, as would their two daughters, both in their early teens. No, his wife would have none of it. Martha de Stoeckl had firmly refused to join her husband for this visit to St. Petersburg, even though it meant that she and the girls would be separated from Edouard at Christmas. She had had enough of the days and nights of seasickness through which she suffered during the wretched Atlantic crossings. And she had had enough of the boring hours of sitting and waiting while her husband attended to the volume of business at the Foreign Ministry or at the several other ministries that did business with the government of the United States, or with firms engaged in trade with the Americans.

Boring? Being in St. Petersburg for her was like being in prison. Even when Edouard was with her during those weeks of hotel confinement she was bored and unhappy. There was little for them to talk about except to wonder how the children were getting on back in Washington with their nanny or for de Stoeckl to go on about the various events that had happened during the day, rattling off stories about people — always men — whom she had never met. His Excellency so and so, Minister this and that, His Royal Highness The Prince of something or other.

So gradually their time together became a time of silence. He would read and shuffle through his papers while she would attack her needlepoint. It followed, or so she thought, that with his advancing years Edouard's interest in touching her, offering acts of physical intimacy, or expressing words of affection had all but disappeared. The once glowing light of love had dimmed, choked off by that powerful, depressing force that enveloped both of them — boredom with each other's minds and bodies. While she silently blamed his advance into old age, de Stoeckl told himself that she had chosen frigid abstinence, probably out of fear of another and, at this late time, a much-unwanted pregnancy.

As his thoughts of Martha coursed through his mind — but only briefly — Edouard de Stoeckl's shoulders moved in an involuntary shrug under the smooth dark sable. That rich fur was a mark of his senior rank in the hierarchy of power that flowed across the Motherland as an emanation of the man upon whom he had been summoned to attend, Alexander, the Tsar of all the Russias.

The shrug was the response to the point at which his rueful thoughts about his unresponsive mate intersected with the image of another woman, a raven-haired beauty whose face forced itself into his mind, causing the features of his wife to disappear the way a magician disposes of the presence of a person behind a puff of stage smoke.

There in his mind's eye lay Anna, her willowy pink-white body silhouetted against the silk sheets, her full lips opened with invitation as her arms reached out for him. What an unbelievable night of lovemaking — beyond any experience de Stoeckl had ever had or believed could be had. He shook his head ever so slightly as his mind reeled with the incredulity of the passion so fresh in his memory. He had torn himself from Anna's amorous embrace in order to bathe, trim his beard and moustache, dress, and be out of the Grand Hotel and into the waiting sleigh to be carried to the Foreign Ministry.

Would Gorchakov notice how haggard he looked? Would the Prince speak to him about his apparent lack of sleep? Behind the sable collar his lips parted in a smile as he decided that his response, if queried, would be that he had spent a fitful night worrying about the issues of the Russian America decision and about his ability to comprehend and adequately respond to the questions that might be put to him by His Imperial Majesty or His Royal Highness. It would be highly inappropriate for him to announce that his condition was the result of a night of frantic love-making. On the other hand, if de Stoeckl were to make such an admission, Gorchakov might look at him with reproof but would undoubtedly conceal a surge of jealousy behind his mask of shock.

De Stoeckl was rudely jolted from his thoughts by a sharp, pungent, heavy smell that blasted, undiluted, full into his fur-covered face, penetrating the sable with the ease of a sharp sword cutting soft lard. The horse on the left had noisily passed a packet of stench that would either sober or strangle any normal mortal. For his sins, de Stoeckl prayed that the animal felt healthily relieved.

3

December 11, 1866
Newbury, England

I'M CONCERNED ABOUT WHAT THOSE BLOODY AMERICANS ARE up to, I must say. That wretched fellow Seward and his Manifest Destiny thing." Lord Carnarvon took a long pull on his after-dinner cigar. Through the cloud of pungent smoke, he politely asked his Canadian guests, "More port, gentlemen? Monsieur Cartier? No. Mr. Galt, a soupçon? Yes. And of course, Mr. Macdonald. Your glass is empty."

"The port is exquisite, Your Lordship." John A. Macdonald smiled as he held out the silver goblet to be refilled by their host, thirty-five-year-old Henry Howard Molyneux Herbert, fourth Earl of Carnarvon and the Colonial Secretary in the unstable government of the day.

The Colonial Secretary, recently in office in succession to Edward Cardwell, was most anxious to grasp what was going on with the Canadians and the Maritimers at their private proceedings in the Westminster Palace Hotel. It was inappropriate for Carnarvon to intrude directly on the meetings. He was already dedicated to the proposition of Confederation of the British colonies in North America. That past summer, during the transitional period of assuming the Colonial Secretary's post, the young earl had concluded that his most important objective would be to strengthen, as far as practicable, the central government of British America against the excessive power or the encroachments of the local administrations.

What better way to have news of the proceedings than to invite the three Canadian leaders — all of whom he now knew through meetings and correspondence — to travel down to Newbury by mid-afternoon train and have dinner and spend the night at his family's hereditary estate, Highclere Castle?

This magnificent stone edifice stood majestically encircled by gently rolling parkland broken by stands and copses of trees. The first viewing of the castle had made a deep impression on the awestruck colonial trio as their two-horsed coach approached Highclere through massive iron gates and proceeded down a red cobblestone lane lined with towering oaks. Their awe had continued even after the warm greeting by the youthful minister and his lovely and even much younger chatelaine. After being shown by servants to their respective rooms, the Canadians had been taken by their host on a tour of the vast mansion with its many wood-panelled rooms, most of them enriched with splendid paintings of Carnarvon's numerous ancestors as well as past and present members of the Royal Family.

"Dinner is at seven for eight," Carnarvon had advised his guests as he guided them at long last back to their bedrooms. Knowing that formal dress was required, the colonials had come prepared.

"About this 'Your Lordship' business," Carnarvon said as he put the port flask on the spindly, lacquered table that stood between the deep, soft, dark-leather chairs clustered around the roaring fire in the library. "I think it would not be untoward, gentlemen, if in private circumstances such as these you might be good enough to call me Harry. After all, we'll see a great deal of one another in the next weeks as we work toward the legislation you need for the creation of a unified British North America. So I would be obliged if, in view of my comparative youth and" — he grinned — "inexperience, you called me by that name."

Macdonald, Cartier and Galt, each looking nearly old enough to be Carnarvon's father, shifted uncomfortably in their chairs as they considered how to respond to this gracious, totally unexpected request. It would be up to John A., the chairman and leader of their London Conference, to respond.

As he listened to Carnarvon, Macdonald sipped his heavy, sweet port. He was already relaxed after several before-dinner scotch whiskeys and the superb Loire Valley white wine served flowingly with the pheasant. The lanky minister had his response at the tip of his eloquent Scottish Canadian tongue. He looked at his host, a man of fine-cut English aristocratic features, his wavy brown hair and full black Victorian beard carefully groomed, his dark brown eyes soft and sincere, his frame slight in build and much shorter than his tall, gangly self.

"That is a most generous offer to us unworthy colonials, sir." Macdonald's Scottish brogue was soft. "On behalf of my respectful colleagues and myself, even though we are not necessarily in comfort about the matter, we accept, Harry. But only on the condition that you call us George, Alex, and John A."

"Agreed!" Carnarvon laughed. "Now tell me, how is your conference going?"

The pugnacious, square-jawed Alexander Galt, his large nose and high forehead flushed pink from the food, wine, and fire, said, "If it please Your Lordship —"

"Harry."

"Harry . . . before we discuss how the conference is going, what's all this about what the bloody Americans are up to?"

"Well, we are all much aware that their anti-British animosity cup is running over."

"That's a mild way of putting it, considering that the bloody Irish American Fenians want to kill us all," Macdonald muttered as Cartier nodded his head in agreement.

Carnarvon pulled a handkerchief out of his left sleeve, staunched his slightly dripping nose, then continued. "I've received word of a Washington rumour that may be significant. Or, it may not. I'll let you people be the judges. But first things first. The conference. Is it going well?"

Macdonald looked toward the leader of the government in Lower Canada, the white-maned, excitable George Cartier. A slight nod invited Cartier to open the response.

"We have had much success, thanks to the strong way in which John A. has held the chair." Cartier paid the compliment easily in his high-pitched voice, the English words spoken with a heavy layer of the unique French Canadian accent.

"Now, now, George, enough of that," Macdonald protested with a grin, his wide-set eyes squinting with pleasure.

Cartier waved, signalling to his colleague to shut up.

"John has taken us through a review, a confirmation review, of the seventy-two resolutions we agreed upon at the Quebec Conference and there have been — how shall I put it — there have been no combats!"

"Jolly good!" Carnarvon was surprised. "No fights, no amendments?"

"That's right," Macdonald affirmed. "No fights. One amendment to the educational clause was put forward by Alex. The clause allows religious minorities in both Upper and Lower Canada the right to appeal to the central government against any law of a provincial legislature that prejudicially affects their educational interests. Right, Alex?"

"Right. My amendment gives all provinces, including the Maritimes, the right to appeal. In that way we hope at least partly to mollify the Roman Catholic bishops who want equality for their religion in educational matters even in the Maritimes."

"So you left that problem to be settled by each province in its own way after Confederation."

"With a right to appeal," Galt explained, "that I expect will never be used."

"Also the Maritimers are insisting on a guarantee by the central government that their beloved intercolonial railway will be built," Cartier said.

"There's been much noise and wind about that, but nothing's settled," Macdonald observed.

Galt added, "And in my bailiwick, the Finance Minister's world, several resolutions that relate to property and finance have been referred to a committee of three financial wizards . . ."

"Of which you are the principal wizard." Macdonald laughed with the others.

"No bloody doubt about that, dear boy!" Galt agreed, slapping his knee in emphasis.

Carnarvon asked, "So I gather that the principles laid out in the Quebec Resolutions will stand? There's no serious challenge to them, particularly those dealing with the specific powers of the provinces and the overriding residual powers going to the central government?"

"Exactly right, Harry," Macdonald confirmed.

"Good. You see, gentlemen, I'm most anxious to get a proper draft of the legislation under way. It's a laborious process, as we all know. So, if you tell me the Quebec Resolutions are going to survive relatively unscathed, I can get the drafting gnomes started immediately. We are pressed for time, are we not, John A.?"

"We most certainly are. The Nova Scotia legislature must dissolve by spring and the seventy-two resolutions of the Quebec Conference still haven't been put to that legislature for confirmation."

Galt added, "The Nova Scotia delegates are here and lawfully empowered to represent their government, which is fully supportive of confederation. But their spring election might well put in an anti-confederation government, and all our efforts would be for naught. So we've got to get on quickly with . . . we have to decide quickly."

"I must also move quickly," Carnarvon said. "Our parliament opens again on February fifth. That gives us fewer than sixty days to prepare and settle the bill so that I can introduce it in the Lords as soon as possible after the opening formalities." He looked to Macdonald. "John A., you'll be back in London tomorrow. I know you and Sir Frederic get on well." Sir Frederic Rogers was the senior civil servant, the Permanent Under-Secretary in the Colonial Office. "I would be obliged if you would arrange to call upon him on Thursday and hand him a note, which I shall write, instructing him to take the appropriate steps to do another draft of the British North America bill. The first draft, the earlier one done by my people, was a disaster. You can explain the urgency."

"Yes, I'd be happy to do that. I know he already has a copy of the Quebec Resolutions."

"Even so, he'll need copies for the drafting staff. Perhaps you could take along half a dozen or so — if you have them," Carnarvon said as he passed the port again. This time all three accepted.

He asked, "So you're still intending to include as much of the British parliamentary system as possible, having regard to your country's enormous distances and regional differences, right?"

"And also having regard to the ethnic and language differences," Cartier was quick to point out. "As, you know, Harry, my Quebec —

Canada East, Lower Canada, whatever — is French. We come from the sixty thousand French who were there when your English army defeated us on the Plains of Abraham. We have kept our own language, religion, culture, and code of civil laws. I am satisfied that with the creation of the Province of Quebec our rights and our distinctiveness will be reasonably protected. But only the passage of time will tell if I am right."

"You shouldn't have any concern about the French language and rights, George," Galt retorted. "Christ, man, what more do you want? After all, I looked after that issue during the Quebec Conference two years ago."

"Well, you made an effort," Cartier acknowledged. "You took a positive step but, again, only the passage of time . . ."

"An effort?" Galt snorted derisively. He addressed Carnarvon. "George has a memory as short as a pig's tit, Your Lordship . . . Harry. It was I myself who took care of the French problem, not George. The member for Sherbrooke, Quebec — that's I — I proposed the language resolution at the Quebec Conference!"

Carnarvon thought for an instant that he should intervene. But this situation promised to be educational and entertaining. It might provide him with a valuable insight into the minds and personalities of these colonial leaders, people who clearly displayed their lower-class origins. He puffed on his cigar, sipped on his port, and listened.

Galt leaned forward, glaring at Cartier. "Remember my resolution, George? If you've forgotten, let me remind you. It was carried unanimously. Even you voted for it!" Galt shouted.

Carnarvon softly suggested, "I wonder, Alex, if you might be good enough to recite the purport of your language resolution. Can you give me the thrust of what it said?"

Lowering his tone, Galt spoke: "I can give you the thrust and I can also tell you what the resolution didn't say." Eyes intense and fixed on Carnarvon, he put his port goblet down. Clenching his thick fingers together, he spoke. "My resolution was in no way a statement of the general principle that the British American federation was to be a bilingual or a bicultural nation. Not at all. Canada West and the Maritime colonies are not French. Quebec is French except for the large English numbers in Montreal and around my Sherbrooke base.

"But there had to be some strong recognition of the French language by the central federal government, because it will oversee the affairs of national interest."

Macdonald was becoming impatient and showed it. "For God's sake, Alex, tell Harry what your goddam resolution was."

"All right, all right. By faulty memory I may leave out a word or phrase but this is the way it went. I moved 'that in the general legislature and its proceedings . . .'"

"By general legislature," Carnarvon broke in, "you mean the upper, appointed federal body together with the elected House of Commons, the confederated House — as opposed to the colonial or subservient provincial legislatures. Am I right?"

"Correct. I moved that in the general legislature and in its proceedings both the English and French languages may be equally employed. And also in the local legislature of Lower Canada and in the federal and local courts of Lower Canada."

Carnarvon was perplexed. "Why did you frame your resolution in such a way? It gives French a place at the federal level and obviously in Lower Canada, Quebec, but not elsewhere in the country?"

"Perhaps I can explain." Macdonald couldn't resist. "Alex's motion, his resolution, recognized that a concession should be made to the French-speaking minority in our new capital city of Ottawa in exchange for a like concession to the English minority in Lower Canada."

Carnarvon admitted, "Perhaps it's the wine and port, but let's see if I have it right. The proposed legal status of the French language in your asked-for national parliament will not be extended to the legislatures and courts of any of the confederating provinces other than Lower Canada. Am I right?"

"That's right, sir," Macdonald continued. "Canada as it now stands — Canada West and Canada East — is bilingual only insofar as the debates and records of its legislature and the proceedings of the courts of Canada East are concerned. The French language has no legal standing in the courts of Canada West, nor in the courts or legislatures of any of the Maritime provinces, even in New Brunswick."

"Even though New Brunswick has a large number of French-speaking people," Cartier added.

"But they're only a minority of the population." Galt had to make that point.

"Yes, yes, of course," Cartier agreed.

Macdonald, ever the moderator, decided it was time to move away from the highly sensitive issue of French language and culture. In any case, the conference had put the matter to bed. Rehashing it further over port and cigars in the presence of the Colonial Secretary would only increase antagonism and enmity.

"So, Harry," he said, "while the conference is going well and the Maritime representatives seem to be getting along with us strange folk, the British in Upper Canada and the French in Lower Canada — we folk who seem to be able to live together notwithstanding our racial, cultural, religious and language differences — I must add that some unforeseen element, emotion, or event may yet appear that will destroy our purpose to unite all the British colonies in America in a single confederation."

"John, you're just a bag of wind who can't resist making a speech." Galt couldn't avoid taking the friendly shot across Macdonald's boozy bow. "And what he didn't say, Harry, was that uniting all the British colonies will eventually include the Northwest Territories and those on the Pacific coast, Victoria Island and British Columbia."

Macdonald grunted his agreement, saying, "Those two, Victoria and British Columbia, are critically important to us. Without them, and without the Territories, our goal of a single unified nation from sea to sea will be lost."

The Colonial Secretary's cigar was down to a two-inch butt, having been consumed with pleasure as he listened to the three Canadians speaking, each with his own accent. In that splendid library Henry Carnarvon was hearing a hint of the multitude of languages and races that might someday be found in that land so large that an Englishman sitting on his tight, powerful little island with its empire cast all over the world like a golden net could not intellectually grasp or conceive of its enormous size. Even if he had visited there, which Carnarvon (like virtually all the members of the Lords and Commons who would have to vote on the British North America legislation) had not, it would have been nigh impossible to comprehend the vastness, the kaleidoscope of the terrains of the British possessions in America.

"Well, now, the mention of Victoria Island and British Columbia, and for that matter, the Northwest Territories, brings me to what I said earlier about Seward and the Americans."

"We hadn't forgotten about that," Macdonald assured him. "You called it a Washington rumour."

"Indeed, that's all it is, a rumour. But it's a very disturbing one, particularly from the point of view of your objective, which is also mine — the creation of a unified British North America from the Atlantic to the Pacific."

"And the Arctic," Macdonald added. "The Arctic is a frozen wasteland, but it is land. The Hudson's Bay Company is there and has possession of it, but the Arctic must be ours."

"It must indeed," Henry Herbert agreed. "The rumour comes by way of Her Majesty's most able envoy in Washington, Sir Frederick Bruce."

Cartier nodded. "We all know Sir Frederick. He travelled to Quebec to visit with us last summer. An impressive man. Speaks French, Parisian French, without an accent!"

"Splendid. The rumour Sir Frederick has reported, if true, could have serious consequences for your confederation plans. I have to put it as bluntly as that, gentlemen."

"For God's sake, Harry, what are you talking about?" Galt's voice was at an impatient near bellow.

"Well, Bruce, through his diplomatic network, has heard that the Russian ambassador to Washington has been called back to St. Petersburg to talk with the Tsar and his advisers about the purchase of Russian America by the United States. It seems that the Tsar wants to talk about selling it because Russia is in dire financial straits. That's what Bruce has heard and I thought you people should know about it."

Their brain power muted by the evening's long drinking session, the Canadians did not respond immediately to what they had heard. There was an extended silence as they absorbed the implications of

Lord Carnavon's words.

Finally Macdonald brought his hands together, fingertips touching, and rolled his eyes upward in a prayer-like position of frustration, saying, "Those bastards! That Seward sonofabitch. He's going to buy Russian America and force British Columbia and Victoria to join the United States as part of his Manifest Destiny expansion."

The colonials well understood the concept: the United States should expand to embrace all of North America. Indeed, at every opportunity it should reach out and take in the Atlantic islands on the east and whatever it could find in the Pacific.

"If Seward gets Russian America," Cartier pronounced. "He'll get Victoria and British Columbia. I mean, my God, why would the people of those colonies stay with us, join us thousands of miles to the east, if they are not connected in any way except by a treeless plain and an impenetrable mountain range?"

"And the Northwest Territories?" Galt's mind was reeling. "If Seward gets Russian America, he will gobble up everything west of Lake Superior. Everything!"

Cartier said what everyone else was thinking: "If Sir Frederick's rumour is true, our plan for a British America confederation from sea to sea could be completely derailed. British Columbia, Victoria Island, and the Territories will fall to the United States either by persuasion or by aggression. And who's to stop it?"

"We are!" Macdonald was emphatic. "We should offer to buy Russian America!"

Carnarvon had to say, "Who are *we*? The only entity that could make an offer is Her Majesty's Britannic government. You people have no status until the British North America bill is passed."

"No status and no money," Galt, the guardian of the Province of Canada's treasury, affirmed.

"However, you're absolutely right, John A.," the young Earl agreed. "We, all of us together, with my government as the proposed purchaser, must get into the bidding for Russian America . . . whether or not the rumour Bruce has heard is true."

Carnarvon stubbed out his near-dead cigar. "And odds are it is true. We do know that about six years ago the Americans, led by one

Senator Gwin, put a proposal — in the interests of businessmen and entrepreneurs in the Pacific northwest states — to the Tsar through the Russian ambassador."

"The renowned de Stoeckl. We've heard about him. He was in the thick of things, the Russian fleet in American ports during the Civil War . . ."

"Yes, John A. The renowned de Stoeckl. It was an offer to buy out the interests of the Russian American Company and the Hudson's Bay Company's licence to operate in Russian American territory. That offer was rebuffed, but only after careful consideration by Tsar Nicholas, the present Tsar's father."

Carnavon paused for a moment, then continued. "Now the Russian American Company is losing huge amounts of money, and the Tsar's brother, the Grand Duke Constantine, wants to have the Company dissolved. The subsidies to the Company are draining Russia's coffers and killing the Russian navy's opportunity to expand the way that its Grand Admiral, Constantine, insists it should expand."

The Earl stood and went over to pull the tasseled cord hanging from the ceiling near the tall, ornately carved French fireplace. "I'm sure a touch of cognac would not be inappropriate, gentlemen."

A servant appeared instantly through the library door bearing a bottle of golden Courvoisier and four crystal brandy snifters on a silver tray.

As the cognac was being served, Carnarvon settled back into his chair. "You should know, gentlemen, that at this moment de Stoeckl is in St. Petersburg. He arrived there on the American ship *Union Eagle* out of New York. The information reported by Sir Frederick is that his meeting with the Tsar will occur within the week."

Macdonald threw the last of his cognac back, enjoying the searing movement of the powerful liquid flowing down his throat. "Let us be profoundly realistic, Harry." His Scottish burr had been intensified by the alcohol he had consumed. "We canna go off half cocked over a wee rumour. But what we can do — and mind, we have a duty to do for the sake of the nation we are attempting to birth — what we can do is take the rumour seriously, as if it was a proved fact. We must prepare a plan of attack."

"Agreed!" Galt interrupted.

"And so we have no choice but to put together two schemes. Yes, two, as I see it," Macdonald said.

"And they are?" Carnarvon encouraged him.

"The first scheme is for the purpose of driving a wedge of distrust between the Tsar and the White House, or between de Stoeckl and Seward. I don't know what the tactics would be but that's the strategy. If we could do that, those two would never make a deal, even though Russia and the United States are close friends."

"And, each of them, for their own reasons, detests Great Britain," Cartier observed.

"Your point is well taken, John A. I can get the Foreign Secretary, the Earl of Derby, and his people to devise the tactics. They're experts at that sort of thing. Now what's your second scheme?" Carnarvon asked.

Macdonald tipped his glass to his mouth for the last drops of cognac. He did not protest as his host refilled the delicate crystal snifter.

"My second scheme? Ah yes. Well, as I said, we should prepare an offer to buy Russian America."

"Since the Hudson's Bay Company has been a licensee of the Russian American Company for God knows how long," Galt suggested, "perhaps we could get their cooperation or advice on putting an offer together and presenting it?"

Macdonald shook his head. "No, if we're going to do anything, we're the ones who should put together an offer. But, as you said, Harry, the offer must be made by Her Majesty's government. The governments of the colonies can be silent partners and can agree to repay the British government over a period of time."

"John A.'s right," Carnarvon observed. "And whatever is done must have the Queen's personal imprimatur."

"Why is that?" Cartier asked.

"Because it is her equal . . . in royalty terms . . . Tsar Alexander the Second, who will make the decision whether to cede Russian America. And so the offer must be signed by Queen Victoria. Otherwise it's a waste of time."

"Harry, would you be prepared to assume the leadership of this matter for us?" Macdonald put the question in his most persuasive tone.

Carnarvon did not hesitate. "Yes, of course. My first step will be to have a chat with the Foreign Secretary." As the colonials knew, the Foreign Secretary was also the Prime Minister. "If he's agreeable, then we'll set up a small secret team, headed by his Permanent Under-Secretary and mine. They can work on the details and the four of us can provide policy direction. How does that sound?"

"First class," Macdonald announced, with his colleagues nodding their agreement. "The amount of money to offer, and how it'll be put together, will be difficult." Galt was such a fuss-budget about his bloody finances, Macdonald thought.

"That's a matter for the Prime Minister and Mr. Disraeli — and, of course, Her Imperial Majesty. I can assure you, gentlemen, that the Queen pays close attention to affairs of the state, particularly since she lost her beloved Prince Albert."

Henry Herbert stood, walked to the still-roaring fire, and turned his buttocks toward it. Holding his coattails aside to allow the heat to better penetrate to the skin of his lean frame, he said, "So, gentlemen, you have given me much work to do. As I said, I will write a note to Sir Frederic Rogers instructing him to work in close concert with you people in preparing a proper British North America Act based on the Quebec Resolutions. And as soon as I come down to London later in the week, I will attend upon my good friend and Prime Minister, Lord Stanley, the Earl of Derby, to enlist his support in acquiring Russian America."

Macdonald stood, swaying slightly and intoned, "And thereby put the boots to that conniving bastard Seward and his dreams of Manifest Destiny."

Alexander Galt applauded, clapping his hands slowly, and said "Well spoke, John A., well spoke. Now while you're on your speechifying feet, why don't you compose a few rapturous words to tell His Lordship about the beautiful young miss you met on Bond Street."

"Very good, John A.!" Cartier exclaimed. "How old is she? You're still young and virile at fifty-two. Ah, *l'amour, je pense*, I think it is marvellous, even if I haven't heard your story yet. Is she really beautiful, John? Has she big breasts, wide hips?"

"Oh, for Christ's sake, George, you lecherous old frog. Leave off!" John A. Macdonald's ugly face turned a shade of deeper red. He flopped back down in his chair, crossed his long legs and waved the black half-Wellington boot of his lifted foot. "Harry, a week ago last Monday, I met this lovely young creature — on Bond Street, as Alex says. She's tall, almost as tall as I am, and carries herself like a queen. She has a wonderful smile, brown eyes and dark wavy hair. And I know her family. Know them very well."

Cartier was astonished. "What a coincidence! How old is she, John A.?"

Macdonald replied. "She's closer to thirty than she is to thirty-five."

"What are your intentions, John A.?" Harry had lit another cigar as he stood before the fireplace. He judged that the evening was about to become longer than he had anticipated. He was anxious to join his wife in bed upstairs, especially since dinner she had given him their secret signal that her hands were lusting to have his body that night.

"My intentions? If the truth were known, I would take her to wife in an instant, if she would have me."

"But you've only just met her."

"Well, no . . . as I told you, I know the family. Her brother, Lieutenant Colonel Hewitt Bernard, is a member of my staff, and he and I once shared accommodation in Ottawa. When his mother, Madame Bernard, and his sister, Susan Agnes, came to live with him in Ottawa, I saw a great deal of them. But at the time I had no eye for Agnes. As you may know, Harry, my dear wife passed away nine years ago, and since then I've been alone with my politics, my law practice — but without the comfort and care and love of a woman. I've also been alone with too much drink. But that's changed. Since meeting Agnes, except for a tiddly moment of falling off the postillion tonight in the presence of my dear colleagues and a noble host, except for that, I have been the model of behaviour."

"Indeed," Galt agreed. "Your performance as chairman of this London Conference . . ."

"You highly intelligent, perceptive colonials appointed me chairman unanimously!" Macdonald snorted.

"Yes, well, mark that down as an error. Anyway, your performance has been devoid of any blemish of drink — and the results have been spectacular. You've handled the sessions and all of the sensitive personalities around the table with remarkable patience and leadership."

"Alex, leave off all this bullshit!" George shouted. "I want to hear more about Agnes. John, you'd probably like to bed her, but what are the chances that an out-of-practice fifty-two-year-old like you could do such a thing in this highly moral, painfully Puritan age without marrying her?"

"And that, my dear George, is exactly my intent, to marry her if she will have me. That's the rub. What if she refuses me? I've been with her three times since we met on Bond Street, always at dinner and always with her mother or brother or both in attendance. They watched me as if I was an ancient hawk circling to steal their most precious chick."

"Who can blame them?" Galt roared, again slapping his knee with delight.

"Who can indeed?" John A. could only agree. "Well, chaps, I shall soon put the question. Thursday, to be exact. Agnes is dining with me. Not her brother, not her mother. Just Agnes alone. I'll do it then. I'll work up my courage and propose!"

The fatherly Cartier cautioned, "Just don't work up your courage with drink, John."

Macdonald allowed, "That would be the quickest way to lose my wonderful Agnes. I have enough handicaps as it is, God knows."

"And George and I are two of them." Galt laughed as he stood up saying to Carnarvon, "Well, sir, it's been a long day."

"But a productive one," Lord Carnarvon told him, "and there are still other matters we haven't covered this evening."

Macdonald struggled to his feet. "Perhaps we can address them in the morning after breakfast?"

"Yes, of course. I'm anxious to talk with you in your capacity as Canada's Minister of Militia Affairs about the military threat from the United States in general and the Fenians in particular."

John A. straightened his long frame. "I bid you goodnight, Harry, and thank you for your gracious hospitality." He held back a belch. "I shall be happy to give you an appraisal of the American threat, which continues unabated, and of those Irish madmen."

4

December 12, 1866
London

EVER THE CONSUMMATE HOST, THE EARL OF CARNARVON HAD insisted on driving with his honoured colonial guests to the sparkling new railway station at Newbury. It would have been impossible for Henry Herbert to simply see his guests off from the front entrance of Highclere Castle.

So it was that on the morning of December 12 he escorted his three visitors to board the waiting train amid the whistling vapour clouds and pulsing puffing noises of the powerful steam engine as it vibrated with energy waiting to be unleashed like a racehorse to get on to the next stop.

Carnarvon had said farewell to Galt and Cartier, adding that he would see them in London on the weekend or by Monday at the latest, and admonishing the two ministers to ensure that the work of the confederation conference went smoothly.

Then he turned to Macdonald. "Now, John A., be a good chap and take care." He frowned as he spoke in a low, not-to-be overheard voice. "Keep a watch out for the Irish, those abominable Fenians who want us out of Ireland. They've been infiltrating London, setting off bombs again, terrorizing the city." Carnarvon's face showed his concern. "Scotland Yard is doing its best, but the Fenians are killing prominent British citizens when they think it will assist the cause of independence."

Carnarvon hesitated. "What I'm saying is that you should be very careful about your personal safety. You could well be a Fenian target."

"In London?" Macdonald was incredulous, and the arching of his eyebrows showed it. "That can't be! I mean, we're thousands of miles away from the American Fenians. Surely they wouldn't attack us here in England."

"And why not? Your presence here is well known. If the Fenians of Ireland — they're in league with the lot in America — if they came after you and did you in, it would be a great victory that might well destroy the plans for Confederation, right? Let's face it, John A., without you the plans would collapse."

The call to board the train was ringing in their ears. Cartier and Galt were already settled facing each other in the first-class compartment.

"I understand what you're saying, Harry, and I will keep an eye out for anything suspicious."

"Good. If there is anything, any problem, get in touch with Scotland Yard straightaway. And, John A., that's wonderful news about Agnes."

Macdonald climbed into the carriage and he pulled the door shut behind him. He then turned, lowered the door window, put on his grey stovepipe hat, and stuck his arm out the opening. Grasping Carnarvon's hand as the first whistle signalled movement of the train, he shouted, "Thank you for that, Harry, and wish me luck!"

"You have it!"

✦

FROM THE TIME CARNARVON ASSUMED THE OFFICE OF COLONIAL Secretary during the summer of 1866, Macdonald had been in constant communication with the new minister about the plans for Confederation and the Fenian raids. The two men were able to exchange messages rapidly by means of the magical transatlantic cable that had just been laid and put into operation.

Macdonald also reported his concerns about the enormous Grand Army of the United States, almost a million men still in uniform after the end of the Civil War six months earlier. There had been a gnawing fear in the British American colonies that as soon as the Union armies had defeated the Southern Confederacy — of which Britain had been steadfastly supportive — the entire fury and force of the victorious troops would be turned north to wreak vengeance on the British. Such an assault and conquest would be consistent with the ideas of the powerful William Seward, Lincoln's and then Johnson's

Secretary of State who made no secret of his belief in the Manifest Destiny of the United States.

As for the Fenians, there was a strong possibility that any attack they might make across the border into British America would be the spark to ignite a serious confrontation between Britain and the United States, which could readily escalate into another war.

The Fenian Brotherhood united all its Irish American members into a strong emotional force with one intent: to free Ireland from British "subjugation." To further that cause, the leaders of one militant branch of the American Fenian movement, filled as it was with veterans of the Civil War, had decided to go to war against the British in North America.

The Fenian movement — the main political manifestation of the Roman Catholic Irish who had flooded into America since the 1840s — was motivated not only by the traditional anti-British emotions of true sons of Ireland but also by the belief in the Manifest Destiny of their new-found nation, which they could assist by conquering British America. Thus the Fenians began assembling in Buffalo and Detroit in early 1866. With much public show they started to parade and train, sure that word of their presence and intended attack would seep across the border and put the fear of God into the British colonials.

Rumours abounded in Canada that the Fenians would strike on that most symbolic of Irish occasions, St. Patrick's Day, March 17. Macdonald's intelligence network was certain that an assault across the Detroit and Niagara rivers would occur on that day.

It did not. The attack came many weeks later, on the night of May 31, when Colonel John O'Neill led a strong force of fifteen hundred Fenians across the Niagara River north of Buffalo. On the morning of Saturday, June 2, near Ridgeway, O'Neill's 'army' was confronted by a column of eight hundred and fifty Canadian militiamen. In the ensuing battle nine Canadians and many Fenians were killed, scores injured. On Sunday, learning of new British forces soon to arrive, O'Neill withdrew his men back into the United States.

That Fenian assault, combined with two other incursions and rumours of more to come that summer, convinced the British American colonies of the urgent need to seek military assistance from the United Kingdom. Finally, on August 27, on the advice of Macdonald and Sir John Michel, the General Officer commanding the regular Imperial forces in Canada, the Governor General, Lord Monck, sent off an urgent cable to Carnarvon appealing for immediate reinforcements. It was a request that was not answered by the sending of more troops.

The Fenian raids also solidified the intent of Canadians and Maritimers to combine their colonies into one nation loyal to the British Crown, safe from the threat of Seward's Manifest Destiny.

✦

THE TRIP FROM NEWBURY TO PADDINGTON STATION TOOK MUCH longer than scheduled because a thick you-could-cut-it-with-a-knife fog had settled on London, reaching as far west as Slough. The train finally entered the cavernous station at nine-thirty that evening, three and a half hours late. It took an additional hour and a half to cover the short distance from Paddington to the Westminster Palace Hotel, as the cab driver and his lively young horse cautiously picked their way through the classic thick, dark London fog.

It was well past eleven o'clock when the three weary travellers entered into the anteroom that led to their separate rooms on their second-floor suite, their bags hefted in behind them by the night porter and his assistant.

Macdonald, exhausted, bade his companions goodnight, but not before saying to them, "I must have said this a dozen times today. I'm really worried about the sale of Russian America to the Yankees. I'd like to brief the conference on the situation as soon as possible. Alex, when can you have ready a rough draft of the financial terms really?"

"First, I have to know how much we are . . . the British are prepared to offer, if anything."

"The main number?"

"How much are you prepared to offer?"

Macdonald's brow furrowed. "Use ten million dollars U.S. as your calculating base. If a higher or a lower figure is decided on, it'll be easy to recalculate." I'll talk to Carnarvon when he gets back to

London. He can open the Prime Minister's door for me as well as the Chancellor of the Exchequer's."

"Next Monday, the seventeenth," Galt said. "I'll need until then. Eight-thirty, here in our anteroom. I'll get breakfast organized. All right, George?"

Macdonald smiled. "Have a good sleep, chaps."

Moving with hesitant care in the darkness, Macdonald entered his bedroom, the dim wavering light from the hall candles giving his tired, searching eyes nearly no aid in finding his way across the carpet to the foot of the bed. But once he reached it his hand groped along the soft edge of the eiderdown until his fingers felt the table at the bedside, then the candle that would bring the room alive with its flickering flame. He fumbled for a match from his waistcoat pocket. There it was, its slim wooden shaft moving warmly between his thumb and forefinger, which were far more used to holding a glass.

He shoved the head of the match down to the rough underside of the tabletop, and moved it swiftly across the coarse surface, his favourite place for match-striking in this comfortable high-ceilinged corner room. The first attempt was unsuccessful but the second brought a spark of light as the sulfur started to burn. Then, with a billowing burst of yellow-white flame and a rush of sound from its minuscule explosion, Macdonald's match was alight.

His shaking hand — that shaking had just recently started, nothing severe and only in spurts — held the match to the candle's waxed white cord until the shaft of blue-tipped light was transferred completely to it. As the candlelight spread, Macdonald stood for a moment, his eyes transfixed by the dancing fire. Then he blew out the match flame as it nearly reached his fingers. Looking around the room, he saw with pleasure the pile of newspapers on the bed, the *Times* on top. Good. The concierge, as he had been asked to do, had delivered all the day's papers so that Macdonald would have them to read upon his return from Newbury. Newspapers were the most important documents — that's what he called them — in Macdonald's life. From their pages he absorbed information, facts, and opinions the way a sponge soaks up liquid. Newspapers were the stuff that John A. Macdonald, by his own account a workaday politician, thrived on.

It was time to get into bed and read those beckoning journals. He went to the water closet down the hall, then back to his room, shutting but, as was his custom, not locking the bedroom door. After all, this was London, the most civilized city in the world and the most crime-free. Carnarvon's words of caution had already been forgotten.

Macdonald undressed, put on his flannel nightshirt, left his socks on to keep his feet warm, and, climbing into bed, grunted with satisfaction as the bedclothes enveloped his long, tired body. He reached for the *Times* while slipping his spectacles onto the bridge of his slightly bulbous nose.

Lying back, his large head on two pillows, he held the *Times* in both hands, eyes scanning the headlines of the front page. There was, of course, no news from British North America. There never was anything about the colonies in the London papers. It was as if they didn't exist. But as to what was going on in the United States and Europe, that was a horse of a different colour.

Macdonald was keen to obtain any information out of Washington: what was the Congress up to? What was the incompetent President, Andrew Johnson, doing or thinking, especially about U.S. relations with the British colonies to the north? And Secretary Seward, the Manifest Destiny man, what news of him, all the more important now if the Russian ambassador to Washington was in fact in St. Petersburg to get instructions from the Tsar about selling Russian America to the United States?

Macdonald, eyelids drooping, started to read the column headlined "Impeachment of U.S. President Possible." As he read he turned for comfort onto his left side, folding the newspaper the better to focus on the Johnson column. His mind, slipping fast into sleep, told him he had to blow out the candle just inches away from his face. Then John A. Macdonald was sound asleep.

It was the searing heat against his right shoulder that wakened him. He couldn't believe what was happening. There was fire all around him. The newspaper, the bedding, the curtains over the window, were ablaze; vicious yellow-orange flames crackled and roared as the fire consumed them, spewing acrid black smoke that was billowing and filling the room.

In the split second that it took to assess the danger, Macdonald knew what he had to do if he was to survive the growing inferno. He thrashed his way out of the bed, throwing off the flaming newspaper, doubling the eiderdown over on itself to smother the flames that were ravaging it. As his feet hit the floor he reached for the far part of the window covering not yet burning and hauled on it with all his considerable weight. The whole curtain, its rod and centre core in flames, came crashing down. Macdonald grabbed for the huge water jug on the washstand. and poured its full contents onto the curtain's still blazing remnants extinguishing its fire immediately.

Turning to the bed, he threw the burning eiderdown to the floor, ripping it and pillows open. He later described the scene to Susan Agnes Bernard as pouring "an avalanche of feathers on the blazing mass." The feathers were enough to cut off the oxygen feeding the fire and the flames disappeared.

But Macdonald needed more water to finish the job. He hurried through the common sitting room he shared with Cartier and Galt and banged on their doors, not loudly because he did not want to create an alarm throughout the crowded hotel. A shout of "fire" would have caused pandemonium. Macdonald knew he had the fire under control, but he wanted his colleagues' help and their water jugs to extinguish it completely.

Opening Cartier's door after knocking on it, he said in a calm voice, "George, are you awake? I need your help. I've had a fire."

He could hear the bed squeak as Cartier sat up. "A fire? Mon Dieu!"

"Bring your water jug right away, and your candle so we can see what we're doing." Macdonald went to Galt's door, repeated the process, then hurried back to his smoke-filled room. Cartier and Galt were on his heels, lugging their heavy water containers and their lighted candles.

"Here, let me do it," Macdonald said, taking Cartier's jug, pouring its precious contents on the smoldering portions of the eiderdown. "How does the curtain look, Alex? Will you check it out?"

Galt, jug at the ready, went to the blackened, sodden heap that had been the curtain. "Looks as though you got it all, John A."

"Good. And I think I've finished this one off. Would you mind opening the window, please, George? Better shut the door first. Just put your water jug over there on the floor in case I need it."

Macdonald was pouring the last of Cartier's water when Galt came up to him saying, "Your shoulder — you've been burned, John. Christ, it went through your nightshirt. Let me take a look."

"Be careful, Alex. It hurts like hell."

"It looks like hell," Galt said as he gingerly lifted the charred edges of the near-circular eight-inch hole in the right shoulder of Macdonald's nightshirt. "It's blistering already. "We'd better get a doctor. I think there's one staying in the hotel."

"No, I'll be all right. Really. The main thing is to get this mess cleaned up. If you'd fetch the night porter, he'll do it."

"And we'll get him to bring some sheets and pillows and a new eiderdown. What happened, John?"

Macdonald shook his head. "I don't know. I'm sure I blew out the candle before I dozed off. I'm sure I did."

"But obviously you didn't," Cartier said. "You must have fallen asleep with the candle burning. The newspaper you were reading probably fell on your night table . . ."

"Next to the candle," Galt added, "and away it went."

"But I blew it out," Macdonald insisted. "I blew that goddam candle out! I know I did."

"Sure, John A., sure. I'll get the night porter." Galt went to the tasseled call cord by the door, pulled it twice, and turned toward Macdonald. "I'm going to get a doctor, John A., whether you like it or not."

Macdonald muttered as he wearily lowered himself into the bedroom's sole stuffed-leather armchair. "You're probably right."

"Y'know, we can't have you incapacitated. You're doing such a marvellous job as chairman of our conference, putting out all the fires, so to speak."

Macdonald laughed, then grimaced. "God, Alex, I'm having enough pain from my shoulder, let alone your humour."

"Ah, well, I'm only trying to make light of the matter. Where's that bloody night porter? Probably asleep."

As Galt spoke there was a knock at the door. "Come in!" he roared.

The night porter opened the door, his eyes widening as he took in the charred remains and the stench of the fire.

"Cor, luv a duck. Wot's 'appened 'ere, sirs?"

"Just an accident, Ben," Macdonald replied. "Just an accident. I'll deal with the manager about the damages. I'll see Mr. Gates in the morning."

"Right, sir. Sorry I was so long in comin', but me night assistant he jus' up an' quit not more than ten minutes ago and, well, like I 'ad to look after an earlier call."

"It's all right, Ben. Can you clear this up for me and bring me sheets and pillows and an eiderdown for the bed?"

"Certainly, Mr. Macdonald. Right away, sir. If my assistant hadn't quit . . . those bloody Irishmen. You can never tell what they're going to do next. Kelly'd only started with us day before yesterday and he up and quits in the middle of the bleedin' night."

"Kelly? Obviously an Irishman."

"As Irish as Paddy's pig."

"Who hired him?" Macdonald's mind was locking onto Carnarvon's cautionary words about the Fenians, words he had dismissed with a wave of the hand.

"I did, sir. He seemed a likely lad. Anxious to work. Full of the Irish blarney and all. Knew there was a lot of Canadians staying in the 'otel. Said he'd relatives in Canada and the U.S. Had experience in other London 'otels, the Strand an' such. Bright lad, sir. Good worker. We got on well. No idea why he quit."

"Where is he now?"

"I don't know, Mr. Macdonald. All I know is he couldn't get out of 'ere quick enough. Only about ten minutes ago or so. Got out of his uniform, put on his civvy clothes, said, 'We'll get all you British bastards out of Ireland yet,' and he was gone. Didn't even ask for his pay!"

Macdonald grunted. "His pay was the privilege of putting the torch to this room, the honour of killing me as I slept, a Fenian killing me for the honour of Ireland. And he almost succeeded."

"You mean Kelly started this bloody fire?" Ben's mouth was agape with astonishment. He couldn't believe his ears. Nor could Cartier and Galt, both of whom were uncharacteristically speechless.

Macdonald struggled to his feet, his hand clutching his right arm just below the area of his burn. He was in deep pain, his face twisted by it as he stood.

He looked intently at his colleagues and the night porter. "Not a word about how this fire started, gentlemen. Not a goddam word. But there'll have to be an explanation about the fire and the burn."

"Of course, John A." Cartier understood immediately. "If this man Kelly was a Fenian . . ."

"He was, make no mistake about it. Carnarvon warned me about them when we were getting on the train at Newbury."

"But you didn't tell us," Galt protested.

"Of course not. I didn't think anything of it. No need to get you two alarmed, that's what I thought. And I was wrong."

"Almost dead wrong. I'll go and fetch the doctor."

"Good. And remember, this was an accident. I fell asleep, didn't get the candle blown out. The newspaper caught fire. You hear that, Ben?"

"Yes, sir, Mr. Macdonald. I hear you strong, I do. I'll clean all this up straightaway, sir. Cor, wot a bloody mess."

5

December 14, 1866
London

THE DELEGATES HAD DECIDED TO TAKE FRIDAY THE 14TH OF December as a break. The burn-injured Macdonald was at the Bernard flat for most of the day. There, to the amusement of his colleagues, he was continuing his wooing of Agnes. All silently wished him well, even the bellicose but softening Robert Wilmot.

But for Alexander Galt and George Cartier, it was a heavy working day, to say the least. The two men met with merchant banking groups in the City to discuss an urgent financial matter.

With Cartier at his side, Galt had the difficult, painstaking task of raising the preliminary funds for the construction of the railway line to Quebec and Ontario from the Maritime provinces which those hard-nosed Maritimers had made a principal condition of Confederation. During the discussion with the largest banking firm in the City substantial progress was being made when suddenly, without prior discussion with his shocked colleague, Cartier, Galt said to the bank's chairman, who was also its managing director, "You know, Sir William, if we're successful in completing the financing of the inter-colonial, it is only the beginning."

"Oh, really. You mean you have other railways in mind?"

"Of course. We must move quickly to bring the colony of British Columbia into our new Confederation."

"And the price they'll demand is a railway?" Sir William was quick.

"Precisely. It could well be the longest railway yet built. It would run from Ontario west across the Northwest Territories through the Rocky Mountains to Vancouver and the Pacific."

"What sort of distance are you talking about?"

"Something in the range of two thousand miles."

Sir William's eyebrows shot up as he contemplated the tens upon tens of millions of pounds that would be needed to undertake such a monumental project.

"So long as you have Her Majesty's government covenant to guarantee, Mr. Galt, we'll be happy to do business with you. When would you be needing money for the Pacific railway?"

"It's difficult to say. It'll take some time and effort. First, we must have the Colonial Secretary's support for our plans to bring B.C. into Confederation. We've started negotiations with Sir Frederic Rogers. He's the —"

"Yes, I know him. He's the Permanent Under-Secretary of the Colonial Office."

"In fact we've been negotiating with him off and on for the past ten days."

"But why are you negotiating with Sir Frederic? Doesn't British Columbia have a governor or a legislature? Won't you have to deal with them?"

"Of course, Sir William. But if we can convince Rogers and the Foreign Office that Canada's offer to British Columbia to join our Confederation is practical and realistic, then he can recommend it to his government."

Sir William was dubious. "But if you're going to build a railway all the way to Vancouver and the Pacific that is thousands of miles long and costs millions of pounds, it will take years and years!"

"Probably fifteen or twenty years," Galt acknowledged.

"How long will it take to start construction?"

"Perhaps a year, eighteen months, to get the British government to agree to a deal for us to bring B.C. in."

"And then?"

"Maybe another year to convince the B.C. legislative assembly to join Confederation."

"Next?"

"Collateral to all this will be the negotiations with you people here who will put up the money, so long as Her Majesty's government *and* the Canadian government are on the guarantor's covenant."

"How long for that?"

"You're the best judge, Sir William."

"Probably no more than six months after the B.C. government or the British approve, whichever is the later. Then it's a matter of laying out the route. How long for that phase?"

"Likely a couple of years. Then the preparation of tender calls and the actual callings. Receiving and analyzing them would be next, followed by the legal paperwork. Try nine months for that phase. No, better settle for eighteen months."

"What about the approval of the proposed Canadian government?"

"Well, we haven't been able to really deal with that issue yet. We're not sure of a confederation approval, let alone the confederation date. Probably next spring or summer."

"The upper house will have to be appointed. Who will do that?"

"The first Prime Minister."

"And who will that be?"

"We don't know yet. It will be up to Governor General Monck. He will appoint the Prime Minister to take office on Confederation Day. The Prime Minister will then appoint the senators and call a general election to take place within a month or two."

"If the Prime Minister's party loses the election?"

"Then he's out and the leader of the majority party becomes the P.M."

"Are you a candidate to be the first Prime Minister, Mr. Galt?"

Galt snorted. "Everybody is — my colleague Mr. Cartier here and others like Tilley and Tupper. It's whoever Monck thinks has the strongest political party likely to win the most seats in the first election, the person who is the proven best leader and best understands the political and the parliamentary processes."

"Who d'you think that will be, Mr. Galt?" Sir William pressed.

"I've just described John Alexander Macdonald!"

"D'you agree, Mr. Cartier?"

"There's no doubt in my mind. How else are we going to build the Pacific railway and the intercolonial too? How else is British Columbia going to be brought into Confederation — and Prince Edward Island

and Newfoundland — unless Mr. Macdonald is the Prime Minister?"

"I must confess" — Galt smiled — "I think Macdonald has a hankering for the job."

He stood to thank the banker so that Cartier and he could take their leave. "In the meantime, Sir William, we really must get on with the business of keeping British Columbia out of the clutches of the Americans. And that means building a railway to the Pacific. We thank you for your interest."

"Gentlemen, you have my attention and my interest," Sir William said cordially. "But it's your interest that I will be looking for if we finance you. Your interest payments — guaranteed."

6

December 16, 1866
St. Petersburg

BOTH SIDES OF THE TALL, ARCHED DOORS TO THE ANTEROOM swung open to reveal the Emperor's principal secretary. The wizened old man's eyes, more shortsighted than ever, searched the expansive waiting hall until they stopped at a blurred figure in the distance.

"Minister de Stoeckl?" came the tentative query.

"It is I, Oleg Vladimir Ivanovich," de Stoeckl replied.

"Good. His Imperial Majesty will see you now."

De Stoeckl, broad-shouldered, heavy-set, neither tall nor short, strode the length of the marble-floored waiting room, the heels of his polished black leather boots making a loud, reverberating clacking, so much noise that he knew it would be useless to speak to the hard-of-hearing old man until he stopped next to him.

"Oleg, old friend. It's been two years since I saw you last. How are you keeping? I must say the time has touched you lightly."

The ancient retainer chuckled. "Lightly? Perhaps. But with a brush that has lightly diminished my sight, lightly curtailed my hearing, but, even so, has increased my enormous attractiveness to the opposite sex."

De Stoeckl threw back his head and laughed heartily. "If they're after your body, Oleg . . ."

"Yes, minister, I know. If they're after it, let them have it. But then there are so many that I've had to consider rationing."

De Stoeckl became serious. "Speaking of many, are they all here?"

The secretary motioned him inside the anteroom, then shut the doors behind them. "Yes." He nodded. "The Tsar, the Grand Duke, Foreign Minister Gorchakov, the Minister of Finance, Mr. de Reutern, and

Vice Admiral Krabbe."

As the old man spoke, de Stoeckl's eyes took in the paintings of the Tsar's ancestors that adorned the silk-covered walls. It was appropriate that all who had received an audience with His Imperial Majesty should be made to understand or, indeed, be reminded of his powerful lineage. De Stoeckl stared at the huge portrait hanging to the right of the door leading to the conference room. It was of Peter the Great, whose striking face of physical strength, vast intelligence, and extraordinary determination inspired de Stoeckl on the rare occasions when he was privileged to see it.

He walked slowly beside Oleg, who began to shuffle his way across the deep Persian rug toward the entrance to the Tsar's chamber.

"I expected everyone but Krabbe. Why is he here?" de Stoeckl asked.

"Simple, my dear minister." Oleg's reedy voice was lowered as they approached the door. "Minister Gorchakov thought that the Admiral should be present because as Marine Minister he has special knowledge of the affairs of the Company which, as you know, is in dreadful condition."

"Dreadful indeed," de Stoeckl agreed.

For decades the wealthy and powerful Russian American Company had developed and controlled the expansion of the business of hunting the valuable sea otters and seals and latterly whales and fish, as well as trading in those and other commodities along the northwestern shores of North America. Moreover, the Company possessed and claimed sovereignty over those lands and waters in the name of the Tsar.

But now the Company was in dire straits. In 1857 the value of a share of the Company stock had been a gratifying 500 rubles. In the intervening nine years disaster had befallen the organization. The herds of seals and sea otters in Russian America had been depleted by uncontrolled hunting almost to the point of extinction. Trade with the Americans had virtually ceased during the American Civil War when most of the resources of the United States had been concentrated on the resolution of its bloody conflict. The Company had fallen on such hard times that its shareholders could get no more than 75 rubles for a share and were lucky if they could find a buyer. In reality the Company was bankrupt and its principals had had no choice but to plead with the Tsar and his ministers to have the government take it over.

The plight of the Russian American Company was only one part of the question that the Tsar's secret "Committee of Tomorrow" would have to resolve at this meeting. More importantly the Committee would also have to decide the fate of the Tsar's North American territorial possessions. Should Russian America be retained and strengthened and the Company taken over by the government — or should the North American territories be sold and the Company terminated? There was no question in de Stoeckl's mind as to what should be done, but it would be His Imperial Majesty's decision alone after he had received the advice of his senior ministers.

As was the custom, Oleg knocked on the door three times and waited for permission to enter. At the sound of the Tsar's word "Come!" the old man pulled the door open and stood aside to allow de Stoeckl to enter.

The chamber was a corner room designed in order to enable the now-long-forgotten architects to utilize the two outer walls for broad windows that stretched from the floor to the relatively low, ornate gilt ceiling. The windows were lightly draped so that on that brilliant day they allowed shafts of warming sunlight to fall across the room. The other two walls harboured massive fireplaces, each leaping with flame as they and the sun's heat made the Tsar's chamber passably warm against the piercing wintry cold.

Dominating the room was a long conference table with seating for ten on each side. At the far end was the high-backed, elaborately carved chair in which the Tsar now sat, with the Grand Duke on his right side, Gorchakov on the left. All the chairs to the right of the Grand Duke were empty out of deference to his station. To Gorchakov's left were de Reutern and Krabbe, the Vice Admiral in full uniform while the others at the table were in their high-collared shirts and black cut-away business suits in emulation of His Imperial Majesty.

De Stoeckl, his valise in hand, walked to the table and made a deep bow toward the Tsar, who acknowledged the salute with a curt nod of his head, then motioned de Stoeckl to sit next to Krabbe. Like the others, the Vice Admiral, monocle clenched in his left eye, was engrossed in reading a document, a copy of which had been passed to each of the participants before de Stoeckl's arrival.

There was, however, no copy for de Stoeckl, so he took his reference papers out of his valise and busily arranged them in order on the table as the Committee members continued to read — with the exception of Foreign Minister Gorchakov. The Tsar's most influential minister sat back in his chair, his large stomach touching the table's edge. His face was upturned toward the carved and figured ceiling. He had gazed at it unseeingly countless times during interminable conferences and meetings over the past two decades of his power at the left hand of the Tsar. Gorchakov's ever-present pince-nez were clamped to the broad bridge of his bulbous nose. That was the predominant feature of a round, pink, flat, and heavily jowled face made further unattractive by a pate bald except for a few feathery wisps of grey hair. In his mid-sixties, Gorchakov was gross of body, brilliant of mind, and weary of the heavy burdens of his office, the never-ending dealings in battles and wars, diplomacy, and the petty politics of the court.

The document the rest were looking at was Prince Gorchakov's analysis of the Russian America territorial problem, the Russian American Company debacle, and the presentation of his solutions.

When the Tsar finished reading he turned to his brother, asking: "Well, what does His Imperial Highness think?" The brothers never called each other by name in the presence of non-family members.

The Grand Duke Constantine, as was his wont, stroked his graying brown beard and ran a finger across his moustache — a sign that he was giving serious thought to the question. With his pale blue eyes and straight, grey-flecked brown hair he looked remarkably like his older sibling, Alexander.

Constantine tapped the document he had just read. "I cannot fault Minister Gorchakov's the line of reasoning, which is the usual position I find myself in with regard to his advice." He smiled across the table at the trusted Foreign Minister. "Let me say, Your Majesty, that as I have striven to rebuild your navy —"

"With astonishing accomplishment and success," the Tsar broke in.

The Grand Duke modestly dropped his eyes for a moment and gave a slight nod of acknowledgement. "Your Majesty is most kind. In rebuilding the navy and having sailed to every one of your Pacific ports and those in the Sea of Okhotsk, I have become most anxious that all effort be made to concentrate on strengthening our forces in those areas, so far distant from St. Petersburg. I think, Your Majesty, that you should bend every effort, do everything possible, to devote the entire solicitude of your government to your possessions there and on the Amur River. Those possessions form an integral part of the Empire and in every aspect offer more resources than the northern coasts of our American possessions and are readily accessible by land, whereas Russian America can be reached only by hazardous crossings of the North Pacific."

Gorchakov's huge head bobbed in silent agreement as Constantine continued. "Not only are our American territories inconveniently distant from the Mother country, they have no real trade or resource importance for Russia — at least not in these times when the furs taken there have so diminished and where our trade has been so curtailed by events."

The Grand Duke's eyes moved to those across the table to look for signs of approbation. He certainly knew where Gorchakov stood. And de Reutern, the financial expert, could not help but follow in this logic. As for Krabbe, he might react negatively to his next statement.

"As I say, the necessity to defend Russian America against the Americans — or the British — will continue to be as difficult as it is expensive. Perhaps nearly impossible is a better description than difficult."

He could see Vice Admiral Krabbe shifting uncomfortably. Constantine went on. "As you are aware, Your Majesty, the affairs of the Russian American Company, particularly in regard to control, discipline, and administration at Sitka, became so inadequate that it was necessary to install a naval captain as governor. He has had to be supported by a substantial group of naval personnel and ships and stores that, because of urgent commitments and requirements on the direct coastal perimeters of the Motherland, we can ill afford."

Constantine looked at Krabbe, whose eyes immediately turned

away. After all, what Constantine was proposing would amount to a diminution of the role and power of the navy, even though that lessening was being proposed by the very man who had restored the Imperial navy to the strength and stature that it had achieved more than a century before under Peter the Great.

"Therefore, Your Majesty, the grounds that I proffer — the near-impossibility of defending your American possessions and the cost of sustaining and maintaining the now bankrupt Company — on these grounds I consider it is urgent that you cede your American territories to the United States . . . that is to say, sell . . ."

"If you recommend that we sell to the United States, why not offer to the British as well?" the Tsar asked.

The only minister at the table who had the stature to intervene without being first invited by either the Tsar or his brother did so.

Gorchakov said, "If I may be permitted, Your Majesty, there is no doubt that, from a business point of view, when an object is offered for sale the best price will be received when there are two bidders therefor. So it might indeed be better to offer your American possessions to both the United States and Great Britain. Certainly the British would be prepared to pay handsomely for much the same reason that would motivate our American friends. It is the natural need for territorial expansion of one's boundaries, particularly so if one can do so by negotiation and purchase rather than by war."

Gorchakov paused and looked around the table. Satisfied that he had everyone's attention, he continued. "The colony of British Columbia needs to be supported by the government of Her Britannic Majesty. Your American possessions lie immediately to the north of that colony, so it would be a perfectly natural acquisition that would strengthen the colony and in particular the Hudson's Bay Company. You will recall, Your Majesty, that we were able to negotiate a treaty with Britain that grants the Hudson's Bay Company the right of passage to the Pacific on rivers that flow from British North America — the border between your lands and the British being some twenty miles inland from the coast."

The Foreign Minister adjusted his pince-nez. "For that matter, the treaty grants all British vessels the free right of access and transit on those rivers and streams between their possessions and the Pacific. This was all in consideration of the British recognition of the neutrality of your American possessions during the war between us and the British."

"Quite so," the Tsar acknowledged. "And what about the intelligence you mentioned to me the other day about the British colonies in the eastern part of the continent negotiating for the right to have their own parliament?"

"Our information is that the political heads of the various British colonies in North America are negotiating in London with my counterpart, the British Foreign Secretary, and with the Colonial Secretary, for legislation that would unify all the eastern colonies into one under a federated form of government. The intent is that the sovereignty of the British Crown in North America will be solidified ultimately from the Atlantic to the Pacific and thus would eventually embrace British Columbia and Victoria Island."

"And if that is so," the Tsar observed, "it follows that the British and . . . what is it they call themselves?"

"I'm not sure, your Majesty." Gorchakov turned and looked down the table "De Stoeckl?"

"They call themselves Canadians. What the new federation will be called remains to be seen."

Alexander was satisfied. "So the British and their colonials in America as well as the prosperous Hudson's Bay Company will be most anxious, to say the least, to purchase from us."

Constantine responded. "Oh, but Your Majesty, can you really contemplate giving the British anything of an advantage over the Americans? After all, we have just been through a bloody, humiliating war with the British in the Crimea. We're still licking our wounds from that one. Their hostility toward us and their arrogance continue. I respectfully suggest that it would be totally unacceptable to the people of Russia if your American possessions were offered to the English Queen."

Heads around the table nodded in agreement as Constantine paused.

"On the other hand," Constantine continued, "there is a strong bond between us and the Americans. There have never been any differences between us. Indeed there have been continuing acts of friendship, not the least of which was the safe harbouring of our entire fleet in American ports during the Crimean War."

Gorchakov took off his pince-nez to emphasize the point he wanted to bring to bear. "Furthermore, Your Majesty, de Stoeckl reports that certain high officials in the American administration have expressed serious interest in Russian America. As for the British, there has been no expression of interest whatever."

The Tsar leaned back in his chair, fingertips before his face, as he contemplated what he had just heard. It was his customary signal that all talk should cease while he thought. In a few moments he leaned forward: "It seems to me, gentlemen, that you have assumed that I have made a decision to sell. But I have not heard from all of you as to your respective positions. So perhaps, Minister de Reutern, you might be good enough to let me have the benefit of your views."

The Minister of Finance was a tall man, gaunt with deep-socketed dark eyes and a hank of white hair that hung over his forehead. He would have preferred not to have to say anything at all. He was extremely apprehensive and nervous whenever he was in the presence of his Emperor and doubly so when he was required to express an opinion. However, he was prepared for this question. Rather than leave it to chance, he had written out his response. His hands shook slightly as he took the folded paper from his pocket and spread it open on the conference table.

The Tsar was amused. He had seen this same performance many times before and was sympathetic to the man's discomfort.

De Reutern spoke hesitantly. "If it may please Your Majesty, I prepared a brief statement setting out my position from the viewpoint of my responsibilities as Minister of Finance."

Taking Alexander's silence as permission, de Reutern read: "The Company to which the exploitation of the American colonies was confided has been unfortunate or inept. It is maintained at this time only by artificial means which will scarcely be able to prolong its existence."

De Reutern glanced at the Tsar, then continued: "As I see it, Your Majesty, the Imperial Government has two alternatives. It is obliged either to come to the assistance of the Company, which is near bankruptcy, with considerable financial aids, or to take on itself the administration of the Company's affairs which will involve sacrifices no less burdensome.

"For these reasons and having regard to the state of your national treasury and the requirements of your Imperial government and the Russian people, I recommend, Your Majesty, that a disposition of your American possessions be undertaken with the greatest possible haste."

De Reutern folded up his sheet of paper, adding gratuitously, "I have no comment, or at least I don't have an opinion, as to the question of whether the territory should be offered to the British as well as the Americans. But I will say this: As we all know, when gold was found in the region near Sitka, thousands of Americans made their way north and into your territory, Your Majesty. The only reason they did not stay and take de facto possession was that the gold find did not prove to be valuable enough. The point is, the way things are going, one of these days the Americans will probably take possession whether we like it or not and we won't be able to do anything about it. Nothing. So why not sell to the United States or, for that matter, to the British? As Finance Minister I say, Your Majesty, that your treasury urgently needs money, and we should get as much as we possibly can out of such a transaction."

De Reutern cleared his constricted throat, unused as it was to the utterance of so many words one after the other. "And I say to Your Majesty that, on the other side of the coin, there is an urgent need to cut off the huge amounts of money already being spent to support your American possessions, let alone those that will have to be made if the Company is to be salvaged."

De Reutern had been as articulate without notes as anyone at the conference table had ever heard him.

"We are grateful to you, Minister de Reutern," said the Tsar. "You made your points effectively and persuasively."

It was Vice Admiral Krabbe's turn to speak. Acknowledging that he was in the presence of the Grand Duke Constantine, father of the modern Russian navy, he merely said that he could not usefully add to the statements of the Grand Duke. Neither the Tsar nor Constantine commented upon Krabbe's lack of contribution. He was usually strong, vocal, and forthright. Perhaps it was a weakness in the man they had not seen before.

Then it was on to de Stoeckl, who (the secretary Oleg noted in the minutes he was scrupulously taking) did not hesitate to state his case in a robust fashion.

"On more than one occasion, Your Majesty, I have reported to Minister Gorchakov on the inconveniences that the possession of our American colonies present and on the little security they offer. In case of war, these colonies will be at the mercy of any hostile power, and even in time of peace they are not protected from American vessels that swarm the Pacific for fish and fur. To the complaints that we at the Imperial Mission at Washington have more than once made on the subject, the government of the United States has invariably responded that it cannot assume the responsibility of guarding our coast. It is for us to take the necessary precautions against these marauders."

"Not an unreasonable position," The Tsar agreed. "But surely they can restrain those American vessels?"

"Perhaps they could, Your Majesty," de Stoeckl replied, "but they do not. So these controversies, always disagreeable, may do harm to the good relations between our two countries. And as Minister de Reutern said, we are vulnerable to occupation by either American forces or their people, as happened during the Sitka gold rush."

"Surely there must be some alternative to these confrontations?" Constantine wondered.

"I remind you, Your Majesty," de Stoeckl nodded wisely, "that some years ago the Americans proposed the purchase of our colonies to me, as in the past they bought Louisiana from France and Florida from Spain; and lately Texas and California from Mexico. It is my belief that the American government could be induced to renew this proposition to us."

To de Stoeckl's brief words Gorchakov added these. "While I concur with what Minister de Stoeckl has said, Your Majesty, I would like to make this additional recommendation, if you would be so kind as to hear it." He waited but a fraction of a moment. "I strongly suggest that it is essential that the negotiations be managed in such a way that the initiative be taken by the United States. Or if it is your wish that the British might bid, then the initiative must also come from them."

At that point Alexander was satisfied that he had heard what he considered to be a consensus. He took a moment to consult the notes that he had made during the discussion, and to one line that he had underscored in particular.

He gave his reasons and his decision. "Pray know, gentlemen, that we are pleased to have your collective advice on this vexing matter. But before we state our decision there is one consideration that has not been discussed on the question of whether we should entertain any proposal from the British."

The Tsar looked down at his notes before continuing, in slow, modulated words so that Oleg could record them accurately.

"All of you are familiar with the terms and obligations of the Paris Peace Treaty of 1856 after our defeat by the British in the Crimea. Those terms and obligations must be set aside at all costs. Because the Treaty is still in effect between Great Britain and us, we cannot authorize initiating negotiations for Russian America with the Queen of England or any of her representatives. However, should the British — or the Canadians, if they form their own government — take the initiative and open discussions, it must be made clear that as part of any protocol, the first consideration must be that the Paris Peace Treaty be nullified."

Like his brother, His Imperial Majesty had the habit of stroking his beard, which he now did for a moment as he chose his words.

"Now, Oleg, write this down: It is our decision that our Russian American possessions be authorized to be ceded to the Government of the United States for an amount in gold coin to be determined by the Grand Duke Constantine in concert with Minister de Reutern and upon such terms and conditions as the Grand Duke and Minister Gorchakov together shall decide. And that is our decree. So be it."

The Tsar turned to his brother saying, "We did not discuss a price. Do you have a recommendation?"

Constantine looked across the table at Gorchakov and then replied. "Yes, Your Majesty, I have. I recommend that the monetary compensation must not be less than five million United States dollars in gold."

Tsar Alexander's eyebrows arched in surprise. "That's a mere pittance!" he protested. Then he lifted his hands in a gesture of futility. "Again, so be it."

7

December 17, 1866
London

THE THROBBING PAIN IN HIS RIGHT SHOULDER WAS EXCRUCIATING. The burned flesh, blistered and festering, was not responding to the salves. The doctor carefully applied new dressings each morning and it was agonizingly painful when the old ones were removed, taking pieces of skin with them.

When at the conference table Macdonald had stoically displayed little outward sign of his suffering. On the morning after the fire he had taken his chairman's place as usual, determined to carry on as if nothing had happened. The doctor had tried to persuade him to stay in bed and rest, but the stubborn Canadian would have none of it. The work of the conference was of critical importance. It had to succeed and was succeeding and time was of the essence.

As chairman he had the responsibility of keeping everyone around the table talking and agreeing, or at least reaching a consensus on the multitude of points that had to be resolved. Macdonald believed that if he wasn't present there would be disagreements and squabbles that would destroy the work of the Quebec and Charlottetown conferences and other meetings that had led to this final conference in London.

There was no one else to whom Macdonald could entrust the job of chairman, no one who could control the tempers, passions, and regional loyalties that sometimes erupted at the table like an unexpected wind ripping at the sails of an unstable boat. Macdonald had no choice. He had pressed on, burn or no burn, pain or no pain. As he had written to his sister Louisa on Thursday morning following the fire: "So I got it dressed and thought no more of it." Now, four days later as he and Galt met after the afternoon conference session, the pain surged through him as an intense reminder of that awful fire.

That morning, Galt was to have presented to him and Cartier a financial plan of an offer to purchase Russian America. But Galt had not been ready. He had had a problem with a difficult senior civil servant in the Office of the Chancellor of the Exchequer where funding would have to receive preliminary approval. The civil servant had taken a personal dislike to the pugnacious colonial, and, in any event, could not see the rationale for the British government to give its good money to the detestable Tsar in order to purchase valueless frozen wasteland somewhere in the uninhabitable Arctic. Idiocy!

As a result Galt had been obliged to call upon the good offices of Carnarvon to obtain an appointment with the Chancellor himself, and the meeting had taken place at three o'clock that afternoon.

Galt reported to Macdonald that he had had a good — no, excellent — meeting with the Chancellor. Carnarvon had attended. "It looks as though we might have a deal, John A. But I have to do some more calculating and find where I can steal a dollar here and a pound there out of my operating and capital budgets."

The pain-wracked Macdonald said, "That's fine, Alex. All I want to know is when you will have something we can all look at."

The Finance Minister reflected briefly. "It will take me a few days to complete it, so let's say the afternoon of the twenty-first. Our colleagues won't even notice that I'm not at the conference."

"Rubbish, Alex. They'll think you've slept in again." John A. managed a smile.

His jibe was ignored. "I'll have my recommendations by noon."

"Perfect. You can present them directly to the conference."

"I thought you wanted me to let you and George see my financial analysis first."

"It's too late. We haven't said a word to our colleagues about Russian America, so it's going to come as a surprise — shock is a better word — when we give them the news."

"Then when we start the two o'clock session I'll open with what Carnarvon told us, the Bruce rumour about the U.S. purchase of the Russian territories, its potential consequences, and its threat to our Confederation dream.

"And then I'll tell them the solution. We will put in a bid to purchase Russian America, with the British government and the new Canada combining resources to make an offer." Galt announced. "I know what the Brits are prepared to contribute."

"Is it enough?" Macdonald asked.

"It's more than enough money. But there's one snag."

"Which is?"

"The Treaty of Paris." Galt shook his head. "The Prime Minister told Carnarvon it's not negotiable."

"We'll see about that. We will indeed. I'll go and see the Prime Minister. Without changes to that Treaty we'll probably never make a deal with the two-headed Russian Eagle."

Galt grunted. "Eagles. You're up against two proud, friendly eagles, John A. Friendly with each other, that is."

The intense pain from Macdonald's shoulder made him wince as he agreed. "I hadn't thought about it before, but you're right. I'm against eagles — those two, at any rate."

"And you and I, John A., and all of us here must do everything in our power to defeat the American eagle and its Manifest Destiny while we convince the Tsar of all the Russias that his powerful two-headed eagle should deposit its Russian American egg safely — and at an enormous price in gold — in our Canadian nest."

Macdonald paused, then announced, "After that flight of oratory in the presence of excruciating pain, Alex, I think I deserve a tumbler of the best whisky. But I cannot. Agnes is joining me for dinner tonight. I must be on my best behaviour. More's the pity."

8

December 17, 1866
London

"Isn't it strange, Agnes, it's as if I'd never met you before, even though I've known you for years. Suddenly we meet on Bond Street and I'm looking at you as if I've never seen you before. You're beautiful, and intensely attractive to me. You know that."

Susan Agnes Bernard looked straight into Macdonald's blue eyes and said, "Oh, John A., I love it when you make your little speeches. And, yes, I know you're attracted to me and that pleases me very much, very much indeed."

He smiled. "And do I detect, even slightly, that you, that you — well . . ."

"Yes, I do. I find you most pleasing to be with, a most intelligent man." Her eyes turned away from his briefly, then came back. "I can remember very well the first time I saw you, John A. It was nine years ago in Toronto at a concert at Shaftesbury Hall."

Macdonald's mind was immediately flooded by memories of his dear Isabella and of the agony of her death nine years before. Painful memories. But he put them aside and studied her as she spoke. Her face long like her brother Hewitt's; her dark hair was pulled back neatly in a bun; her full red lips moved invitingly as she spoke.

Agnes had lived a sheltered life after moving to England in 1851. She and her mother Theodora had settled in with relatives who lived in the vicarage in Lacock, a small village close to Bath. There they had been comfortable, but with a restricted income from the Jamaican estate. Theodora was not able to travel around England with Agnes as much as she would have liked for her own pleasure and for the edification of her fifteen-year-old daughter. Agnes had concentrated on her religious studies and her singing and art lessons, especially watercolours. What excitement then when the letter from Hewitt had arrived in early 1854 inviting them to join him in the mysterious, distant town in Canada West called Barrie.

After their ship docked at Quebec City, they had travelled by boat along the St. Lawrence and across Lake Ontario to the bustling harbour of burgeoning Toronto. There they were joyously greeted by a now-bearded, tall-as-ever Hewitt, who swept them off to the nearby railway station. They had spent a few talk-filled hours on a new (so different from British) railway car of the recently built Ontario, Huron and Simcoe Railway, before the puffing train delivered them to the Barrie railway station on the western shore of Kempenfeldt Bay of Lake Simcoe.

Agnes, now eighteen, was already a well-educated woman by the standards of the day, and her years in Barrie with its summer activities on the water and snow in the winter gave her a strong affinity to the outdoors. Then it was on to Toronto for Agnes and her mother when Hewitt had become John A's private secretary. Over the years there and later in Quebec City, where Hewitt moved to accompany his chief when it was that city's turn in 1859 to be the capital of the Province of Canada, Agnes had been in John A.'s presence at myriad social events. Those were part of the lifestyle of a legislature that brought its members together from enormously long distances for sittings that lasted for weeks on end.

But in those days no spark of love had ignited between them.

"Shaftesbury Hall," Macdonald said. "Yes, I remember that concert. The singing was dreadful." He paused, pulling nervously at his silk cravat. "Agnes, these past few days, seeing you so often and getting to know you so well, I . . . Agnes, I love you. I know I'm much older than you are and I have my handicaps . . ."

Agnes was nothing if not forthright. "It's too much whiskey from time to time. But I must say, John A. you've been on your best behaviour."

"I've tried, and being with you has made all the difference. Agnes, I'm asking you to marry me. Will you?"

Fearful that the answer might be no, John A. put off hearing her response. “Before you tell me yes or no, you should know that I come from a humble Scottish immigrant family of not much account and while I’ve made my way as a barrister and a politician, I’ve not been able to accumulate much money. Very little, in fact. So I cannot offer you much . . . how shall I put it?”

“Much security in case things go bad?”

“Aye, lass, that’s it. So will you have me, Agnes?”

In their secluded corner of Claridge’s darkened dining room, lit now only by the table candles, Susan Agnes Bernard delayed giving her answer to the question she had known for days would be put to her by this unusual man she had come to love.

“Before I give you an answer, John A.,” she smiled as he took both her hands in his, “there’s one condition I must make. No, I don’t want you to stop drinking, although that would please me.”

“Then what is it?”

“That shoulder of yours — the doctor says you should be in bed with it exposed to the air. And I know it’s giving you dreadful pain. The condition is that I want you to do what the doctor tells you and go to bed for as long as it takes for that horrible burn to start to mend.”

“My sweetheart, I’ll do exactly as you say. The business of the conference should be finished tomorrow. We have one final and most important matter to deal with in the afternoon, then we’re done and I’m for that bed.”

“And I’ll come and visit you.”

“With your mother as chaperone, of course.”

“Of course. You don’t think that a reputable young maiden would be seen visiting the hotel room of a handsome man all by herself, do you? I wish I could.”

“I wish you could, too. If your answer is yes, the next question is, when will the wedding be? It can’t be too soon, which means it should be while I’m still here in London trying to shepherd the Confederation legislation through Parliament.”

“How long will that take?”

“Probably until some time in March.”

“Then we’ll do it in early February. It will take that long to make all the proper arrangements, the church, the bridesmaids, the reception . . . So the answer is yes, John A. Yes!"

"The honeymoon? Would Oxford be alright? I know a delightful inn there."

"Of course. Anything you say. You should know, my sweet John A., I look forward to our honeymoon more than I've ever looked forward to anything in my life."

9

December 21, 1866
London

MACDONALD'S SHOULDER GAVE HIM MUCH LESS PAIN WHEN HE wakened on the morning of Friday the 21st of December. Perhaps it was because joy and happiness filled his mind as he remembered that he was an engaged man, a man whose proposal of marriage had been accepted by Agnes, beautiful *young* Agnes!

Hewitt Bernard had heard the news from his sister the night before. He banged on his chief's door as Macdonald was finishing dressing.

The private secretary was about to become a brother-in-law and he wanted to congratulate John A. and tell him how pleased Theodora and he were. The change in status did not, of course, alter the formality that existed between the tough, intelligent lawyer, leader, employer and the resilient, but pliant, lawyer, follower, scribe and secretary. There was not even a hint that Hewitt might be given the privilege of calling John A. Macdonald by his first name. Not even a thought let alone a hint.

Over breakfast, Macdonald, beaming with pleasure, confided in Cartier that Agnes had accepted his proposal, whereupon the ebullient First Minister of Canada East was on his feet to make the announcement to the entire dining room, filled as it was with virtually all of the participants in the conference. They responded by giving the newly engaged minister a standing ovation which he graciously accepted, his smiling face beet red in happy embarrassment.

The morning session got under way at nine o'clock. The conference had disposed of nearly all the Quebec Resolutions by this time. As soon as Macdonald brought the meeting to order, Tupper suggested that the subject of "sea coast and inland fisheries" be taken out of the list of provincial powers and given to the federal parliament. Better that the federal government be responsible for the protection of the inshore fisheries from the predations of Yankee fishermen now that the Reciprocity Treaty had been abrogated by the Americans, the abrogations thereby terminating their inshore fishing rights along the coastlines of British America. Tupper's proposal was discussed and accepted.

Then the unexpected happened. An issue, probably the thorniest to be dealt with by the conference and one that had been dealt with and at least temporarily disposed of on the 13th, was raised again by two still-disgruntled reformers, W. P. Howland and William McDougall. The issue was the seventh resolution of the Quebec Conference, which established the regional composition of the legislative council, a body that had yet to be given a name. Some were already calling it "the Senate" in the American style. Whatever — it would function as a check on the House of Commons rather like the House of Lords in Britain. Tied with the seventh resolution was the eighth, which set the number of members of the appointed legislative council at seventy-two, and the eleventh, which provided for their appointment for life by the central government.

Howland and McDougall wanted the legislative council to be elected, not appointed. They railed against this "irresponsible chamber of crown appointees." They proposed that the members be elected for a term of years by their provincial legislatures.

Their arguments had gained support from some of the New Brunswick delegation and certainly from William Henry of Nova Scotia. He was also concerned that there be a way to increase the size of the legislative council when circumstances dictated the necessity. It was he who had raised again the legislative council matter. When Henry asked the chair for leave to further discuss the issue, Macdonald groaned inwardly but, statesmanlike, allowed the Nova Scotian to carry on.

The sum of Henry's eloquent dissertation came in these words: "Do you wish to stereotype an upper branch irresponsible both to the Crown and to the people, a third body interposed unaccountable to the other two? The Crown unable to add to their number. The people unable to remove them. Suppose a general election results in the election of a large majority in the lower house favourable to a measure, but the legislative council prevent it from becoming law. The Crown should possess some power of enlargement."

As the discussion raged on that morning it was apparent to Macdonald that, like it or not, Henry's argument was compelling. The Crown could not, should not, be given unlimited power to appoint. The Crown, in practical reality, would be the Prime Minister of the day. But to avoid a deadlock between the two houses, surely there could be provision for the addition of just a handful more members in equal proportion from each region.

Again, as on the 13th, there was no final consensus and the issue was left to be settled during the later drafting stage, likely toward the end of January when the advice of the Colonial Secretary and the Colonial Office could be sought and given weight.

As he brought the morning session to a close, Macdonald said, "Before we adjourn I must say a word about the absence of our colleague Alexander Galt."

"Probably nursing a bloody great hangover," the Honourable Samuel Tilley of New Brunswick was heard to mutter.

"Not so, Samuel. Alex has taken on a major and urgent task at my request. He has spent the last two days completing a report that he will present to the conference immediately after the noon meal. Gentlemen, we are adjourned until two o'clock."

Macdonald went to Galt's room and found him just finishing his report.

"I'm all done, John A.," Galt said as he stacked his sheets of paper together and stuffed them in his leather file case.

"Good. You can brief George and me over lunch. I've reserved a table for just the three of us."

"You'll probably have a hell of a time concentrating on all of this."

Macdonald looked surprised. "What are you talking about?"

"Well, I mean a newly engaged person will be able to think only about his anticipated marital delights. The affairs of state will be shoved right out of his daydreaming mind."

John A. grinned. "What bullshit. Let's go. I'm starving for a good lunch."

"And a sasparilla?"

"*Only* a sasparilla."

✦

FORTIFIED BY TWO LUNCHEON GLASSES OF THE NON-ALCOHOLIC BEVERAGE and a plate of pork kidneys, chutney sauce, and fried potatoes, Macdonald took his usual seat at the head of the long conference table down upon which the young Queen Victoria — orb in hand, crown on head — looked from her flag-flanked portrait. Overhead hung three gas-lit chandeliers, their thin brass arms resembling the legs of a spider.

The time being two minutes past the hour of two, and satisfied that there were no late stragglers, Macdonald raised his voice above the room's conversational chatter. "Gentlemen, may we come to order, please? Thank you."

He did not look down at his notes. There was no need.

"The First Minister of Canada East and Minister Galt and I have been privy to a rumour that we heard from the Earl of Carnarvon when we visited with him and his lovely chatelaine last week. We reported to you all of the salient aspects of our conversations with the Colonial Secretary except for one matter. The purport, the significance, and the potential negative impact of that on our confederation discussions and negotiations are such that we decided to keep its contents confidential until we prepared at least the bare bones of a countermeasure to lay before you to balance the weight of the rumour."

Macdonald could see that Galt, sitting on his immediate left, was becoming characteristically impatient, the signs being his near-twitch body movements. Galt would have to wait. The preamble to the rumour itself was of too much psychological importance to cut short.

"The rumour — and we must act upon it as if it were fact and not simply gossip — is that the Tsar's ambassador to Washington has been called to St. Petersburg, where he will advocate and expect to receive instructions from His Imperial Majesty to offer to sell Russian America.

"The critical importance to us of such a sale is that the all-important colony of British Columbia would be at risk of loss to the power- and land-hungry administration currently camped in the White House."

"You mean Secretary of State Seward, don't you?" Charles Tupper was two places away from Macdonald's right hand. "That bastard has only one objective in mind: he wants the U.S. to grab Canada lock, stock, and barrel."

"And anybody else's territory he can get his hands on." It was William Ritchie of Nova Scotia. "Seward would do anything to get Russian America, anything. And his timing couldn't be better if he wants to knock our confederation plans into a cocked hat."

Macdonald tapped the table. "I want to clarfify one point. The rumour is about what the Russians are going to do. There's no indication that Seward is a player yet."

Ritchie persisted. "That may well be, John A., but I can tell you, I've met that banty rooster. Seward hates us British because we gave aid and succour to the Confederacy during the Civil War. If the Tsar's man . . . what's his name?"

"De Stoeckl."

"If de Stoeckl arrives in Washington with a proposal that's within reason, Seward will go after it like a hound after a fox. Mark my words!"

"Marked. Ah, by the way, Hewitt, my brother-in-law-to-be . . ."

"Poor chap," someone at the far end of the table offered to the amusement of all.

" . . . I forgot to tell you. I want all of this off the record, so stop writing and tear up what you've already written. Gentlemen, this information is completely confidential — no word of this to anyone. Our dream of confederation might well be destroyed if it becomes public knowledge that Russian America is for sale and that we — the four British American colonies — are going to do something about it."

"We are?" New Brunswick's Charles Fisher spoke up. "What in God's name can we do?"

"We can do nothing unless you, all of you, agree to do something — assuming the rumour is true."

"So who's the source of this great goddam rumour?" William Henry's question received nods of approval.

"Her Imperial Britannic Majesty's ambassador to Washington, Sir

Frederick Bruce."

More nods of approval. Many delegates had met Sir Frederick.

"Sterling chap," Cartier said. "He has developed an intelligence net in Washington that's the envy of every major world power. One of his beautiful chambermaids planted in the Russian embassy is probably sleeping with the First Secretary of the Tsar's mission to America!"

Macdonald was ready to move on. "Well, gentlemen, now you know what the threat is. The question is: What do we do about it? That's what Alex and George and I have been trying to sort out since we received the rumour from Carnarvon."

"What are you proposing?" Henry asked, adding, "It had better be good and it had better have the approval of the British government . . ."

"And the Queen," Galt added, anxious to get into the fray.

Macdonald held up his hand, a signal for patience. "The Foreign Office is working on schemes to sabotage the current friendly relationship between the Americans and the Russians, whose whole bloody fleet turned up without warning in U.S. west coast and east coast ports, San Francisco and New York, right in the middle of the Civil War. Looking for safety from the British navy as we all know."

"And what else?" It was Tilley's question.

"The relationship between Russia and Britain is still hostile after the defeat of the Russians during the Crimean War . . ."

"And, in the Treaty of Paris, the Russians promised the sky in compensation payments to Great Britain," Tupper said. "Astronomical amounts!"

"What else?" Macdonald repeated Tilley's question. "George, Alex, and I are proposing that we — ourselves plus the British government — put together an offer to buy Russian America and that we put the proposal to the Russians as soon as possible."

"Why not present the offer here, to the Russian ambassador to the Court of St. James?" Peter Mitchell of New Brunswick ventured.

Galt responded. "Because we can go directly to the Tsar or his ministers. No need for an intermediary."

"If they're prepared to receive you in St. Petersburg. What if the Tsar won't negotiate?" Mitchell persisted.

"We'll cross that bridge when we get to it," Galt replied.

Macdonald had been expecting that someone in the volatile group around the table would be against the idea of attempting to buy Russian America, quite apart from the matter of price.

But not a word. The menace to their concept of a new country stretching from sea to sea, safe from the grasp of the avaricious American eagle, was so patently obvious that not one of them challenged the concept.

But the matter of the cost would probably be a quite different kettle of fish.

"The reason for the delay in putting the Russian American situation before you, gentlemen, is that we wanted to look into the matter further," Macdonald explained.

Cartier, on his immediate right, added, "We wanted to — how do you say it in English — sound out, yes, sound out Her Majesty's government. Would the government support the idea of the purchase? Would they be prepared to pay all or part of the offering price — and how much would that be? If it was only part, then how much would we have to contribute?"

It was back to the chairman. "So we asked our efficient, penny-pinching Finance Minister from Sherbrooke to take on the task of finding out the answer to all those questions."

"Which is why I've been absent from so many sessions in the past few days," Galt said defensively. "If you will allow me, Mr. Chairman, I'll explain what Her Majesty's government is prepared to do. The Prime Minister, Derby, is agreeable to putting up the money even though I think the poor old chap has little idea of what or where British North America is, let alone Russian America — or British Columbia for that matter."

"I'll bet he sure as hell knows where Washington is!" Tilley snorted. "And St. Petersburg."

"He does that," Galt agreed. "Let me tell you, gentlemen, that my task of the last week has been one of the most difficult in my career as a public servant. I mean, here I am, a colonial minister in a colonial government having the audacity and the gall to impose upon the crême de la crême — have I got that right, George? — of the high-and-mighty British senior civil servants. As a breed I can certify they're all, every last one of them, arrogant, conceited bastards with noses down which they look at us colonial inferiors — noses as long as Niagara Falls!"

"Do we take it, Alex, that these marvellous people have made it difficult for you?" Macdonald, smiling, reached out to put a compassionate, understanding hand on Galt's shoulder.

Galt almost snarled. "You wouldn't believe the demeaning, the patronizing, the humiliating treatment I've had to put up with!" He shifted in his seat, shook his large head as if to clear it. "Anyway, I've beaten those lah-de-dah snobs at their own game."

"What does that mean?" Tilley asked, amused by Galt's ferocity.

"I played one ego — all very large — against the other. I was the colonial bumpkin, right?"

"We won't argue about that!" Tupper exclaimed.

Galt gave him a friendly glower, then his bushy browed eyes went to his notes. He slipped on his reading spectacles, saying, "This is the deal — subject to the approval of all of you turkeys — and I have in mind my dear friends, especially those from Nova Scotia and New Brunswick . . ." His face took on a happy "I got you" look momentarily.

"The British have agreed to the amount, the theoretical amount, that our chairman gave me as an opening offer. I mean, how can you put a value on Russian America?"

Cartier had the answer: "You have to give the Tsar what he needs to cover his deficits, his shortfalls, whatever he needs to keep his St. Petersburg coffers filled — or even partly filled."

"Exactly, George. Spoken like a true French Canadian."

"So what's the magic number?" Cartier asked although he knew what it was from the luncheon briefing.

"Ten million U.S. dollars, payable in gold in Washington or London."

There were gasps and oaths of shock around the table.

"Dear God in Heaven!" Tilley was aghast. "Where in hell are we going to find ten million? And what about the intercolonial railway you Canadians have agreed to build from Montreal down to us, the link that physically joins us? What happens to that?"

"Just a moment." Galt was on the defensive. "I didn't say we'd have to pay the whole thing. The Chancellor of the Exchequer and his lah-de-dah people, they've agreed to pay fifty percent of the price, whatever it is."

"Does that mean you've got some negotiating room on either side of the ten million dollars?" It was a new voice at the end of the table, George Archibald.

Galt nodded. "Yes. Obviously I can go below ten, but I can also go to fifteen million, if I have to — and if you agree."

Tilley was visibly angry. "Mr. Chairman, the reason New Brunswick is at this table is the commitment given at the Quebec Conference, a commitment cast in stone, that the first priority of the new government is to build the intercolonial railway. That link is absolutely essential to the concept of confederation, just as the ultimate extension of the railway westward beyond Ontario is essential to the Mowat resolution we passed at the Quebec Conference providing for the admission of the Northwest Territories, British Columbia, and Victoria Island. No railway means no nation. The kind of money you're talking about here, Alex — something like five to ten million for our share — would seriously jeopardize our ability to finance even the intercolonial, let alone a line to the Pacific."

Macdonald quietly asked, "Well, Alex, what about it? We've guaranteed Mr. Tilley his railway."

"And if we don't get it, we'll do the western extension — we'll extend our existing railway southwest to join up with the American rail system!" Tilley pounded the table.

Peter Mitchell joined in. "I agree with Sam. We New Brunswickers have a choice and don't forget it for one minute. We can go with Canada or we can go with the United States. If you people take away the intercolonial railway, then you leave us no choice. We would have to join up with the Yankees."

"I hear you, gentlemen. Well, Alex?"

Galt grunted. "I also hear you. And let me tell you the intercolonial railway ranks at the top of our spending priorities. In my opinion, with the guarantees of the British government in our pockets, we can raise money to build the railway by debentures. We can easily raise money from private investors. And we can raise money without a negative impact on any negotiations for the purchase of Russian America."

Tilley kept listening, so Galt went on. "That's the way I see it, Mr. Chairman. In fact, I've persuaded the Chancellor of the Exchequer to agree to put up all the money for Russian America against our promise to pay half the amount over a period of twenty years . . . I heard someone ask what the interest rate would be? One per cent. You couldn't get a better deal than that."

Sam Tilley nodded. "If that is the deal, Alex, I'm satisfied."

"So are we agreed, gentlemen?" Macdonald asked. No one else offered an objection.

Cartier asked Galt, "What about the Treaty of Paris? What if the Russians want its terms cancelled as part of the purchase price?"

Macdonald answered. "Alex and I had a brief meeting with the Prime Minister yesterday on that point but, well, the answer was no, the Treaty of Paris could not be offered as a bargaining tool. Money yes, but not the Treaty."

"What if the Russians say they'll negotiate but only if the Treaty's on the table?"

Macdonald smiled. "If the Russians raise it — we can't — if they raise it, then the P.M., if he's still the P.M., will consider it. No commitment, mind you. But the door is slightly open."

"Assuming we're going to negotiate, how're we going to do it? Will the Brits do it for us?" Langevin asked. "Or are we going to do it?"

As Macdonald felt a burst of pain in his shoulder his face involuntarily contorted in a grimace of agony. His left hand clutched the arm just below the shoulder in a futile attempt to ease his intense hurt.

Cartier, beside him, stood in alarm as all in the room watched Macdonald's suffering. "John A., for God's sake, are you all right? Can we do anything to help you?"

The pain was easing. "A glass of good whisky," Macdonald muttered through clenched teeth. "No. I'm fine. Really, George. This'll be over in a minute."

He let go of his arm and shook his head in relief as the sharp, cutting pain subsided. Smiling apologetically, he said to his concerned colleagues, worry written on all their faces, "I'm sorry, gentlemen. This burn of mine hasn't been healing properly. I had to have a doctor look at it again this morning and he's ordered me to bed, which is where I should be and where I'm going to go as soon as we're finished."

Cartier resumed his seat as Macdonald spoke to Langevin. "Who will handle the negotiations with the Russians? As I said, Alex and I had a meeting with Prime Minister Derby. He's also the Foreign Secretary, as you know . . ."

Galt commented, "I hear Disraeli thinks the old boy's in a region of perpetual funk."

"Well, that description isn't too far off the mark. But Derby is the Foreign Secretary. He thinks it would be better if we Canadians do the negotiating ourselves. As Derby sees it — actually it's Carnarvon's idea — we colonials would present a much less hostile face to the Russians than an English envoy would, or than Sir Andrew Buchanan, the British ambassador to St. Petersburg, would."

"That makes sense," Langevin agreed. "Do you have a plan? Who will do the negotiating and how will it be done?"

"No, I don't have a plan, not yet anyway. First we had to get all of you to agree to make an offer. Now that you've done so, I'll work with Carnarvon and the Foreign Office to put a plan together."

"There's no time to lose if it's true that de Stoeckl is getting instructions to negotiate with the Americans," Cartier said.

"I think I can speak for all of us, John," Tilley said. "We'll leave the matter of the Russians in your capable hands. We think that since we've dealt with all the issues and our work here is pretty much finished, the conference secretary, young Hewitt Bernard here, can write a final report and you can get your ass into bed! I move this meeting be adjourned."

10

December 22–25, 1866
London

HE LAY ABED IN HIS CORNER ROOM ON THE SECOND FLOOR OF THE Westminster Palace Hotel for three long days and nights. At first his wound felt nearly as hot and red-yellow as the flame that had caused it. He had to be on his back or his left side so that the skin of his raw, exposed right shoulder could heal more rapidly without the pressure of a dressing, a nightshirt, or even a sheet.

And not a drop of whisky crossed his lips the whole time. Not that he didn't hanker for a wee dram. What he hankered for much more was the warm, stimulating presence of his beloved.

Agnes came every morning and stayed through lunch. She would return in late afternoon and have dinner with him, her vivacious wit, her beauty, and her touch giving John A. much comforting pleasure. Visitors trooping into his room to give encouragement, to seek advice, to give opinions, to discuss the wording of this resolution or that, helped to fill the hours when Agnes was not there.

Each day Hewitt Bernard arrived at the hotel with Agnes. In the sitting room that Macdonald, Cartier and Galt shared, under the close supervision of his chief, he would work on the preparation of the document that came to be known as the London Resolutions.

So the days passed. Despite all the visitors John A. found time to read and edit the drafts Hewitt prepared in his fine, flowing script, avidly read the daily newspapers, and respond to messages from Ottawa asking for decisions or directions — much of the time with dear Agnes knitting by the bedside.

"Knitting what?" John was bold enough to ask one morning.

"Your Christmas present, my darling."

"My God, it is almost Christmas, isn't it? And I haven't done anything about a present for my son. I must send a cable to my sister Lou in Kingston straightaway. Hughey must have a proper Christmas gift."

John A. had wanted to get up on the 23rd, but the doctor, though being well pleased with his skinny patient's progress, had said that the wound was by no means fully healed, and, with the danger of infection still present, it was necessary to continue the confinement until Christmas Day.

Macdonald was up early that morning, waiting for Hewitt to come and fetch him in a splendid closed carriage.

It was but a short ride to the Bernards' flat. Macdonald, about to become part of the family, spent the day and evening in the loving care of Agnes and her mother and brother, who was now as close to John A. as any man. Agnes played Christmas carols. Then came the exchange of presents. The long sweater that Agnes had been knitting for John A. was finished and carefully wrapped. John A. had managed to purchase his gift for her the day before his unwelcome confinement. It was a delicately crafted gold ring, set with three modest diamonds, the engagement symbol. He chose a moment when they were alone together to present her with the velvet box in which the gold band nestled.

There was nothing but joy and love and peace in the Bernards' London flat as they sat down to what John A. later described as "a happily groaning board of succulent roast beef, incomparable Yorkshire pudding, followed by perfect plum pudding illuminated by sparklers that near danced."

✦

EN ROUTE TO THE BERNARDS' FLAT THAT CHRISTMAS MORNING Macdonald and Bernard made a brief but important stop. They pulled up at the Colonial office to deliver to Her Imperial Majesty's government a Yuletide gift, the formal, completed London Resolutions as prepared and presented by Queen Victoria's loyal subjects in her British North American colonies of Canada East, Canada West, New Brunswick and Nova Scotia. Hewitt, who had laboured for so long over the drafts, placed the precious document in the hands of the attendant at the main door of the office.

When he climbed back into the carriage, John A. took his hand, saying, "Well done, Hewitt. My sincere congratulations, you've been absolutely first class. We couldn't have done it without you."

Hewitt's broad smile showed how pleased he was at his chief's words of praise. "Thank you, Chief. Thank you. But you're the one without whom this conference couldn't have been a success. I'm just the scribe. You're the artist, the sculptor, the creator. The way you've handled the sessions was just superb."

"And I thank you, Hewitt. It's a time for celebration and Christmas Day of 1866 couldn't be a better time. But we have our work cut out for us. Getting the bill for Confederation drafted and navigating it through the House of Lords and the House of Commons will be like building a canoe, then steering it down white-water rapids that one has never seen before."

"An enormous challenge. And then there's Russian America. I've made the bookings to France for you."

"Yes, of course. The Foreign Office has opened all the necessary doors for me, thanks be to God and Carnarvon. My complete itinerary, letters of introduction, and so forth arrived yesterday afternoon."

"And you'll be staying with the British ambassador, Earl Cowley?"

Macdonald laughed, giving Hewitt, sitting opposite, a slap on the knee. "Is Victoria the Queen? So when do I leave? The sooner the better. Time is of the essence, as you well know."

"I do indeed. Your ship sails at high tide tomorrow afternoon. You have a first-class cabin. You have to be on board at Dover by two."

"Good. I'll be there, never fear."

"The Confederation bill has to be ready by the opening of the Imperial Parliament. Have you any idea when that's going to be?"

"I had a letter yesterday from our great friend and Governor, Lord Monck. Without his support I don't know what we would have done. He's at his family's seat, Charleville, at Enniskerry. He confirms what Carnarvon's been saying. The opening is February the fifth."

Hewitt gave a slight shake of his head. "I don't know if Reilly and his people can get the final draft ready in — what — five weeks?"

F.S. Reilly was the main legal expert at the Colonial Office, the man who would draft the bill in association with others on the Colonial Office staff and Hewitt Bernard himself.

"Five weeks. And y'know, Hewitt, we haven't even decided what we're going to call this new country of ours."

"That's right."

"I think it should be Kingdom of Canada. That's what we'll put in the first draft of the bill."

"I'll see to it."

"Good. Now, when do I get back here?"

"By the second of January. I've allowed two days to get there, and two to get back, and one day once you're there."

"I don't know, Hewitt, I may need two."

"I've made provision for two."

"Well done, Hewitt. Well done."

"What am I going to tell your colleagues? I mean, here you are, engaged to my sister. It's Christmas time and you go off to France all by yourself for a week."

Macdonald laughed. "Look. All my colleagues are off with friends or relatives for the holidays. They won't even be back here to put the question to you. Don't worry about it."

"And Agnes. Have you told her?"

"No. I'll tell her today. I wanted to get all my ducks in a row, know that everything is arranged, before I told her. She'll understand."

It was Bernard's turn to laugh. "I'm not so sure. She's one strong young lady."

"She's also like you, Hewitt — intelligent, practical, pragmatic. If she wasn't pragmatic, why in hell would she even think of marrying an older fart like me?"

"Because, as they say, and as I've found out, to know you is to love you. But for Christ's sake, Chief, it's Christmas!"

"And I'm entitled on this wonderful rainy, foggy day in Londinium to have just a wee drop of whisky to celebrate, am I not, Hewitt?"

Bernard's face lost its smile. "Why not, provided it doesn't lead to one of your illnesses. You know what I mean."

"If I had an illness now, I'd likely lose Agnes . . ."

"She knows about your illnesses — when the bottle is too much for you."

"Most everyone does, I suspect."

"But she's never seen you up close when you've been ill, so she doesn't really know what happens to you. You don't get nasty or violent, that's the main thing."

"Thanks be to God. Not to worry, Hewitt. I love Agnes more than anything in this world. I'll not do anything, not take too much whisky, not do anything foolish. Not this day anyway."

11

December 29, 1866
Paris, France

The British ambassador who greeted John A. Macdonald upon his arrival in Paris was a bulbous, pear-shaped person, massive of girth, with jelly-like jowls at the bottom of a round face rather like that of the squat British bulldog. A man of similar height to Macdonald, His Excellency made it perfectly clear from the outset that he looked down on the Canadian colonial. Macdonald was determined to soon change the ambassador's attitude.

The Right Honourable Henry Richard Charles Wellesley, Earl Cowley, Her Imperial Majesty's representative, had been instructed by the Foreign Secretary himself to meet this Macdonald person at the Gare du Nord railway station and to grant him accommodation in the embassy. Well, those instructions were almost too much.

On top of that, Earl Cowley had been obliged to grovel to obtain an appointment for Macdonald to meet with Prince Gorchakov, one of Russia's highest placed persons, who was visiting the French capital. Fortunately, the ambassador had met Gorchakov several times over the years, a factor that persuaded the Russian to agree to see Macdonald on short notice.

He, Earl Cowley, had done what his buffoon of a political master had required of him, and the vacationing Prince would receive this colonial person who had travelled from America to discuss a terrain of mutual interest.

The Earl's uniformed aide, who had searched out the easily recognizable Macdonald on the station platform, took the Canadian's single travelling case and guided him to the ambassador's elaborately carved, gold-embossed carriage, the British coat of arms emblazoned on its doors and on the snow-dusted blankets that covered the backs of the two white horses ready to draw their vehicle at a brisk pace.

Inside the stuffy but cold compartment, Earl Cowley greeted him, offering a limp hand of introduction, nodding his white wigged head slightly. His elaborate curls were capped by a plumed tricorn hat. Macdonald was conscious of beady eyes appraising him from within the cocoon of rich black fur that enveloped the ambassador.

"My dear Minister, welcome to Paris." The shrill voice grated on the travel-weary Macdonald, but he managed to respond.

"Thank you, Your Excellency. I am obliged to you for your courtesy in meeting me. After all, it's teatime in Paris."

"Well, I can tell you it isn't every day that I come all the way down here to this railway station." He sniffed. "It is such an inconvenience. But never mind, you're here on an important mission all the way from America and I have instructions from my minister to offer you every assistance."

Macdonald could hear Earl Cowley's reluctance in every word he spoke in his upper-class English accent.

The aide, standing in the light, still-falling snow, reached into the carriage to throw a blanket over John A.'s long legs. The Canadian, well used to heavy snows and intense winter cold, was prepared for the unusually wintry Paris day. His heavy, long red underwear covered every inch of his lean frame except for his feet, which were encased in thick socks under high-laced leather boots, and his hands, which were in muskrat fur gloves. His ears, which tended to protrude from under his bushy hair, could be a problem in bitter cold, especially if, as a matter of protocol, one had to wear a tall stovepipe hat. For such an emergency, John A. had for many years carried special raccoon fur muffs designed to slip on and fasten snugly over each ear. Now he turned up the beaver collar of his fur-lined coat, reached into one of the pockets, and pulled out the ear muffs. Carefully, without removing his stovepipe hat, he put them on.

"I say, Mr. Macdonald, you seem to be well prepared for survival in this wretched French winter climate. Well done."

"Well, Your Excellency, I come from a country where the winters are much more severe, so I'm used to this kind of weather. Having

Scottish roots I have a natural instinct for protecting myself."

"My dear chap, if you indeed have such an instinct, I suggest, I really do, that you hone your skills for your meeting tomorrow."

The heavy carriage lurched as the driver put the whip to his horses. The piercing squeal of metal coursing over fresh snow and patches of ice sent a shiver down Macdonald's spine as he listened intently to the diplomat's caution.

"That's rather a sober warning, Your Excellency."

"Hah! That's one of the things I must caution you about."

"What is?"

"That sober business. The Prince — he's getting on, you know — the Prince likes his vodka. Any Russian aristocrat, any Russian for that matter, likes his vodka. How are you with vodka, Mr. Macdonald?"

"Never touch the stuff myself. I tried it — tasteless so far as I'm concerned. I prefer good, pure Scotch whisky. Nothing like it."

"Well, now you'll have to protect yourself against the Prince's vodka, whether you like it or not. By the by, I share your opinion of the stuff. Tasteless fish pee is what it is. But powerful, Macdonald, powerful. Near straight alcohol, I tell you."

Macdonald smiled. "I've had a wee bit of alcohol in my time. It's often been my solace, my friend in times of grief, in times of loneliness, in times when I've been beaten to a pulp in the legislature or on the hustings."

"Indeed. Well then, I'd say all of us — politicians, diplomats — have something in common."

Macdonald changed the subject. "The Earl of Carnarvon told me that you are the best man for this post, given the post-Crimean War difficulties between Great Britain and a never-satisfied France. And, of course, relations between Russia and Great Britain are still greatly strained."

"Strained? Almost to the point of snapping. My job is to ensure that they don't snap. Now, let me tell you how to protect yourself from the Prince's vodka."

Macdonald listened carefully, noting all the vodka cautions and instructions that His Excellency recited.

"Now, even more important than the vodka is Gorchakov. He is the right hand of the Tsar. He has been Foreign Minister for this Tsar's father and has just continued on.He's bright, Macdonald, and a tough, shrewd, hard bargainer. So be on your guard when you're dealing with him."

The ambassador peered out the frosted window of the swaying carriage to identify where they were in relation to the embassy.

"Ah. We're almost there. For your information, Minister, we are travelling on one of the world's great thoroughfares, the Champs Elysées. You will find the architecture of the buildings — you'll see them in the morning — in a word, majestic. The palaces, cathedrals, residences are in my opinion graceful and superbly proportioned. Many of them are tall, four and five storeys, would you believe? Hard to get up to the top floor for fifty-odd-year-old legs, what?"

"I should think so," Macdonald politely agreed.

"And there are wonderful shops on the Champs Elysées, lots of them. Theatres, yes, and restaurants, excellent restaurants. The street is always filled with people and carriages from early morning to late at night, even in the dead of winter."

"Yes, I've been amazed at the traffic and the number of people."

"Pity you won't have time to see much of the city. Two days in Paris are nothing. And so much of your time will be taken up with meetings."

"I hope so. If I can get the Prince's favourable attention, if he doesn't throw me out in the first half-hour, I'll need the two days for negotiating and trying to get everything down on paper."

"Gorchakov is pretty good at getting things down on paper — if it's to his advantage."

"What about an interpreter? I understand the Prince speaks French but not English, and I don't speak French."

"You don't?" The ambassador raised his eyebrows in surprise. "My God, I thought everybody in Canada spoke French."

"French in Quebec, yes. But I'm from Upper Canada, English Canada, where the French language isn't spoken, just as English isn't in most of Quebec."

"Then how does your legislature work, and your courts?"

"With difficulty. Those language problems have been some of the greatest difficulties to overcome in agreeing to a new form of confederation. That's what we've been trying to do in London this month, and we've done it."

"Yes, of course. I have that in the briefing note from the Foreign Office. You'll have to explain it to me . . . Ah, here we are."

The bouncing, rolling carriage turned into an arched gateway toward what Macdonald could barely make out to be a huge greystone building. Lights could be seen through nearly every window as they approached the structure's wide porte-cochère.

"My valet will see you to your rooms, Minister. Then if you would be so kind as to join the Countess and me in the library at half past six, we can have a tot before dinner. Over cigars and port after dinner you can explain what you want to get out of Gorchakov and the Tsar."

The carriage came to an abrupt stop under the porte-cochère as Earl Cowley added, "Ah, yes, you asked about an interpreter. Who better than I, Her Imperial British Majesty's ambassador to la belle France? Gorchakov has approved of my presence with you."

The door of the carriage was being opened from the outside and the ambassador was throwing off his fur blanket when he added, "Oh, I forgot to tell you. You're in luck, Mr. Macdonald. The Prince will receive you not at his hotel as set out in your itinerary. He will meet with you instead at the Russian embassy."

"Marvellous!" John A. exclaimed, in surprise and pleasure.

"Bloody marvellous, I should think," Earl Cowley shouted. "You're privileged, Minister, for what reason I'm not sure."

"Why's that?"

"We British, the enemy, we're not usually welcome at the Russian embassy. I've been there but once — when I arrived here two years ago. Oh, yes. It was a ball to celebrate the Tsar's birthday. Must've forgotten to strike me off the list." He turned to ease himself out of the carriage, walking stick in gloved hand, the other reaching for the steadying arm of his military aide who had opened the door.

Having safely guided the ambassador out of the carriage, the young aide performed the same service for Macdonald, then hurried ahead to open the huge wooden door for his master and the guest.

The Earl ushered John A. into the vestibule where coats, hats, and the other accoutrements worn against the bitter cold were removed.

The aide then threw open the double French-style English oak doors to reveal a magnificent hall that John A. judged to be some thirty paces in length and nearly as wide. From the high vaulted ceiling hung a huge, multi-armed, brass chandelier filled with a hundred crystal-encased candles glowing in special honour of the Canadian minister's arrival. The floor of inlaid, intricately designed dark oak, the walnut-panelled walls adorned only by the flag-flanked portrait of the young Queen Victoria, the grand, curving staircase — all gave John A. the feeling that he was in a baronial English mansion, far from the cold heart of an intensely foreign city.

"My, this is splendid!" he said as his admiring eyes took in the calculated splendour of the great hall.

The ambassador was pleased. "This was one of the first things I did when I arrived here. This hall was an absolute shambles. Disgraceful. London balked at the expense, but it had to be done."

"Magnificent."

"Yes. Well now, I have things to do down here. If you will follow my aide here. Peter, please see Minister Macdonald to his room. We'll meet again at six-thirty in the library."

"Which is where . . . ?"

"Ah yes. Through that door on the right. And, by the way, Minister, it is my practice during an unusually cold winter's day in Paris to provide a decanter of golden cognac from Jarnac to warm my freezing guests. You'll find it on the small table by the fireplace, which ought to have a roaring fire in it, eh, Peter?"

The aide picked up John A.'s heavy valise, responding as he did so, "Indeed, Your Excellency, and the fires aren't the only things that roar around here."

His master roared with laughter. "Well done, Peter. Well done."

John A. decided that at least the ambassador had a sense of humour.

The dinner passed pleasantly. Countess Cowley was a gracious hostess who showed particular interest in the agricultural prospects for Canada. The Earl was more interested in knowing about the Red Indians and, oh yes, the Fenian Brotherhood — were they really a threat?

After dinner the two men retired to the library. Over several glasses of delicious port — John A. declined the rich Havana cigar — he outlined the purpose of his visit, hoping to elicit as much advice as the ambassador could offer on how to negotiate with Gorchakov, and what to expect from the Russian mind. But Cowley repeated that he had had precious little opportunity to meet with the Tsar's ambassador or his embassy staff because after Russia's defeat in the Crimean War, relations between the two countries were far from cordial.

"It may well be, however, that the special treatment you're being offered, John A." — the two men had agreed with port-induced conviviality to allow the use of first names — "is that you're a North American; British, yes, but only a colonial. You're not really English . . ."

"God, I'm certainly not. I'm a Scot and proud of it!"

"Of course, but you understand what I mean. Either way you're not carrying the resentment, the baggage, of the Crimean War."

"Yes, and that may be a factor. But could it also be the possibility that I'm a messenger of money?"

The Earl sucked thoughtfully on his cigar, relishing its delicious, unique smoke. "Quite likely, old boy. Quite likely. But then, we'll see, won't we?"

"We will indeed," John A. agreed as he finished off his third glass of port. A small glass, he told himself. "What about de Stoeckl? Have you been able to find out anything? Is Russian America going to be offered to the United States? As you undoubtedly know, that was the rumour from Sir Frederick Bruce."

"Well, I can tell you, my dear chap, that de Stoeckl left St. Petersburg before Christmas. He has been here in Paris for two weeks. I learned this from a senior French diplomat, a friend of mine. De Stoeckl might go to Austria for a week."

"His native country?"

"Yes. God knows how an Austrian could get to be the Tsar's ambassador to Washington. But there you are."

Earl Cowley filled John A.'s glass. "Evidently he intends to leave for America some time around the middle of January."

"To discuss Russian America, I suspect."

"Haven't a clue. My French friend was in St. Petersburg about two weeks ago and saw de Stoeckl at a reception at the Austrian embassy. Apparently he was in a — how did Marcel put it — he was in an exuberant mood. I gather he had seen the Tsar and received new marching orders. He was a happy man. But no mention of Russian America."

The ambassador paused. "I say, old boy, I've been wondering. Do you have a family, wife, children? This is rather a poor time to be away from them. Christmas, New Year's, and all."

"It is that. I'm a widower, Henry. My wife passed away nine years ago after a long illness and much suffering."

"What a shame! Sorry about that."

"Time heals, and only time. I'm well over it now. I have a son, Hugh John, a fine lad of sixteen years. He's with my sister in Canada, in Kingston, my home town. I don't see enough of him, of course, but he's getting on well enough. And you won't believe this — I scarcely do myself. I'm engaged to be married!"

Earl Cowley, delighted, reached over to slap John A.'s knee. "Bloody marvellous! Tell me about her."

Macdonald wasn't reluctant. "First of all, she's twenty-two years younger than I."

"Which means she's . . . ?"

"Thirty."

"What is she like, John A.?"

"Quite handsome indeed. She's witty and intelligent as well. Her name is Susan Agnes Bernard. Her brother is my private secretary."

"Then you must have known her for a long time."

"Yes, but until a few weeks ago I hadn't seen her for about two years. She has changed a lot in that time."

"Enough to catch your eye."

"And fill it!"

"You're engaged already. You must be a swift and persuasive suitor, John A. How could you bear to be away from her now? By the way, have you set the date yet?"

"We are hoping to be married in the middle of February, but it's very difficult because my colleagues and I are drafting legislation for the Confederation bill."

"But, as I was saying, it must be difficult being away from your loved one at this festive time of the year?"

"True, it isn't easy." John A. paused a moment. "We did have Christmas together, and I gave her an engagement ring. But I absolutely had to come to Paris to meet with Gorchakov. Agnes understands."

"I'm sure she does, old chap."

"You see, Henry, if Canada — or whatever Her Majesty decides to call our new country — if Canada loses British Columbia and Victoria and perhaps the Northwest Territories to the Americans, the entire concept of a new British nation from sea to sea will be finished."

Macdonald's voice was rising, his face reddening. "And if the Americans acquire Russian America, then British Columbia is bound to be overrun by Americans searching for gold or furs or fish. We simply must do everything in our power to prevent the Americans from getting that Russian territory!"

"Of course you must."

Macdonald finished off his port again. The ambassador immediately refilled his glass.

"I had to undertake this mission in secrecy, Henry. I didn't want the press, and certainly not Seward, to know anything about it. If I'm successful, the Americans will know about it in due course — *after* we complete our deal with the Tsar."

"Is it so easy to keep your trip a secret?"

"My conference colleagues in London think I've just gone to France for a short vacation by myself."

The Earl snorted. "Surely they'll wonder why Agnes isn't with you?"

"Well, the obvious answer to that question is that my dear sweetheart and I are not yet married. The morals of our society may become permissive over the next hundred or hundred and fifty years. But today in this twenty-ninth year of the reign of Queen Victoria the moral standards are akin to unlockable chastity belts."

"Unlockable except by the vows of marriage."

"So the record will show, Henry, that I'm on a solitary vacation in

Europe. Only Agnes, her brother and her mother, as well as Carnarvon, and a handful of people on the Foreign Secretary's staff know that I am in France."

The ambassador nodded. "So much for the record, John A. I suggest we retire to the upper reaches of this draughty edifice to get some much-needed sleep. You'll need to be fresh for your meeting with the great Prince Gorchakov tomorrow."

"And his vodka."

12

December 30, 1866
Paris

THE APPOINTMENT WITH PRINCE GORCHAKOV WAS SET FOR TEN o'clock. It would be bad form to keep the third most powerful man in the Tsar's empire waiting. The carriage ride to the Russian embassy would take about ten minutes, and to provide a comfortable margin, Earl Cowley and Macdonald left the British embassy at twenty-five minutes past nine.

No sooner were they out of the embassy gates than the Earl opened the soft brown leather valise next to him on the seat. "Here we are, John A. A loaf of fresh, white bread for each of us. Here's yours. Now eat up, man. Get as much into your stomach as you possibly can. Gorge yourself."

"Is this really necessary?" Macdonald plaintively asked. He had already had a large English breakfast.

"Absolutely necessary. As I explained to you, the bread will absorb the vodka, soak it up, then let it out slowly, very slowly, into your system. That way you don't get drunk and fall over in a heap while your Russian adversary, who has just negotiated you out of your last quid, is still standing. If you drink the vodka on an empty stomach — even if you've had a big breakfast — the vodka will go straight into your bloodstream in no time. So eat up, my dear chap."

John A. Macdonald did as he was told while Earl Cowley provided a running commentary on nearly every building, statue, monument, park, and edifice they passed en route to the Russian embassy. He was particularly expansive when it came to the description of various war memorials.

"It seems to me that in Europe there's nearly always some kind of war going on or about to go on or just finished," John A. observed as he viewed yet another edifice glorifying one of Napoleon's victories.

"True. With the diversity of races, languages, religions, and the many monarchical and military powers that exist on this civilized continent, it's difficult to conceive of the situation ever being anything but bellicose in some region or another. Ah, we're almost at the embassy."

What Macdonald saw ahead was a massive structure, its background of green setting off handsome white columns and golden stucco molding. Countless sculptured figures stood below the flat roofline.

"Magnificent, isn't it?" the Earl said as they approached the entrance gate. "Wait until you get inside. It's the baroque masterpiece of an architect by the name of Coutant sometime at the end of the 1750s."

John A. Macdonald was indeed awed by the splendour of the embassy. Coming as he did from a new frontier country, he could not have imagined that such architectural opulence existed.

Once inside, they were saluted and guided down long arched corridors, up two flights of marble stairs, along more corridors, and finally arrived at the upper-plated doors to the conference chamber. An attendant took their coats.

They made a strange, formidable-looking pair as they waited to be admitted. The Right Honourable Henry Wellesley, Earl Cowley, was resplendent in his ambassador's uniform. He wore a black jacket, with a high collar and epaulettes; the gold braid decorating it was enhanced with royal reds and blues. A crimson velvet sash crossed from the right shoulder to the opposite hip; half a dozen medals on multicoloured ribbons were pinned on the left side of the jacket, over the ambassador's chest. Below them sat the star of his rank with which his Queen had vested him. His black trousers bore wide gold stripes down the outside seams. Those stripes disappeared into highly polished half-Wellington boots.

A short ceremonial sword in an elaborately engraved and embossed scabbard hung from a broad gold-decorated belt that encircled Earl Cowley's considerable girth. On his head sat, foursquare, a large black cocked hat covered with more gold braid, its forward point jutting straight out from his wigless wide forehead. Across the hat's crest several white feather plumes danced in total lack of unison. That ornithological decoration announced Earl Cowley's ambassadorial rank to all and sundry who saw it.

By contrast, Minister John Alexander Macdonald was modestly garbed in his favourite black cutaway, tailed dress coat, pearl grey vest, and four-in-hand black tie on a white winged-collar shirt. Tight-fitting grey trousers and a fashionably tall, grey stovepipe hat completed his formal attire.

As they stood on the deep Persian rug outside the conference room, Macdonald was once again in awe of the magnificence of what surrounded him, this time the powerful portraits of some of the ancestors of His Imperial Majesty all looking down imperiously from their silk-covered wall perches. Macdonald couldn't identify any of them.

Earl Cowley nudged him and nodded toward the enormous painting hanging to the right of the conference room door. "That's Peter the Great, the Tsar who founded St. Petersburg."

Macdonald handed the attendant his stovepipe hat, but the Earl insisted on carrying his cocked hat with him. Crooked in his left elbow it was, after all, an important part of his British uniform.

The two visitors were ready.

The attendant hauled on the pull cord beside the doors. In a few long moments the handle turned and the left-hand door swung open.

"Good morning, gentlemen. I am Vladimir, the Principal Secretary to His Royal Highness Prince Gorchakov." The words were in French, the first translation test for the ambassador, who momentarily forgot that it was his function, but then repeated the words in English for Macdonald.

The bespectacled secretary was a slender man of mid height with a long neck and narrow, sallow face who looked to Macdonald rather like a blue heron. After the ambassador announced his name and that of John A., Vladimir motioned them to follow him as he moved to shut the door.

"Marvellous," John A. muttered as the secretary addressed the solitary figure sitting midway down the conference table: "Sir, I present His Excellency the Earl Cowley, ambassador of Her Imperial Majesty, Queen Victoria, and . . ." He turned and whispered anxiously to Cowley, who said "Macdonald." ". . . Yes, and Minister Macdonald from the British colony of Canada in North America."

Unnoticed, the secretary then padded out of the room through a small servants' doorway.

There was no need for Earl Cowley to translate that which Macdonald could not have avoided understanding. However, from that moment on, the ambassador was the instantaneous, unfailing translator.

Prince Gorchakov stood, then waddled toward them, his large stomach rolling with each slow step, a gold-toothed smile on his pink flat face, pince-nez firmly in place on his large nose.

"Welcome, Your Excellencies, welcome." He shook the hand of each man in a short pumping motion. "Come, we will sit at the conference table . . . I will sit in the middle in my customary chair. If you will sit opposite, please."

His quick eyes assessing the room, Macdonald took in the parquet floor of many woods, the wide, tall windows, the sleet falling beyond them like a flowing sheet in a wind. The chamber was marked with the heavy touches of Rastrelli gold, brilliantly contrasted with walls of soft blue enhanced by crimson, lapis, and alabaster. Fires in two enormous high-mantled fireplaces, with dense yellow-green-red-orange flames leaping from the stacked logs, warmed the large room. The elaborate gilt ceiling covered with paintings of human figures loomed perhaps twenty feet above. The superbly carved oak table, its unblemished surface polished to perfection, had been cut from a single massive tree trunk, long enough to comfortably receive eight or ten chairs on each side. And the breathtaking chair at the table's far end! Was it there for the Tsar, should ever he visit? It was elevated on a low dais, the seat in royal purple velvet with the twin-headed Imperial eagle embossed on it in golden thread, the back cushion a mirror reflection of the seat. Above it was the most elaborate wood carving Macdonald had ever seen. Again it was a representation of the Russian royal symbols, the double-headed eagle, the globe, and other accoutrements. The top of this spectacular throne was capped by a graciously proportioned crown, a wooden replica of that placed upon the head of each Tsar or Tsarina at the occasion of coronation.

John A. Macdonald was in the presence of a force he had never before encountered. He was uplifted and at the same time intimidated by the raw statements of absolute power that enveloped him in this most regal bastion of all Russian bastions outside the Russias.

"Please, Minister Macdonald, please be seated so that we might drink a toast." Gorchakov waved to the chair directly opposite the one into which he carefully lowered his overtaxed self.

The last item that took John A.'s attention was actually the first thing he saw when he entered the chamber. It was a bottle (probably at least forty ounces, as his experienced eyes measured it) of clear liquid that could have been water from a crystal spring. Vodka. Next to the bottle stood three long-stemmed, cut-crystal goblets ready to receive the mind-altering liquor upon which Russian society relied from the Tsar's court downward.

Thanks to Earl Cowley, John A. Macdonald was not only ready for, but was also prepared for (there *was* a difference between being ready and being prepared, so far as the Canadian was concerned) the vodka manoeuvre of the senior Prince. John A. silently praised God and Henry for the loaf of bread he had consumed in the carriage.

"So, Your Excellency, you are to function, with great skill of course, as the interpreter this morning?"

"That is correct, Your Highness."

"And also to share in the vodka, in the toasts." Gorchakov smiled knowingly.

Cowley returned the smile. "I might offend if I failed so to do, sir."

"Ah, the Earl Cowley fail? Never." Gorchakov looked at Macdonald. The Canadian was outwardly calm as a good barrister is trained to appear while inwardly wracked by nervousness and the stress of the moment. "So, Minister Macdonald, you have come a long way, many thousands of miles, all the way from America, to honour us with your presence and, as I am informed by the British government through its distinguished ambassador to France," — he nodded graciously toward the Earl — "to bring with you a most important matter for discussion."

Gorchakov, with decades of experience holding conversations through interpreters, had paused several times during the speaking of those many words to allow Earl Cowley to translate. That would be the pattern as Macdonald quickly discovered.

"I have indeed come a long way, Your Highness," Macdonald began. "But I must confess, when I sailed for London in November I had no hint, no expectation, that I would have the privilege of being in this beautiful city of Paris, let alone of being in your august and much-famed presence, Prince Gorchakov."

The delighted Prince pounded the table after hearing Cowley's translation. "A good speech. A very good speech! Now a toast to welcome Minister Macdonald."

Gorchakov picked up the bottle, pulled out the cork, and, with aiming skill perfected over a long lifetime, he filled the three goblets — Macdonald guessed that each held two, perhaps three ounces — to the brim.

The Prince stood to hand to his guests across the wide table the first of his ceremonial offerings.

He remained standing, glass in his right hand, ready to propose the initial toast. Macdonald and Cowley got up, their glasses in hand, as they looked down from their enviable heights on the squat nobleman whose gimlet eyes were peering over his pince-nez directly into the unblinking, unwavering orbs of the Canadian.

"A toast to the new nation you are attempting to create in the vastness of North America!" Gorchakov raised his glass in a short pumping-motion salute, then threw back his head as he poured the vodka, all of it, down his throat in a single gulp.

His guests followed his example exactly, even to the point of wiping their mouths with the left sleeves of their jackets.

Macdonald could feel the powerful alcohol coursing down his gullet toward the secret sponge of bread. The vodka did have a taste to it after all. Rather tart and biting but by no means unpleasant. Powerful? Probably — no, undoubtedly — devastating if it went into an empty, unsuspecting, inexperienced, unprotected stomach.

Uncoached but intuitively Macdonald reached for the vodka bottle. He filled the glasses in the still-steady hands of the Prince and Cowley and his own.

Staring into Gorchakov's eyes, he solemnly intoned: "A toast to His Imperial Majesty Alexander the Second, Tsar of all the Russias, and to Her Imperial Majesty Queen Victoria."

Emulating the Russian's salute, he tossed back the vodka in a single swallow, as did the others.

Gorchakov then sat down, motioning to his visitors to do the same.

As if by some unseen signal, Vladimir slipped into the room to take a seat two removed from Gorchakov's right, where the secretary had earlier placed his quill pen, ink, and linen paper.

"I have taken the liberty of arranging for Vladimir to take notes on our deliberations so that the record will be certain. If that is acceptable? Good. Now, Minister Macdonald, you wish to discuss Russian America."

"Yes, Your Highness, it is my mandate to discuss with you in the broadest terms what His Imperial Majesty the Tsar intends to do with his territorial holdings, his remote holdings in North America which are costly to maintain and to govern. If there is any possibility that His Imperial Majesty might be giving thought to ceding those lands, then I am here to advise you, Your Excellency, that the governments of Her Majesty's colonies in America would welcome the opportunity to negotiate for us the acquisition of Russian America."

Gorchakov summed it up: "You want to buy Russian America."

"If it is for sale."

"It is not up to me — I am but a servant of His Imperial Majesty — to say whether it might be available. That question can be answered only by my master." Gorchakov paused, studying Macdonald, looking for some evidence of the effect of the vodka on the Canadian. "But if I was so bold as to put the question to him, he would be disappointed if the question was not clothed."

"Clothed?"

"Yes, of course. Such a question must not be naked. It must be clothed in the terms and conditions you might offer His Imperial Majesty as he considers whether or not Russian America might leave his domain. Yes?"

Macdonald nodded his understanding. "Indeed, Your Highness, if I might be so privileged as to be the dresser of the naked question?"

"But of course." Gorchakov smiled. "And perhaps I can be your assistant."

The British ambassador quickly added in both languages, "You will need a tailor in this process, gentlemen. I have had much experience in stitching things together."

"Good. Good." Still smiling, Gorchakov slapped the table. "Now, let us begin with the underwear, that body-warming garment so necessary in the frosty, ice-filled, snowy climate of Mother Russia."

"So, what is the underwear?" John A. asked, knowing full well what the answer would be. He could feel the tongue-loosening, protocol-softening vodka beginning to reach his brain. Thank God for the Earl's bread!

"It is money, my dear Minister. You must first clothe the naked question with money. That underwear of money must stretch from ankle to neck, not from knees to chest, if you follow my dresser's perception?"

Macdonald rose. He picked up his glass, newly recharged by Gorchakov. "A toast." The Prince and the ambassador struggled to their feet, vodka in hand. Vladimir remained seated, without vodka. "A toast to the spirit of Russian America. May it be clothed always by the strength of a powerful majestic sovereign."

To which Gorchakov instantly added, "A sovereign who might well wear the garments and trappings of an elected head of state and government . . . I would wish to include our dear friends and allies, the Americans. To the spirit of Russian America!"

Down went the vodka.

Macdonald, sitting at the same time as the Foreign Minister and the ambassador, put his empty glass down next to the bottle, in which the quantity of liquid was fast diminishing. It was the frugal, penny-pinching Scot who spoke. He was authorized to offer much more but his opening bid would be low: "The underwear, the money, is seven million dollars in United States currency terms of gold."

Gorchakov took his nose between his index fingers, elbows on the highly polished conference table, his eyes shut momentarily behind the pince-nez as he absorbed the words. Then his eyes flew open as his hands dropped. "United States dollars?" He was astonished. "You are British! The money you are offering —"

"The clothes, Your Highness."

"Yes, yes. The clothes are in American dollars, not in British pounds, not in the currency of the most powerful economic and naval realm in the world! Why not?"

Macdonald smiled lightly as out of the corner of his eye he could see the Earl Cowley bursting to respond to that question as he translated it.

"The reasoning is simple," John A. explained. "If indeed there are negotiations with the Americans —"

"There are none."

"You would be dealing with them in terms of their own currency in gold. So rather than offer you pounds sterling and have to go through the difficult variables of a currency conversion I thought it would be much easier if . . ."

Gorchakov waved a hand. "Yes, I understand. So that's the money. It will be offered and paid by your government, Your Excellency, and not by this colonial power, Canada, correct?"

"Correct, Your Highness," Cowley answered. "It has been so authorized by Her Majesty's government."

"Which is undoubtedly prepared to go higher?"

"I have no knowledge of that, sir."

"But Minister Macdonald undoubtedly does, eh, Minister?"

John A. thought for a moment. "The answer to that question can be given only if there is some positive indication that the underwear is almost big enough, subject to some slight adjustment here and there — perhaps at the buttocks."

"Or the crotch!" Gorchakov shouted with laughter. "Assume that the underwear is almost a perfect fit . . . it would have to be His Imperial Majesty who would give that answer."

"But would you be prepared to present that sum for his serious consideration?"

The wily old Foreign Minister slumped back in his chair, the crystal-clear vodka slowing his quick mind. "I might, well . . . yes, I might well be prepared. However, you have offered only the underwear."

"What else can I offer?" The Canadian sounded puzzled.

"*You* cannot offer anything more, I'm sure. But His Excellency here can offer a splendid suit, vest, cravat, silk shirt, and a diamond stickpin to adorn the cravat — the clothes to cover the underwear."

Cowley looked shocked. "I do not follow you, Prince Gorchakov. What do you mean?"

The Russian snorted. "My dear Ambassador. If you do not know what I mean then I have seriously overestimated your prowess as a diplomat."

The Earl Cowley was not going to allow any slur on his capability as one of Her Imperial Majesty's most competent ambassadors. "The Treaty of Paris," he said in a flat voice.

Feigning ignorance, Macdonald urgently asked, "What does the Treaty of Paris have to do with this?"

To which the ambassador's reply was: "You'll find out soon enough."

"Exactly, Your Excellency," Gorchakov said. "In any negotiations with Her Britannic Majesty the matter of money would indeed be important, but the Treaty of Paris would be much more important."

Cowley was most anxious. "I assure you, Your Highness, I have no authority whatever to offer any negotiations on the Treaty of Paris."

Gorchakov's face showed his skepticism. "Come now, Ambassador. The people in your Foreign Office are probably the best in the world at predicting and assessing the issues that one of their most skilled diplomats would have to confront — or be confronted by — in a negotiation with a recently defeated enemy whose neck has been stepped upon by the full, unforgiving weight of your British Imperial lion."

"With the greatest of respect, I have had no instructions concerning the Treaty of Paris."

After he had listened to the translation Macdonald added, "Nor have I, Your Highness."

"Very well." Gorchakov accepted what he heard. "I will tell you this: there can be no possibility of ceding Russian America to Great Britain for and on behalf of your colony of Canada without the cancellation of some of the provisions of the Treaty of Paris."

"Not all of its provisions?"

"No, Your Excellency, just Articles Eleven, Thirteen and Thirty-three. To the Tsar those terms imposed by Britain are dishonourable and humiliating. It is His Majesty's principal diplomatic objective to free Russia from the shackles of those articles."

The ambassador was clearly uncomfortable under the force of Mikhail Gorchakov's vehemence. "If I may have a moment, Your Highness, I would like to explain to Minister Macdonald —"

"No. I will explain. That way I will be satisfied that he understands."

"As you wish."

"Good . . ." Gorchakov led Macdonald through his version of the Crimean War, in which in 1854 Great Britain and France had invaded the Crimea in order to gain control of the Strait of Bosporus between the Black Sea and the Sea of Marmara, and the Dardanelles, which connects the Marmara and Aegean seas. The objective was to cut off the Russian navy's access to the Mediterranean Sea and therefore to the oceans of the world.

"Finally a peace treaty was negotiated in Paris and signed on the 30th of March, 1856. I remember the date and the event very well. I did not sign the document of defeat — yes, that's what it was, a document of awful defeat for Russia — but I was there.

"Article Eleven neutralized the Black Sea. This is *Russia's* sea and Great Britain forced us to agree to a neutralization! And in perpetuity. No Russian warships or any others on its waters."

Gorchakov reached for the vodka bottle and poured a full glass for himself. Nothing, not even a gesture toward his guests. The deep resentment that he felt had surfaced during his account, causing him to forget his usual courtesies.

"Article Thirteen went even further. It decreed that the maintenance or establishment of military-maritime arsenals on the Black Sea coast was unnecessary and purposeless, and accordingly the Tsar was forced, Minister Macdonald, *forced* to agree to those shameful terms concerning Russia's sovereign coast on its own Black Sea."

As Gorchakov tossed back his vodka, John A., uninvited, reached for the bottle to pour the dregs for Cowley and himself.

"Then there is Article Thirty-three, the ultimate humiliation. Remember, Minister, that Russia is a Great Power, and that article prohibits us from fortifying our Aland Islands, which lie at the entrance of the Gulf of Bothnia. These strategically important islands command the great Swedish port and capital city of Stockholm. And we are now prohibited from exercising our sovereign rights over our own lands."

He turned to the scribbling secretary, saying curtly, "Vladimir. Vodka." Whereupon Vladimir removed the empty bottle and scuttled to a nearby chest to produce a full one which he expertly opened and quickly placed on the table in front of the Prince, who poured for all.

John A. and Cowley downed their stimulating potions. Each of them was blessed with a high tolerance for alcohol in most of all its invented forms.

Prince Mikhail Gorchakov's tone of excited belligerence began to subside. "Minister Macdonald, my apologies . . . and to you, Ambassador. The Treaty of Paris and its denigrating terms wound my monarch's heart. So if you are to clothe the naked question of whether the Tsar would cede Russian America to a British colony you would perforce use a cloth woven of more than gold, enhanced as it must be by the undoing of the shackles of the Treaty of Paris. Am I clear on that point?"

Cowley asked: "If it is accepted that Great Britain is but one of the several signatories to the treaty, would you be prepared to accept a 'best efforts' pledge from Her Majesty's government?"

The Foreign Minister's reply was vehement. "No, goddam it! Your Excellency. I want an unconditional pledge from Great Britain. Do you hear me? And I want it before there is any discussion about money! Never mind France. The French will follow whatever the British do."

"What about any offer the Americans make?"

The Foreign Minister grunted happily. "With our American friends, who gave succour to His Imperial Majesty's fleet during their Civil War — and with whose Congress and President we exchange regular declarations of mutual national affection — we do not have expensive treaty baggage to get rid of."

Gorchakov's slitted eyes focused with some difficulty on Macdonald. "However, as I said, the Tsar has not as yet received any offers from the United States." He was not about to tell his guests that de Stoeckl had been authorized to draw the American Secretary of State into negotiating for the Russian territories.

It was the careful manner in which Gorchakov phrased his statement that caused Macdonald, the experienced courtroom cross-examiner, to ask, "While you have had no such proposals from the Americans, has His Imperial Majesty authorized such negotiations to take place should they express an interest in acquiring Russian America?"

The Russian foreign minister was an admirer of those who could frame a question that forced him to tell the truth, lie, or obfuscate.

"In my presence my royal master recently indicated that should the Americans express such an interest he would be open to receiving such an expression."

"And open to considering it — open to negotiating?"

"My dear Minister, if the Tsar is prepared to let his foreign minister receive representations from Great Britain, surely it follows he would extend a similar courtesy to a most amicable ally — would you not agree?"

Macdonald pressed on: "I agree, Your Highness. Does it also follow . . . let me put it this way. I'm sure that you, sir, with your vast knowledge of what is being said and done in foreign capitals, are aware of Secretary Seward's belief in Manifest Destiny. He wants his country to possess all of the North American continent north of Mexico, and any other lands — islands included — that he can get his hands on. You're aware of all that?"

Mikhail Gorchakov would not admit otherwise. "Of course I am — just as I'm aware of your concept of Canadian confederation, which might well be dashed if Seward were to harvest Russian America. Which is why you're here drinking the Tsar's vodka." He laughed as he reached for the bottle. Again he filled all three glasses.

John A.'s tongue was loosening under the influence of the alcohol. "If there are negotiations with the Americans, I assume the Tsar's ambassador to Washington would be charged . . . would be responsible for those dealings?"

"Of course, of course. De Stoeckl is a highly trusted envoy, one of the very best. His Imperial Majesty has every confidence in his abilities, in his judgment — as do I. And the ambassador knows Seward and, for that matter, President Johnson as well as all the major figures in Washington."

Gorchakov turned his glass in his hands. "In fact, Minister Macdonald, should Her Britannic Majesty's government in London decide to authorize you to continue to make representations — those which we've just discussed — then I think it would be better for you to deal directly with His Imperial Majesty . . ."

"And with you?"

"Yes, with me."

Gorchakov looked at the Earl Cowley. "Do you think the Foreign Secretary or the Prime Minister would have any difficulty with the protocol of having Minister Macdonald deal directly with the Tsar . . . through me, of course?"

"I should think not, Your Highness, particularly since he would have at his elbow Her Majesty's ambassador to the Tsar's court at St. Petersburg, Sir Andrew Buchanan. He's very experienced, an excellent man."

"As is Her Majesty's ambassador to the Republic of France. A toast to you, Your Excellency and to you, Minister Macdonald."

"And to you, Prince Gorchakov," Earl Cowley responded as all three lifted their glasses. The vodka was down their throats in an instant.

"By the way," Gorchakov, said as he wiped his lips with the back of his hand, "de Stoeckl is here in Paris for a few days. He intends to retire here, you know. Vladimir, when will de Stoeckl be back in Washington?"

"He told me he expected to be there by the first week in February."

"There you are, gentlemen. And what about you, Minister? When do you leave Paris? There is so much to see and do in this magnificent city."

"I am booked on a mid-afternoon train to Calais, then by ferry to Dover. I must get back to London as quickly as possible."

"Pressing affairs of state, no doubt?" Gorchakov asked.

Cowley responded: "And of the heart. Minister Macdonald has just become engaged to marry one of London's most lovely ladies."

The Russian's dour face lit up in a broad smile. "Wonderful, wonderful. A toast to the bride-to-be!"

13

January through February 5, 1867
The North Atlantic

As always happened, or so it seemed to Edouard de Stoeckl — the Baron, as he was commonly referred to throughout Washington's diplomatic and political circles in which he moved with such distinguished ease — the rough voyage back to the thriving port of New York during the deadly weather months of January and early February was a form of pure marine torture. The ship that carried him and some one hundred other passengers from Le Havre thence to Liverpool and then across the Atlantic was a British flag vessel in which its owners prudently carried cargo as well as passengers. It had the most modern coal-fired steam engines which, when augmented by the looming array of square sails and jibs that were hoisted during clement weather, carried the cumbersome craft at a gratifying speed. But the ship had a never-ending, nauseating roll that tore at the Baron's innards and caused a devastating seasickness that lasted for the first half of the three-week-long voyage.

In the middle of the treacherous mid-winter North Atlantic, the ship, its mainsails furled, was ravaged by a massive storm with gale-force winds laden with driving snow.

As for the passengers and all manner of objects on the ship, they were thrown around like "corks in a bottle." Most people huddled in their bunks, hanging on for dear life, venturing to take steps not for food or drink but only for the release of body waste or the product of pervasive seasickness.

The Baron, being compelled to move from his bunk for both reasons, had safely reached his cabin's toilet. Having successfully performed all things that his body required of him, he was slowly making his way back to his place of rest, and only three or four steps away from it, when a mighty lurch of the vessel threw him to the cabin floor. His extended taut legs smashed against the side of his bunk.

The result was that the muscles in the Baron's right foot were badly torn — sprained, as the ship's doctor reported it. He was confined to his bunk even after the storm had abated, but some three days following his injury he was allowed to hobble about on crutches. He even made his way to the ship's dining room for his meals, albeit with some difficulty because of the vessel's incessant roll even in a relatively calm sea. By good fortune his cabin was on the same deck as the dining room, otherwise he would not have been able to participate in the conviviality at the young captain's table.

The Baron's seasickness had dissipated so that he was able to begin to enjoy the voyage and to take critical but appreciative note of the attractive things about the ship. Indeed, the most impressive attractive aspect was one of its passengers, whom de Stoeckl had seen when she had boarded at Liverpool. He had been much taken by her appearance; below a sweeping natural straw hat he saw mischievous blue eyes, nordic blonde hair, a smooth face — a pretty woman bordering on the beautiful. De Stoeckl was instantly sexually attracted to her. His interest was further heightened as he studied her body in its tight-fitting, clearly expensive woolen coat that revealed she was full bosomed.

He had been able to get a closer look at her on deck as the crew was casting off and the passengers were waving excitedly at loved ones and friends who had come to see them off. She was not waving to anyone, simply standing alone watching the scene of milling people shouting their last goodbyes across the widening stretch of water as the ship, its sails clutching at the sparse wind, moved out and away on the tide.

De Stoeckl had approached her from the side, and tipped his wide-brimmed black hat with a grey-gloved hand, his other holding his gold-lion-headed ebony walking stick. It matched the colour of his cutaway morning suit and complemented the grey vest that was meant to conceal somewhat the bulk of his broad chest. It was also intended to diminish a stomach that, after twenty-nine years of diplomatic service, had advanced to the outer ramparts of the chest above it and then perhaps an inch or two beyond. Edouard de Stoeckl, for all his girth, felt confident that he presented a sufficiently fine and elegantly tailored figure that he might arouse sexual interest in the opposite sex.

"Pardon, madame. I gather that like me you have no one standing on the dock waving goodbye. No loved one, no relatives, no children, no husband, no lover?"

She had turned as he spoke, her eyes lifting up to look into his heavily moustached face and startlingly dark eyes. From the expression on her face it was clear to him that she liked what she saw.

"No one, sir." She had smiled, her unflawed teeth gleaming through pink lips. She tilted her slender, high-cheekboned face toward him. "I travel alone, sir."

Then she had looked back toward the still-waving figures on the dock rapidly receding in the distance as the propeller of the long, narrow ship began to bite into the flat water of Liverpool harbour, jet-black thick smoke billowing out of the smokestack and trailing behind it through darkstained sails like a flowing ribbon against the winter's lowering afternoon sun.

"Allow me to introduce myself, madame. I am Edouard de Stoeckl, ambassador to the United States of America for His Imperial Majesty Alexander, Tsar of All the Russias."

"The Russian ambassador? Oh, I am impressed." Her eyes were wide, looking up at him this time with greater interest. He was waiting for her to offer her name but she only said, "Your accent. You're the Russian ambassador, but your accent sounds, well, it sounds German to me."

It was de Stoeckl's turn to smile. "Yes, dear lady, you're right, or almost right. My native tongue is Austrian. I am Viennese born and educated, but I have been in the service of Tsar Alexander and his late father for the past twenty years. So I speak both Russian and English with an Austrian accent, I'm afraid."

By remarkably convenient coincidence the cabin of the lady, the Honourable Pamela Collins, was next to the Baron's. The door between them was, of course, firmly locked. This wealthy lady, he had learned, was from Windsor, west of London. In her mid-thirties, recently separated, she was off to America to visit her sister and brother-in-law, a banker in Boston.

At first Pamela did not take her meal in the dining room, so it was not until de Stoeckl emerged from his cabin on crutches and took his usual place at the captain's table at dinner that he had another opportunity to talk to Pamela Collins, who finally took her place beside him. It was quickly apparent to the captain and his other guests that the two were quite taken with each other. Their conversation, which virtually excluded the rest at the glittering table, was animated and became more intimate as they explored each other's background, likes and dislikes, interests and activities. The Baron couldn't keep his eyes off her turned-up nose, her pouty, inviting lips, and that deep alabaster decolletage into which he was totally unable to resist the temptation to gaze.

The fetching Pamela was pleased as she sat close to this powerfully male, ruggedly handsome, cultured, elegant man. His knee discreetly touching hers from time to time thrilled her, as did the gentle touch of his fingers on the back of her hand as he emphasized a remark or made a light-hearted, laughing rejoinder.

Between the main course and the dessert, the Baron made the appropriate polite excuses to leave the table, including a respectful nod to the captain. Pamela was puzzled that de Stoeckl did not leave the dining cabin as she had expected. Instead he sought out the sommelier who was conducting his duties at the aft end of the cabin. After speaking with that worthy in confidential tones, de Stoeckl returned to Pamela's side. He gracefully lowered his well-proportioned, as she saw it, figure into his chair while unavoidably, yet ever so lightly, touching her arms and legs with his in the process.

"Now, my dear lady," he said, lifting his crystal wine glass filled with newly poured red Burgundy, "as I was telling you, I was deeply honoured by His Imperial Majesty Tsar Alexander just before I left St. Petersburg."

"What happened?" her blue eyes were wide in expectation.

"His Majesty made me a Knight Grand Cross of the Order of Romanov."

"That sounds most impressive, Baron. Does it mean you have been given some sort of decoration to wear?"

He smiled, turning his head modestly. "Well, it's certainly important, a high distinction in Russia. I did receive a decoration — a diamond and ruby-studded star, a breastplate of gold. The twin-headed Russian eagle on it is made of the stones. It's spectacular."

"Oh, I'd love to see it."

"I think that can be arranged." De Stoeckl was able to convey his enthusiasm in his smile. He looked intently into her eyes, then let his gaze briefly lower to her large, but not too large, undoubtedly firm white breasts.

She looked quizzically at the Baron. "I suppose you're going to tell me you have it in your cabin, and you have a chilled bottle of white wine waiting to be uncorked. I'll be disappointed if the answer isn't yes. If it's yes, then we'll go as soon as the captain leaves the table."

He shook his head in amazement. "You saw me speaking with the wine steward. You are very observant, dear lady. The bottle will be there and it will be uncorked." De Stoeckl laughed again. "You have to be one of the swiftest ladies I've come across."

She retorted softly, "Instead of 'across' I'd be much happier if you'd tried 'up against.'"

It was his smile that really turned on her desire as he said suggestively, "Before, during, or after I show you the decoration?"

Pamela slowly swung her knee toward him and, deliberately taking her time, she rubbed the calf of her leg against his. De Stoeckl's face revealed nothing of the lust coursing through his body while Pamela's leg stimulated his maleness.

He arched his left eyebrow, saying softly, "I hope this dinner is finished soon because I'm ready."

There was no hidden meaning in her reply. "If you're not, I'll soon make sure you are."

The agony of polite waiting went on for an excruciating fifteen minutes at least.

It was just long enough for de Stoeckl to boastfully confide to Pamela that he was returning to Washington after conferring with his good friend the Tsar. Alexander had personally assigned him a most important mission.

Pamela coaxed him to tell her what it was, using her considerable touching talents to induce him to say, "The Tsar has authorized me to open negotiations with the Americans for them buy Russian America. That's a most significant responsibility for me, for anyone."

"You must be very proud to be the Ambassador and have such an important assignment."

De Stoeckl agreed. "It is with great pride that I carry out such a task. But it is a secret, Pamela, you understand."

"Of course. Of course I understand. But the British — wouldn't my country want to buy Russian America?"

De Stoeckl was surprised. "You sound as though you know something about Russian America. Where it is, for example."

She laughed. "You think I'm just another pretty face with little education and fewer brains, don't you, Edouard?"

"I don't know what to think. After all, I don't really know anything about you."

"I've already told you about myself. It's more interesting to hear you talk. Tell me more about your decoration from the Tsar, which I'll see when we get to your cabin."

It was on the tip of her tongue to tell him why she knew about Russian America, but she decided not to reveal that her elder brother, Sir Thomas, was governor of the Colony of British Columbia.

In that post for some three years, Thomas wrote to Pamela, his uncle, and other senior members of the family every six months, telling them what had been happening to him and the colony, once even enclosing a copy of a Pacific-coast map his staff had made for him. That map had included Russian America immediately to the north of Sir Thomas's colony. In this way she knew about Russian America and Sir Thomas's concern about its impact on the future of British Columbia. Perhaps, Pamela thought, I'll tell the charming Russian ambassador the truth later.

At that moment the captain rose, signalling the end of the dinner. Pamela departed the dining room immediately, with Edouard hobbling after her on his crutches. As de Stoeckl shut the door of his cabin behind him, he had great difficulty in overcoming the urge to take Pamela's shoulders, turn her around, and take her in his arms.

But he decided it was better to do things slowly. Savour the situation.

"So here we are in the ambassador's magnificent cabin," he announced, "right beside yours."

As he brushed by her toward the wine bucket he sensed the physical attraction, a pull as strong as a magnet for iron. Again the compelling urge to take her in his arms was almost too much. He moved quickly to the bucket, saying, "First the wine and then the decoration."

"One of the things I like about you, Edouard, is that you have your priorities right. This cabin is really very nice, much nicer than mine. The bed is very large, very inviting."

He uncorked the bottle, poured the wine, and handed her a glass, saying, "It is big, isn't it? And I can tell you it's comfortable, most comfortable."

She clinked her glass against his. "I'll drink to that." At the same time she slipped out of her high-heeled shoes. Facing him, her body almost touching his, she said, "There, you see, I'm really a lot shorter than you are. Only five four. The male should always be taller, don't you think?"

"It depends on what you have in mind."

"Your decoration from the Tsar. That's what I have in mind. Isn't that the reason you brought me here?" She gave him a teasing smile.

"Of course. The only reason — in addition to wanting to have you all to myself. After all, you're a most attractive lady."

"And you're a most attractive gentleman. The decoration, Edouard."

"Yes, yes, of course. Here we are." He opened the night table drawer and took out a black leather pouch. Unlacing its end, he reached in, and delicately withdrew the glittering breastplate, putting it gently in her cupped hands.

She gasped. "My God, how beautiful! It must be worth a fortune."

"It is worth a fortune," de Stoeckl agreed, then explained the symbolism of the design on the decoration.

"Fascinating, Edouard. Absolutely fascinating." As she handed the gleaming breastplate back, Pamela moved close to him, her full bodice grazing his vest. "We've seen the decoration. Can we get to the important part now?"

The Honourable Pamela Collins lifted her face to his as his arms went around her, his huge hands against the bare skin of her back. The meeting of their mouths was light, probing, for the first moment, then urgent as their tongues found each other.

✦

"WHAT TIME IS IT, DARLING?" CAME PAMELA'S MUTED VOICE. HER head, on the pillow, was touching his shoulder. The length of her bare, warm body was pressed softly against his, as it had been during much of the eight days and nights of their protracted lovemaking. In their near-unending couplings something had been different for both of them. There was no hint of it all being too much, no glimmer of boredom.

But now their lovemaking was almost at an end, at least for the moment. The ship was about to dock in New York in the morning, Tuesday, the fifth day of February, 1867.

"It's six-thirty-five." Edouard grunted as he rolled over to face her in the darkness. Her hand started to move across his chest, then lower. Her skittish fingertips and nails touched lightly, persistently over him.

"Sweetheart, this will be the fourth time tonight. I don't think I can do it. Well, perhaps once more. What time are we docking?

Her voice came from the middle of his heaving chest. "At noon. Don't worry, darling. We have plenty of time to finish packing, if that's what's on your mind."

"It's the last thing, my love."

14

Saturday, January 26, 1867
London

"GENTLEMEN, TIME IS RUNNING SHORT. VERY SHORT." Carnarvon's aristocratic English voice had a ring of urgency in it. "Here we are on the 26th of January still grappling with the first draft of your British North America bill and Parliament is to meet next Friday. We have less than a week to get this done and there's so much to do."

The Earl's face, nearly grey, showed the gouty pain he had been enduring for days now. He sat in front of the tall, mantled, marble fireplace in the centre of the narrow yet cavernous drawing room of his Grosvenor Street home. His aching left leg was elevated on a footstool to prevent the blood settling in the inflamed veins in the ankle. Using his elbows on the arms of his high-backed chair, carved at the top with the family coat of arms, Carnarvon shifted his slender body, reaching for an unachievable position of more comfort.

Carnarvon looked at the frock-coated men gathered in the room sitting on whatever stool or chair they could find, looking like a grounded flock of white-headed blackbirds sitting on their tailfeathers. All the Canadians and the Maritimers were there, with Macdonald and his Quebec lieutenant Cartier front and centre.

As well, and even though it was a Saturday when every parliamentarian or senior civil servant in that island of world economic and naval power should have been in the bosom of his Victorian family, there sat at a table on Carnarvon's right two of the most estimable of the Crown's professionals along with the member of Parliament who was the Earl's spokesman in the House of Commons.

The Colonial Secretary's Parliamentary Under-Secretary, C.B.

Adderley, his balding head bent down, peered at the pages of the first draft on the table before him. Next to Adderley, but at a respectful distance, was Carnarvon's principal adviser, the Colonial Office's Permanent Under-Secretary, Sir Frederic Rogers, his pink, white-moustached face grim as he listened to his political master.

Also present was the horse-faced legal heavyweight, the scholarly solicitor who had finally been able to cobble together a draft bill shaped from the mass of the London Resolutions and the background decisions that had been recorded by Hewitt Bernard at the Charlottetown and Quebec conferences. This was a man most of the British North American delegates had not laid eyes on before but upon whose skills of legal interpretation and literary expertise all of their wordy efforts now depended: F.S. Reilly.

"So, gentlemen, we really must get on with this. Mr. Reilly's first draft was delivered to each of you two days ago . . ."

"Yes, sir," Macdonald said, responding as the primary spokesman for the colonials. "All of us have had time to examine Mr. Reilly's handiwork and we compliment and congratulate him on the high quality of his craftsmanship. A first-rate piece of work, Mr. Reilly."

Someone at the rear of the room was moved to clap, whereupon all joined in, including the smiling Carnarvon. Reilly, obviously embarrassed, stood up partway, gave a stiff bow of acknowledgement, then quickly sat, eyes downturned toward the comfort of his document.

Macdonald went on. "We are particularly pleased, Mr. Chairman, by the way Mr. Reilly has reworked the residual powers clause. As you well know, we have been concerned . . . we've wanted to ensure that the powers of the central government are strengthened against possible encroachments by local administrators, the provinces that is."

John A. looked toward Reilly. "The first draft has achieved that goal admirably. Logically the residual clause is now at the head of the section that defines the paramount powers of the federal Parliament. Then comes a list of the specific enumerated powers for the federal and provincial governments, leaving the residual powers where they should be, in federal hands. This section — what is it, 90 or 91? — this clause is the cornerstone of the bill. On its success or failure our confederation will stand or fall in the next hundred or even two hundred years. Well done, Mr. Reilly."

The document's draftsman nodded his head once to acknowledge Macdonald's compliment.

The Canadian went on. "There is, however, Mr. Chairman, a major problem, yes, a serious difficulty, with Mr. Reilly's draft."

Carnarvon looked shocked. "A major difficulty? What is it?"

Galt gave the answer. Better he be truculent if need be than John A., the ultimate conciliator. "It's the legislative council section. We've started to use the name that the Americans call their upper body — the Senate."

"Yes, well?"

"In the resolutions we submitted to you at Christmas we proposed a Senate with fixed numbers and appointed for life. I tell you, Mr. Chairman, we worked long and hard, argued for hours about this. We finally reached a consensus. And what happens? The Reilly draft ignores our Senate proposal completely."

The Permanent Under-Secretary drew himself up to his full sitting height. His aquiline face with its narrow pursed lips, slitted eyes through thick glasses, looked as though his long, sharp nose had just encountered a most foul odour. Sir Frederic Rogers gave Carnarvon an if-I-may glance. "With your leave, Mr. Chairman, I should like to respond to the Honourable Minister from Canada."

"By all means, Sir Frederic."

"In the long period of development of the parliamentary system of governance during the evolution of Great Britain as it is today, we have learned much through experience. Minister Macdonald, you and your colleagues are making a valiant, yes, valiant attempt to create a system of government that adapts the British parliamentary form to the unique factors at play in North America.

"If I may be permitted to say so without sounding superior, our system is much better than what you propose."

Rogers waited for a hostile reaction. Outwardly there was none, inwardly the colonials were at the threshold of seething.

"You should know, Mr. Chairman and gentlemen, that the Foreign Office, and indeed all the Colonial Office officials who have worked with me so positively in advancing your quest for confederation, all of us have reacted negatively to your proposition on the Senate. We do not believe it appropriate in this enlightened age to agree to the creation of a body of appointed, paid, lifetime oligarchs. We strongly object to a Senate with its numbers fixed and inflexible. Why? Because it could lead to a highly possible deadlock with the House of Commons."

He paused again, eyes nervously moving from hostile face to hostile face.

"There must be some flexibility. In our parliamentary structure when there is deadlock between the Commons and the Lords the monarch may appoint new members to the House of Lords — on the recommendation of the Prime Minister, of course. And he will see to it that only sympathetic persons — to his cause, that is — are appointed."

Macdonald spoke up. "So that is why this draft proposes that after an initial number of years after the appointment of the members of the first Senate, then one-eighth of those members will retire by rotation every year. Right?"

His question was rhetorical. John A. went on: "But that surely doesn't overcome the deadlock problem, does it? Certainly not the way Her Majesty can do it here — appoint new members."

Rogers backed off. "True. But from our point of view the rotational system is far superior to your inflexible number of lifetime members. That is a sure formula for deadlock and the destruction of the ability to govern."

"That may be your superior opinion, Sir Frederic." Galt was back in the fray. "But our colonial opinion is every bit as good as yours. All the delegates here present have an enormous commitment to this confederation process. You and your people are coming in just at the final moments. It is we who'll decide the terms of reference of our Senate, not you people. And if you don't like what we decide, then I suppose you're telling us there won't be any bill, there won't be any confederation. Is that what you're saying, eh?"

Rogers was flustered. This was blunt, unsophisticated, rough talk to which he was not accustomed. "I'm sorry, Mr. Galt, but I do not make policy. That is for the Honourable the Colonial Secretary and the Cabinet. My staff and I only carry out his wishes and directions and those of his Cabinet colleagues. They will decide the terms of reference of your Senate, not I."

Galt, his face flushed with fury, turned his blazing eyes on Lord Carnarvon. "And what is the decision, Mr. Chairman — will it be your Colonial officials or the colonials who decide the question of the Senate or, for that matter, whether there is a new British nation in North America? Tell me, sir, which will it be?"

Carnarvon pulled his gouty leg off the footstool and made to stand, saying, "There will be no decision this day, gentlemen. I suggest that there be further meaningful, cordial discussions, urgent discussions, on this critical Senate matter and any other remaining issues."

"Including what our new confederation is to be called or named — if I may be so bold." Macdonald spoke the words with a smile.

"Indeed!" Carnarvon returned the smile. "We will meet a week from today, on the second of February."

"Just three days before Parliament opens. Not much time," Cartier observed.

"Time enough, George, if we all put our minds to the objectives and to getting all this done with courtesy and good will, eh, Alexander?"

Under his breath through clenched teeth, Galt muttered a salvo of oaths with, "Between those bloody arrogant Brits and those bloody thieving Americans!" Out loud he said, "Of course, John A. Courtesy and good will. I have a barrelful."

Carnarvon announced, "Thank you, gentlemen, this meeting is at an end. But I would be obliged if Mr. Macdonald, Monsieur Cartier, and Mr. Galt might stay for a moment — and Sir Frederic also."

When the others had left and Carnarvon settled again in his chair with his gouty leg elevated, he said. "It's the Treaty of Paris matter, gentlemen. I thought that with Sir Frederic here we might discuss where the matter stands. Sir Frederic . . . ?"

Rogers did not hesitate.

"I sense, sir, that our colonial friends here are in a state of great frustration coupled with impatience with Her Majesty's government's tardiness in making a decision on changes in the Treaty of Paris in favour of the Tsar. This is quite apart from the Senate issue, Minister

Macdonald, but I sense that the Treaty of Paris–Russian America matter is of deep concern to you." Rogers paused for a long moment. "I wish to advise you that both Prime Minister Derby and his leader in the House of Commons, Mr. Disraeli, are fully if not painfully aware of the negotiations you have so ably opened with Prince Gorchakov, Mr. Macdonald."

John A. gave a slight move of his head by way of notice.

"However, it is only three weeks since you arrived back in London, Mr. Macdonald. That's a short time to provide such a complex answer to such a simple question: Is Her Imperial Majesty prepared to release Tsar Alexander from his covenant of neutralization of the Black Sea? In all fairness, Mr. Chairman, the question would ordinarily take many weeks of consultation amongst various interested ministers and their respective permanent under-secretaries."

"When, then, do you think we might have an answer?" Macdonald quietly asked.

Carnarvon spoke up. "John A., you must also take into account the fact that the British Cabinet is in a state of near paralysis because of an internal dispute over the Derby-Disraeli parliamentary reform bill, which would strip the House of Lords — where I dwell — of most of its governing powers. I'm against it, of course. So the focus of the government, of the Cabinet, is on the reform bill and indeed on its own survival. It's not on the Treaty of Paris . . ."

"Or, for that matter, on our Confederation bill," Cartier remarked.

Carnarvon shrugged. "What can I say except that you might reasonably expect an answer on the Black Sea by the end of February."

The colonials exchanged looks of anger and increasing frustration as Macdonald reacted. "We are obliged to you and Sir Frederic for your views, Mr. Chairman. Is there any clue you gentlemen can give us? Can we be optimistic about the outcome?"

Carnarvon deferred to Sir Frederic. "My personal opinion, is there is reason to be optimistic so far as the Cabinet is concerned. But then . . ." He hesitated.

"But then what?" Galt persisted.

"But then there's Her Majesty, Queen Victoria."

"What does that mean?" Cartier asked.

It means, my friend, that even if the government does agree to amend the Treaty of Paris to accommodate the Tsar and open the door for your negotiations with him, Her Majesty might well be of a different view."

"She might say no?" Cartier's voice had a hue of incredulity.

"Of course she might," Carnarvon answered. "And if she does, that would be the end of the matter."

"But if the Cabinet said no and Queen Victoria said yes, what then?" It was Galt.

"Her Majesty has no power to say yes when the government says no. But there is no doubt she could lawfully say no to the Cabinet's yes." Carnarvon was tired. "So you see, John A., even if the government approves of amendments to the Treaty of Paris, the magnificent lady in Buckingham Palace could stop you in your tracks."

In obvious pain Lord Carnarvon struggled to his feet, saying, "I think it's time for you to be presented to Her Majesty, John A. It would either help or hinder your cause. Help, I'm sure. I'll see what I can arrange."

15

February 2, 1867
London

SURELY YOU CAN TELL MOTHER AND ME WHAT'S HAPPENING, John A.!" Agnes was looking at him between the shafts of four half-burned white candles across the dining room table where the dessert plates sat empty. She spoke for Theodora, sitting at the head of the table, with John to her right and Hewitt at the opposite end.

It had been a most enjoyable dinner. John A. was totally relaxed, his stomach full of roast beef and Yorkshire pudding, capped as it was with a delicious jelly and chocolate-crossed trifle. He luxuriated in the warm, loving presence of his fiancée, whose teasing toe had playfully touched his legs several times. During dessert the toe hadn't merely touched his scrawny right shin, it had actually, to John A.'s delight, pressed against it then rubbed up and down for a few titillating moments.

Now it was time for coffee and talk. And some sweet, special port for John A. Agnes had long since warned him — no, emphatically told him — that in their house there would be no going off after dinner to the library for port, pipes, cigars, and man-talk that women surely couldn't understand, let alone take part in.

When Agnes delivered that dictum John A. thought back to many such post-dinner men-only sessions in many libraries in his own land and here in hospitable, social London.

"Well, my darling Agnes, of course we can tell you and Theodora what's happening, can't we, Hewitt?"

"Where to begin?" The tall, long-faced Hewitt stroked his elegant wide moustache, black in contrast to his thinning brown hair.

"Can you tell us about the Senate question?" Agnes asked. "Have you settled it with Rogers' people or are you still at an impasse?"

Macdonald said, "Hewitt?"

The man responsible for recording the London proceedings shook his head. "It was a struggle, not monumental but a struggle nevertheless. Both sides gave in, so we were able to settle the issue today. A numbers game — that's what it turned out to be."

Theodora was listening intently. "But, Hewitt, you haven't told us what happened!"

"Quite so, Mother, quite so. The Senate will have a fixed number of members and they will not be forced to retire at seventy-five. The Crown — that is, the prime minister of the day — on recommendation to the Governor General . . ."

"Lord Monck," Agnes said.

"Assuming he's still the Governor General when all this is said and done. In the event of a deadlock, the Crown will be able to appoint additional senators. The circumstances are not specified. It's understood there would have to be a confrontation — a crisis."

"But that's not written in?"

"No, it's not, Mother."

Agnes asked, "How many will the Crown be able to appoint, Hewitt?"

"Carnarvon and his people wanted no fewer than twelve additional break-the-deadlock members, but we colonials would have none of it. Finally they took half that number. Six was all they really wanted and that's what they got."

"So the Senate matter is settled." Agnes still wasn't satisfied. "But what about the name? What's this splendid new confederation to be called?"

John A. shifted uncomfortably. He sipped his port delicately. No throwing it back in a gulp in front of Agnes. Hewitt said nothing, so his chief began.

"The name will be Canada. No quarrel about that. The name was proposed by a Maritimer — who was it, Hewitt?"

"Robert Wilmot."

"Ah, yes, good old Robert Wilmot. Canada West will become

Ontario and Canada East will be called Quebec."

"And the colonies of New Brunswick and Nova Scotia will become provinces within the new nation," Hewitt added.

"But what will it be?" Theodora's inquisitive mind was at work. "Will it be a republic? Will it be like the United States — the United Provinces of Canada?"

"Believe it or not, Mother, that's what Carnarvon's minions had written into the first draft. They wanted to call it the United Province — not Provinces — the United Province of Canada."

John A. harrumphed. "But we would have no part of that. One of the first things we decided here in London was to call our new country the Kingdom of Canada. So we crossed out 'United Province' and put in 'Kingdom.'"

"Then what?" Agnes wanted to know.

"Simple," Macdonald responded. "The English governing class decided that the proud title 'Kingdom' was not only premature but pretentious as well. Who did we colonials think we were anyway? Imagine the Queen's representative in Canada being called a viceroy! What cheek!

"And on top of that, Adderley, who is Carnarvon's parliamentary assistant in the Commons . . . Adderley has let it be known that 'Kingdom' and 'viceroy' would create too open a monarchical blister on the side of the United States."

"Too bloody bad," Hewitt muttered.

"Too bad indeed," Theodora echoed.

"Well, like it or not, the Americans have a strong influence on our British masters. Her Majesty's ambassador to Washington, Sir Frederick Bruce — I'll be dealing with him, that is, if we get approval to negotiate with the Tsar — Bruce recently sent a cable to the Foreign Office reporting that the title 'Kingdom of Canada' had aroused remarks of an unfriendly character in the Congress."

"How would the Americans know about the word 'Kingdom' when it's only being discussed here?" Agnes wondered.

John A. shrugged. "Some newspaper report, I suppose."

"So if the title 'Kingdom' is not acceptable, have you settled on something?"

"We have indeed. Tilley came up with the solution. Bear in mind that our London Resolutions have made provision for bringing British Columbia into confederation as well as the Northwest Territories. That's our dream — if the Americans don't get British Columbia first."

Agnes thought his mind was not focusing. "So the name. What did Tilley come up with?"

"Ah," John A. laughed. "Tilley. Yes. With the vision of what we all see Canada becoming, Tilley found these words of the Seventy-second Psalm. I've written them down." He fumbled in his waistcoat pockets. "Here we are." He opened the slip of paper he had found in one of his suitcoat pockets. "I hope all of you are ready for this."

"We are." Agnes spoke for all.

"The Seventy-second Psalm, verse eight: 'He shall have dominion also from sea to sea, and from the river unto the ends of the earth.' From sea to sea is from the Atlantic to the Pacific. Dominion of Canada, that's the title. It's been settled. Carnarvon tells us the Queen has approved."

Agnes shook her head. "My God. Are you happy with that name, John?"

Macdonald shrugged. "It's the best we could do."

His outspoken fiancée made her opinion known. "It sounds rather insipid to me."

Her brother added, "And to at least one person highly placed in Britain."

"And who is that?" Theodora asked.

"The Prime Minister, the Earl of Derby."

John A. guffawed. "The man Disraeli says is in a state of perpetual funk."

"More than that. From my private sources," — Hewitt smiled knowingly — "whose names I will never disclose to you, Chief, my private sources have informed me that the Prime Minister wrote to Disraeli yesterday — ladies, you should know that neither of those worthies has any real interest in British American affairs, let alone our proposed union — and in the letter he said, and I am paraphrasing to some extent, he said, 'I do not know that there is any objection to the term

"Dominion" though it strikes me as rather absurd.'"

"Can we go from absurdity to reality, please," Agnes asked, "and talk about the most important event in my life?"

"Our wedding?" John A. ventured.

"There is nothing else. John A., what about the banns?"

"Ah yes, the banns. I have an appointment to see the Archbishop of Canterbury on Tuesday. It could be a sticky wicket."

"Why?" Hewitt asked.

"We haven't enough time to have the banns read in the customary way. After all, the wedding's only two weeks away. So I must attend upon the dear old Archbishop to beg his leave for a special licence."

"D'you expect any problem, John?" Agnes was concerned. "I mean, after all, the invitations are ready to go out and even that's short notice. The arrangements for the wedding breakfast have been made. And there's my wedding dress . . ."

"Now, now, sweetheart." John A. reached across the table to take her hands in his. "I'm assured that there'll be no problem. This is simply a formality. What about your wedding dress? How's it coming along?"

She smiled. "Very well, indeed. It will be ready in time. But I'm not going to tell you what it looks like."

"Of course not. What about the bridesmaids' dresses? Let me see if I have it right. Your bridesmaids will be Emma Tupper, Jessie McDougall, Joanna Archibald, and Georgina Mayne. Right?"

"John A.! You remembered!" Agnes threw back her tightly coiffed head and laughed. "Their dresses will be beautiful . . . white silk skirts and white tulle tunics with folds of silk to match their bonnets, two of which will be blue and two pink. So there."

"So there indeed! I can't wait to see them."

"And what about your suit for the wedding, my darling?"

"Ah, it's going to be elegant. For convenience I've selected a superb tailor right across from our church, St. George's in Hanover Square."

"How clever of you. You can have your final fitting, then march straight across the square to meet your fate," Hewitt jestingly remarked.

"Agnes isn't my fate. She's my future!"

"Your future would like to know about something else close to your heart."

"Ah, but Agnes, you're the only thing close to my heart."

"What a perfect response. Perhaps I should have said something else on your mind — that is, your Russian American project."

"Well, I'm waiting for Derby's government to make up its mind whether it will be prepared to remove the Black Sea neutralization clause from the Treaty of Paris — you know all about that. All I can do is sit and wait."

"And when Derby makes up his mind, what are you going to do?" Agnes asked.

"If they say no, that's the end of the matter."

"And you could not persuade Gorchakov to negotiate for money only?" Theodora asked.

"No."

"So, if the government and the Queen agree to change the terms of the Treaty of Paris, how will you negotiate with St. Petersburg?" his fiancée asked.

John A. looked first at Hewitt, then at Agnes, as he answered: "I'll go there myself."

"You mean *you'll* go to St. Petersburg?" Agnes looked shocked. "John A., you can't go before the wedding! We're going to be married in two weeks and you don't even have the marriage licence. How can you even think of going to St. Petersburg!"

"If I get a yes from Derby soon I'll have no choice. It will be my duty to go. No one else can do it."

Hewitt reminded him: "You have your appointment with the Archbishop to obtain dispensation for the marriage licence."

"I can't miss that," John A. acknowledged.

Agnes threatened without a smile, "You'd better not."

"There's a ship, the *Torrance*, due to sail out of Southend on the 6th." Hewitt added fuel to what promised to be a fire. "That would get you to St. Petersburg on the 12th. According to Lloyd's she'll unload, take on a new cargo, and be back at Southend on the 20th."

"So?" John A. asked.

"I've made a conditional booking for both of us."

Agnes was appalled. "But, John, our wedding day is the 16th! There is no way it's going to be postponed. Do you hear me?"

John A. said nothing, his eyes fixed on Agnes's face cold with fury.

"Make your choice, John. It's either Russian America or me. Which is more important?"

"There's no choice, my darling. Hewitt didn't make that booking. The two of us were just teasing you."

Agnes looked relieved but doubtful. "You pair of rotters."

John A. laughed as he took her hand. "As I said, all I can do is sit and wait."

"And twist British arms as hard and often as possible," Hewitt added. "Agnes, your fiancé is expert at putting pressure on people, persuading them to his point of view."

Agnes smiled knowingly. "That ability has not escaped this innocent maiden, I can assure you."

Theodora, deciding this was a good time to leave the table; rang the silver bell for the maid. Hewitt passed the port bottle to John A. To his surprise his chief declined, as did the ladies.

Hewitt said, "Chief, I had some news late this afternoon that I should pass on to you about the Russian American situation. Ladies, I don't want to bore you with all this, but since I'm going to be away until Tuesday I thought . . ."

"Bore us?" Agnes was indignant. "I find the subject fascinating. Or perhaps you think Mother and I won't understand?"

Hewitt quickly retreated. "Good heavens no, Agnes. You know better than that."

"Well, I thought I'd let you know you're getting pretty close to being condescending?"

Suitably brought up short, Hewitt decided to press on. "The Hudson's Bay Company lease of the fur trapping and fur trade on Russian American Company land is up for renewal. Not the islands — just the mainland that abuts the Hudson's Bay holdings to the east in the Northwest Territories."

"And the border of British Columbia to the south," John A. added.

"Yes. A group of American businessmen and politicians are trying to persuade Gorchakov and the Russian American Company not to renew the Hudson's Bay lease, and to give the U.S. group a lease for all of the Russian American territory — all of it."

"If this American group were successful it would be a long nail in the coffin of my negotiations to buy."

"Exactly. The group is headed by an American fur trader, Lewis Goldstone, who just happens to operate out of Victoria. Goldstone's group includes some of the wealthiest and most influential men in California. They have the support of the most powerful politician in the state, Senator Cornelius Cole."

Macdonald was looking for a connection. "They want to lease all of Russian America and they have this important senator. So?"

"Cole read law in the office of a lawyer in a place called Auburn, New York."

"That information doesn't help me at all."

"The lawyer was William H. Seward, President Johnson's Secretary of State, the Manifest Destiny man. They say he has Johnson in the palm of his hand."

"Against whom we'd be bidding for Russian America, if Derby says yes."

"You've got the connection now, Chief."

Macdonald only nodded.

"Good. It's my understanding that Cole has been instructed to make contact with de Stoeckl as soon as the Russian ambassador gets back to Washington."

"Which should be any day now."

"Cole's instructions are to convince de Stoeckl that he should assist in persuading the Tsar to let the Goldstone group have a lease of all the rights to trading, trapping, and other commerce in the whole of Russian America."

"Yes?" Macdonald's eyes were beginning to droop. It was, after all, near the end of a long day. His body was running out of energy.

"The Californians are prepared to top the price that the Hudson's Bay people have been paying, plus paying for missionaries to the Indians.

"What were you saying about Seward?" John A. tried to pull himself together.

"Evidently Seward has persuaded Cole to negotiate with the Russians through the United States minister to St. Petersburg, Cassius M. Clay."

"Yes, yes." Macdonald brightened a bit. "Earl Cowley mentioned him."

"Well, the news is, Chief, that the Russian government — I assume that's Gorchakov — has informed Cassius Clay they won't enter negotiations with him or his California clients until the discussions with the Hudson's Bay Company are completed one way or another."

John A. stifled a yawn, but not without being caught in the act by Agnes. "John A., we should really get you back to the hotel. It's late and you're obviously tired."

He smiled. "If I appear tired, my sweetheart, it's because my imagination's been working overtime thinking about the bliss of being married to you."

To which Agnes retorted, "Combined with the bliss of listening to yet another story about how Seward and those dreadful Americans are plotting to get their hands on Russian America and end your dreams of a dominion from sea to sea."

"While I'm plotting to get my hands on you, my darling."

"And I about being your wife, John A. Hewitt, it's time you took your beloved Chief back to the hotel before he falls asleep here."

16

February 16–19, 1867
London

THE PACE HAD BEEN ALMOST FRANTIC, SOMETIMES ON THE precipice of panic.

The wedding! Such a short time in which to get things done. That was Agnes Bernard's happy lament every day of the final fortnight before the magical, surprising morning of Saturday, the 16th day of February. At ten o'clock she would be taken in holy wedlock by the Honourable John Alexander Macdonald, Attorney General of Canada West and Minister of Militia Affairs for said province.

The surprise was that Agnes had found as her true love a man whom she had known, yet not known, for so many years. A man who was indeed old enough to have fathered her, yet so young in mind and physical presence that she saw no difference in their ages, in their compatibility and mutual passion. And what a man among men! He stood taller than any male Agnes had ever encountered — taller physically, intellectually, and above all as a leader whom others would willingly follow. Not necessarily obey, but certainly follow.

There had been the rush to complete the invitation list: of course the delegates and their wives and children, virtually all of whom had joined their men in England for the gala Christmas and New Year's season. Invited also were such dignitaries as the Earl of Carnarvon, Lord Monck, C.B. Adderley, Sir Frederic Rogers, F.S. Reilly, and their wives and grown children. An invitation had even been sent to Earl Cowley and his lady, diplomatically imprisoned as they were in Paris with little hope of release but undoubtedly pleased at bride and groom's thoughtfulness.

The wedding dress had been a challenge. Fittings, fittings, alterations, adjustments, and more fittings. Agnes had worried: Would it be ready on time? The dressmaker had been so far behind with other orders. But it was completed to perfection! The white satin wedding gown had a short train for the modest length of the church aisle. The veil was of fine Brussels lace trailing from a wreath of petite orange blossoms.

Then there had been the marriage licence with John A.'s obligatory attendance upon that most English of correct personages, the venerable Archbishop of Canterbury. While John A. had assured Agnes that it was a matter of mere formality, he had been apprehensive that for some unpredictable reason the holy leader (after the Queen) of the Church of England might refuse the licence. But his fears were unfounded.

On Tuesday, February 5, John A. had met with the Archbishop in his suite of office at Westminster Abbey. The Archbishop, a man perhaps six or eight years older than his supplicant and only an inch shorter but slightly stooped and portly, had been in fine fettle. His Grace had been far more interested in the condition of his flock in Canada than in the wedding of Susan Agnes and John Alexander. And, by the way, did Mr. Macdonald know that Bishop Fulford was in London? Whereupon John A. had gone directly to the Bishop's hotel to ask him on near-bended knee to officiate at the wedding.

John A. had arrived at the Bernard flat later that morning, waving the marriage licence, to tell Agnes excitedly that the most extraordinary thing had happened. Bishop Fulford, the Metropolitan Bishop of Canada and an old friend who was now in London to visit the Archbishop of Canterbury, had been honoured to accept John A.'s request to perform the wedding ceremony. What great good fortune! The rector of St. George's Church had had his British nose put slightly out of joint, but John A. had said that the priest would survive. However, his wife might have some difficulty with her face, the loss of even a fraction of which made life almost unbearable within the rigid social confines of the Parish of St. George's.

The wedding dress had been one thing but John A.'s regalia for the event had been quite another. The tailor in Hanover Square had not been quite on the mark as he tried to match the cut of the cloth to the angles and height of his client's tall and lanky body.

John Alexander Macdonald

Alexander Tilloch Galt

George Etienne Cartier

The Fathers of Confederation, London, 1866 (Macdonald seventh from left)

Russian ambassador
Edouard de Stoeckl

U.S. Secretary of State
William H. Seward

Prince Mikhail Gorchakov

Captain John Fisher
of HMS *Excellent*, 1883

Agnes Bernard

HMS *Warrior*

John A. had determined upon and been fitted for a superfine black dress coat with sleeve linings, corded silk breast facing, plus a pair of superfine black dress trousers. Furthermore, he had seen to the cleaning and pressing of his diplomatic uniform and gone to the Burlington Arcade to purchase a new case for his sword.

The last of at least eight fittings of his suit took place at half-past eight on the very morning of the wedding. That final fitting was a success. By nine o'clock John A. was on his way back to the Westminster Palace Hotel to bathe and dress for the ceremony that would make his family life whole again.

At the peeling of the bells of St. George's Church at ten o'clock on the morning of February 16, 1867, John Alexander Macdonald with his groomsman, old friend D. Bruce Gardyne, stood at the head of the aisle before the steps to the altar. Waiting with them on the top step was Bishop Fulford, resplendent in his robes and purple velvet insignia, his book of wedding service in hand.

As recorded, when the bride, escorted by her brother Hewitt, who was to give her away, entered the church, there were so many present that she had to pass through an avenue of friends extending from the large entrance door to the very altar steps.

The list of those present in St. George's Church, Hanover Square, to witness and be part of the union of Susan Agnes and John Alexander, impressively demonstrated the extent of affection and respect for the couple. As the Ottawa *Times* published it on March 8, 1867 — the day the British North America Act received its third and final reading in the British House of Commons, needing only Royal Assent before becoming law — the list of notables in the church included, among others:

> ***Lord, Lady and the Honble. Misses Monck; Lieut. Col. the Hon. R. and Mrs. Monck; the Lord Bishop of Montreal and Metropolitan; His Excellency Governor Hincks, C.B.; the Honbles. G.E. Cartier, W. McDougall, T. D'Arcy McGee, Mr. and Mrs. Howland and H.L. Langevin; the Honbles. Mr. and Miss Tupper, Mr. and Miss Archibald, Mr. and Mrs. Ritchie, McCully, Johnson, Henry, Wilmot, Fisher, Tilley and Mitchell from Nova Scotia and New Brunswick; Lieut. Col. Hewitt Bernard, Esq.;***

> ***Messrs. E.R. Bernard, Fearon, Chapman, Lieut. Col. Mayne, . . . the groomsman was D. Bruce Gardyne.***

After the church ceremony, some ninety guests attended a splendid wedding breakfast at the Westminster Palace Hotel. The Ottawa *Daily Citizen*, not to be outdone by the Ottawa *Times*, reported that "The tables were spread with every delicacy by a most artistic *chef de cuisine* and with a profusion of the choicest plants in endless variety in full blossom and perfume. On the plate of every guest was a bunch of violets and snow-drops."

John A., having reviewed the invitation list, had realized that there would be present one of the most formidable clusters of able, long-winded orators since the Romans left Londinium. He therefore had counselled Hewitt, who was in charge of the reception, not to allow more than one of those eloquent personages to make a speech. Hewitt wisely complied. On John A.'s recommendation the invitation to deliver the toast to the bride was extended to Francis Hincks, a longtime admirer of Agnes who had been a welcome visitor to the Bernard home in Ottawa.

Hincks, now Governor of British Guiana, had assisted Macdonald in forming the Liberal-Conservative coalition some twelve years earlier. The two men were old friends and jousters in debate.

Hincks offered light-hearted, moving words about the bride. He spoke glowingly of her knowledge of worldly matters, her tenacity, her eloquence, and her ability to stand her ground in argument. That last quality John A. had surely not missed and likely had made her even more attractive to him.

John A. then stood to put forth his reply to his friend's admirable words, noting in particular that the groom had indeed recognized his bride's ability to debate. But he had to admit he was most grateful that, when he proposed marriage, she had declined the opportunity to argue!

John A. concluded by explaining the rationale behind his marriage to his beloved Agnes, saying, "My public mission in London is in favour of union and, as a conscientious man, I feel bound to carry out my own theory!"

After the reception John A. and Agnes Macdonald retired to his suite upstairs in the hotel, where their travelling clothes and luggage for their honeymoon trip were ready. By three o'clock, exhilarated by the consummation of their marriage and by the magic of the ceremonies celebrating their union, the newlyweds were on the train bound for Oxford and an all-too-brief honeymoon.

17

February 19–26, 1867
London

AGNES AND JOHN A. TOOK SEATS IN THE FRONT ROW OF THE spectators' gallery of the House of Lords along with other members of the delegation from that place to be henceforth known as the Dominion of Canada if . . .

The "if" was if Carnarvon was able to steer the British North America Act (the delegates had already started to call it the BNA Act) through the House of Lords and then if his parliamentary assistant, C.B. Adderley, could do the same in the House of Commons.

The House of Lords was not packed with peers that day. Macdonald thought the chamber perhaps half-filled when Carnarvon stood to introduce the bill for its second reading. This was a crucial moment because if it was defeated in the Lords or moved to be sent back to committee for revisions, this would be the time.

The Canadians knew that the irascible, implacable Maritimer foe of confederation, Joseph Howe, was in London lobbying furiously against the bill. Howe had let it be known that he had gone to the length of organizing a massive petition purportedly signed by thirty thousand residents of Nova Scotia. It purportedly pleaded for the Imperial Parliament to delay dealing with the BNA bill until the upcoming general election in their colony had been held. That petition, if indeed it existed, was about to be lodged with Carnarvon.

Had Howe been able to persuade some influential member of the government to delay passage; or some strong man in Her Majesty's Loyal Opposition? This was of concern to all the delegates.

And the matter of the attempt to acquire Russian America: did Carnarvon have any new information? Because of the crisis in the

Derby-Disraeli ministry, which might fall at any moment over its Reform Bill, just as the Russell government had fallen only nine short months before, Carnarvon and his lady, with deep regret, had not been able to attend the wedding. Indeed, Macdonald had not spoken with the Colonial Secretary for almost a week. John A. was sure that Carnarvon would have communicated any news to him as soon as he saw the Macdonalds arrive in the gallery. But if Carnarvon did have word, he gave no sign. He merely acknowledged their presence with a smile, a wave and, standing up, a bow in their direction.

After the House was called to order by the Speaker, the Earl of Carnarvon stood to introduce the BNA bill formally and soon was in full flight in his speech supporting the measure. Macdonald whispered to Agnes that Harry was doing an excellent job. In fact, John A. was moved to tears as he heard the young Earl's final words, words that spoke to a dream that Macdonald held.

Carnarvon talked slowly, passionately, with palpable conviction as he exhorted the members of the House of Lords to support the bill: "We are laying the foundation of a great State, perhaps one which at a future day may even overshadow this country. But, come what may, we shall rejoice that we have shown neither indifference to their wishes nor jealousy of their aspirations, but that we honestly and sincerely, to the utmost of our power and knowledge, fostered their growth, recognizing in it the conditions of our own greatness."

The second reading was swiftly approved that day. Then it went to committee where it went easily through on Friday, February 22, notwithstanding some perfunctory reference to Howe's petition.

On Tuesday, February 26, the BNA bill finally passed the House of Lords, despite a plea for delay by a Howe recruit, Lord Campbell. It was immediately sent to the House of Commons, where it would have its first reading on Wednesday, February 27, a most significant day in the creative, productive life of John A. Macdonald.

18

February 27, 1867
London

AS THEIR OPEN CARRIAGE PASSED THROUGH THE MASSIVE BLACK, gold-tipped iron gates of Buckingham Palace, Agnes Macdonald burst out: "Oh, John A. I think I've died and I'm on my way to heaven!"

John A. laughed. "You haven't died, my darling, but you are in heaven."

"Absolutely. I'm going to be presented to Queen Victoria! It's too much, John A. I simply can't believe it."

"Not only are you going to see the Queen but our British North America bill — my life's proudest achievement — will be given its first reading in the House of Commons this afternoon."

"If C.B. Adderley doesn't botch it." Opposite Macdonald sat Lord Carnarvon, the carved ivory head of his cane clutched in both white-gloved hands in front of him. The Earl was wearing his full court dress, with his plumed cocked hat, his high-collared and gold-buttoned, embroidered black tunic, his ceremonial sword at his waist, his tight cavalry trousers smoothly tucked into glinting half-Wellington boots.

For his part John A. was decked out in the dark-blue diplomatic uniform he had so wisely had cleaned and pressed for just such a thrilling occasion. His uniform and cocked hat were similar to Carnarvon's but not as elaborate. Even so, John A. felt quite splendid and euphoric.

As well, he felt deeply grateful and obliged to the Carnarvons, who had graciously undertaken to present the newlyweds to Her Majesty. The Earl and his Countess would also present the other ministers from

North America but, because Macdonald was their chosen leader, he and Agnes had the privilege of being first.

They also had the honour of riding from the Westminster Palace Hotel with the Carnarvons in their splendid carriage drawn by four horses and emblazoned with the Carnarvon coat of arms.

Both women were dressed in their best finery, wide-brimmed hats sitting on elaborately swept-up tresses. Beneath their cloaks, their high-collared velvet dresses were adorned with lace and embroidery. Agnes had chosen a medium dark-blue dress to complement her husband's uniform. The Countess, on the other hand, had selected a black costume in consideration of the mourning black that she well knew would be the attire of Her Majesty, who still grieved for her beloved Albert.

This was a special court at which only those particularly summoned would appear. It was not an event open to the customary members of Her Majesty's court. Rather, it was to be focused on the colonial ministers of the about-to-be-created new British nation upon whom Her Majesty had conferred the name "The Dominion of Canada." It was Queen Victoria's wish to bestow a unique recognition of the achievements of the loyal colonial delegates.

As their carriage passed through the gates of Buckingham Palace, Big Ben could be heard in the far distance striking twelve noon. The court was to commence at twelve-thirty and, as all knew, the still-young but tragically widowed Queen was prompt to the near second. Thus it was mandatory for all guests to be in place long before the appointed time for the commencement of the audience.

After alighting from the carriage in the inner courtyard of the Palace, the Carnarvons and their guests were escorted through ornate, cavernous, art-filled halls to a waiting room that John A. later said was as large as the council chamber at the town hall of his home town of Kingston, but far grander. Other delegates had already arrived, convivial, unquarrelling friends of a like mind especially this day when their British North America bill, safely through the House of Lords, was about to be given first reading in the House of Commons. There was Tupper speaking with Tilley, and Galt with Langevin. All were in a happy mood, and as good politicians, all were talking at the same time — or so it seemed to the newcomer to political life, Agnes Macdonald.

Then the minutes began to close in on the moment of which dreams were made, a time never to be forgotten, always to be treasured, recalled, and spoken of countless times in a long lifetime thereafter.

The Queen's private secretary came through the tall doors of the receiving chamber. List in hand, he intoned, "Her Imperial Majesty Queen Victoria begs the presence of the Earl of Carnarvon and his Countess and with them the presence of The Honourable and Mrs. John Alexander Macdonald of the Colony of the Province of Canada."

As arranged, Carnarvon offered his arm to Agnes and with her walked forward, followed by John Alexander Macdonald with the Countess Carnarvon on his arm.

There she was on a throne set upon a wide dais some twenty steps or so from the entrance to the audience room. Retainers around her retired as soon as the Carnarvon party entered. With Her Majesty was her daughter, Princess Louise, still in her teens, young, vibrant, and learning from this experience.

The Carnarvons and Macdonalds approached the throne, halting perhaps three feet away from the Queen. Carnarvon bowed deeply from the waist while Agnes performed a low curtsy. John A. and the Countess to their left did the same thing.

They were in the presence of the most ethereal, powerful, majestic person then alive in the civilized world. She was a petite, beautiful woman with alabaster skin, a broad forehead, and heavy-lidded eyes that were kind and attentive. Eyes that were also touched with the veil of sadness brought on by her early widowhood.

Strength. Intelligence. Majesty. Those were the qualities John Alexander Macdonald saw as he gazed for the only time into the serene face of his monarch. He was almost overwhelmed before she finally spoke.

"My dear Carnarvon, how wonderful to see you." She offered her hand to him. He stepped forward. Gently taking the delicate fingers, he bent to kiss the back of her hand. "Your Majesty, it is always the supreme honour to be in your presence," and with a slight bow to

Princess Louise seated slightly behind and to the right of the Queen, "and in yours, Your Royal Highness."

It was the Countess Carnarvon who next offered her respects to Her Majesty and the Princess, after which she said, "Your Majesty, I have the honour to present to you Susan Agnes Macdonald, the recent wife of John Alexander Macdonald, the Attorney General of Canada West and chairman of the conference on the confederation of Your Majesty's North American colonies."

Agnes curtsied once again as the Queen said, "How delightful to see you, my dear. We wish you every good fortune on your recent marriage to this most excellent gentleman. May your life together be for many decades. Life without one's spouse, without one's love, is scarcely tolerable. You are a most fortunate young woman, Agnes Macdonald."

"Thank you, Your Majesty," was the response during yet another curtsy.

Then the Earl of Carnarvon with eloquent compliments presented the Honourable John Alexander Macdonald.

Her Majesty listened attentively to all of Carnarvon's fine words. When he was finished, John A. stepped forward. The Queen offered her right hand, which he gently grasped. Bowing slowly, he kissed the little hand then, straightening, he stepped back.

"Minister Macdonald, you should know that we are most pleased, indeed delighted, with your splendid work toward creating a federation of our loyal colonies in North America. It is a most important step in ensuring that our American friends are not given the opportunity to acquire our territories. You and your colleagues are to be congratulated for your loyalty to the Crown."

"Our loyalty is to you, Your Majesty."

"Ah." she smiled. "But we are not the Crown. We simply wear it."

The smile left her serene, unlined face. Her eyes were intense with energy. "There are two things we wish to say to you in the presence of our Earl of Carnarvon and his dear Countess. What we say to you will not be said to your colleagues when we receive them."

"Yes, Your Majesty."

"The first is that we have read your bill, the British North America

Act . . . It is being given first reading in the Commons today, is that correct, Lord Carnarvon?"

Carnarvon allowed that it was.

"Good. You should know, Minister Macdonald, that subject to any amendments made to it during its transit through the Commons — which we are confident will be successful — it is our firm and happy intent to give our Royal Assent to the bill immediately it is presented to us."

Macdonald was beaming, his face alive with pleasure. Agnes turned to look up at her husband to share with him this unexpected moment.

He responded, "I am deeply grateful and obliged, Your Majesty. This intelligence will not be shared, I assure you."

"Nor will you share this second intelligence, except with those who need to know in order for you to achieve your objective. We refer to your enterprise in attempting to acquire the lands and territories in North America belonging to His Imperial Majesty Alexander the Second, the Tsar of All the Russias."

Macdonald's surprise showed on his face. He did not expect the subject to come up during an audience with Her Majesty. He turned to look questioningly at Carnarvon who gave no indication or gesture.

The perceptive Queen quietly laughed. "We see we have caught you by surprise, Minister Macdonald. You should know that through the good offices of our dear Carnarvon, and the Honourable Foreign Secretary, Lord Stanley, we have been kept informed about the imaginative initiative you have taken and about the results of your negotiations with the Tsar's Prince Gorchakov."

Macdonald made no response, nor was one expected.

"We know that you have been impatient for a decision on the matter of the relief from the Black Sea provisions of the Treaty of Paris. We understand that such relief was stipulated by Prince Gorchakov as an absolute condition of negotiating a cession of Russian America to us in trust, as it were, for our Dominion of Canada. All of that is quite apart from the monetary aspect which, as we are advised, is a matter which you have in hand with the Chancellor of our Exchequer."

John A. could only nod his affirmation.

"You should know, Minister Macdonald, that in consultation with the appropriate ministers of the Crown we have today approved the relief demanded by Gorchakov. We are prepared to remove the relevant articles of the Treaty of Paris that force the neutralization of the Black Sea — but only as part of an agreement between ourselves and His Imperial Majesty the Tsar for the cession to us of all his territories in North America."

Macdonald was elated. "Your Majesty, this is marvellous news, so unexpected, so welcome."

"We thought you would be pleased." Queen Victoria smiled. "Now, some conditions go with your possession of this information, you understand?"

"Of course, Your Majesty."

"You have authority as a minister of the Crown to allege that you can offer the Black Sea relief, but there will be no written document or evidence from us or our government to that effect."

"Therefore any rumour of such a possibility of relief to the Tsar can be denied by Your Majesty's government. Am I correct?"

"Quite. And for that matter, if you fail in your mission — we are sorry, we should have said — if you do not succeed in your mission, no record will exist of your attempt, which we understand has so far been completely secret."

"Except for those of my colleagues who need to know," John A. admitted.

To which Carnarvon added, "As is the case with my colleagues in Your Majesty's government."

"Splendid. But briefly tell me what the next step is in your pursuit of Russian America."

"I must follow the instructions of Prince Gorchakov and negotiate with the Tsar and him directly. I will go to St. Petersburg as soon as arrangements can be made."

This was not unexpected news for Agnes.

"Will Mrs. Macdonald accompany you?" the Queen asked.

"Yes, if suitable accommodation is available on whatever ship I can find to get me there and back."

Her Majesty looked at the Earl. "Lord Carnarvon, this mission is of the utmost importance to us. We think it would be inappropriate for Minister Macdonald to use a commercial passenger ship. There is so little traffic with St. Petersburg that he might have to wait for weeks for passage and his accommodation would undoubtedly be inadequate."

"Yes, Your Majesty." Carnarvon had no idea what was coming next.

"We wish you to have words with the First Lord of the Admiralty. Surely there is some suitable warship whose crew needs some winter weather training."

Carnarvon added: "And an opportunity to show Your Majesty's flag in the Baltic and the Tsar's capital."

Queen Victoria smiled. "Precisely. Convey to the First Lord our express wish that Mrs. Macdonald accompany her husband, should she wish to do so. God speed, Minister Macdonald and Mrs. Macdonald."

The audience was over.

Queen Victoria again held out her hand to the Canadian, who moved to kiss it. Agnes curtsied and with the Carnarvons they backed out of the presence of Her Imperial Majesty.

✦

THE OTTAWA *TIMES* EDITION OF MARCH 16, 1867, REPORTED ITS version of the event at Buckingham Palace:

> ***The Queen held a court at Buckingham Palace on the 27th ult., which the London papers say was brilliantly attended. Her Majesty was attended by several members of the Royal family and many of the great officers of State and most of the Diplomatic Corps were also present . . . Among those who were presented to her [sic] Majesty on this occasion was Mrs. Macdonald by the Countess of Carnarvon.***

19

March 8, 1867
Washington

His Excellency Edouard de Stoeckl had arrived in New York on the fifth day of February, 1867, still suffering from two inflictions received during the arduous voyage across the Atlantic. One infliction brought pain — a sprained ankle — the other brought ecstasy — the Honourable Pamela Collins.

As soon as the ship docked Pamela had sent a telegram to her sister in Boston saying that she had decided to stay in New York for a few days. She would be at the Madison Hotel and would be in Boston in a few days, perhaps longer. A letter would follow explaining the situation. For his part, de Stoeckl happily had made a similar arrangement for rooms at the same luxurious hotel — on a different floor of course. Appearances had to be maintained at all costs.

After being installed in her second-floor suite and before the first of Edouard's many knocks on her door, the Honourable Pamela Collins had seated herself at her sitting-room desk to write an urgent note. It was addressed to her uncle and guardian at his London house.

Uncle — he was her late father's younger brother — had insisted that she keep him informed of her every move. Her message written, Pamela had given the concierge's pull-cord a respectable tug. Within moments a bellhop had arrived at her door.

He assured her that the letter could be sent by cable and that he would take it to the cable office himself. Satisfied, she gave it to him with money she judged to be enough for the transmission of the message across the Atlantic.

The Honourable Pamela Collins was ready for Edouard de Stoeckl's first knock.

In de Stoeckl's judgement it had been impossible to travel on to that wretched place, Washington. His wounded ankle could not withstand the excruciating pain of such a long trip. Moreover he had needed the ministrations that only the Honourable Pamela could provide.

Thus de Stoeckl had informed his principal secretary at the embassy, the loyal, capable Bodisco, that he would have no choice but to stay in New York until his limb had sufficiently recuperated to allow him to travel. Perhaps a week or ten days and would Bodisco be so kind as to attend upon Madame de Stoeckl to so inform her. There was no need for her to be concerned and certainly no need for her to travel to New York, for he was being adequately attended to at the Madison, where he always lodged while in that city.

"Furthermore," he had telegraphed Bodisco, "I will be able to spend much time here receiving persons wishing to do business and have relations with our mother country. So my time will be well spent. Please be in touch with me at any time as circumstances may dictate."

In the late afternoon on the sixth day of February a confidential cable from Pamela's uncle had been delivered. She had been actively engaged with the Baron in the sumptuous bath and so had not heard the knock on the door to the suite. It had been de Stoeckl who later had found the sealed envelope that had been shoved under her door.

When he brought it to her, Pamela had been languorously half asleep between the white silk sheets of the huge four-poster bed.

"There's a letter for you, Pamela; actually it's from the Trans Atlantic Cable Company."

"Oh, good!" She had climbed from the bed, slipped into a peignoir, taken the envelope from Edouard, kissed him lightly on the lips, then gone into the bathroom, where she shut the door to secure her privacy.

The cable had been long and detailed. The words "delay as long as you can" and "use a nameless simple code," repeated three times, had been unmistakable in their importance.

Pamela had thought about those instructions and quickly decided that she would stay in New York, and right there at the Madison, for at least a full month. She had known she would have no problem persuading her willing paramour to stay with her while making all the necessary excuses to his Foreign Minister in St. Petersburg and, of course, to Madame de Stoeckl waiting patiently or impatiently in Washington.

Although de Stoeckl had his own rooms at the Madison, he visited them only briefly every day during the cold, snow-filled month of February. His true residence during those weeks of "recuperation" was the suite of Pamela Collins.

One thing he did while in New York was make an urgent appointment with Secretary Seward for Monday, March 11, at ten o'clock. Although his acquaintanceship with Seward was quite firm after years of mutual contact, to secure the appointment so quickly he relied upon a powerful friend of both men, newspaper publisher Thurlow Weed.

Another matter he attended to was his report to Gorchakov:

> ***I have the honour to inform you, Prince, that on my return here I was kept in bed on account of my sprained foot. I did not, however, lose time but put myself in contact with the Secretary of State by an intermediary, one of his political friends who exercises great influence over him.***

Finally de Stoeckl's idyllic life had to come to an end. He was compelled by duty and conscience to return to his post and family in Washington. Some fifteen pounds lighter than the day he sprained his ankle and now required to remember that he must affect a demonstrable limp, even though the pain had long since departed, de Stoeckl grudgingly made his way back to the American capital on March 8.

The Baron's children were overjoyed to see their father and welcomed him with much joy and affection. His wife Martha seemed pleased enough to have him back again after such a long absence. But by her method of greeting him — the turned cheek instead of the offering of the mouth for the embrace at the threshold — and by the way she held her body away from his at that moment signalled clearly to de Stoeckl that nothing had changed. Almost nothing, that was.

When he followed the servants who carried up his huge trunk to the master bedroom he found there that his wife had made a change that both pleased and annoyed him. In place of the wide canopied bed they had shared during their sixteen years of marriage there were now two single beds well separated.

De Stoeckl made no remark on this development. Instead he sat and opened his trunk to give gifts from St. Petersburg to his happy daughters, spoke a few words to them and his wife about how pleased he was to be with them again. Then it being only mid-afternoon, he called for his carriage, kissed each of them on the cheek, and promptly left the house, saying that there was much to do at the embassy, which indeed there was.

In his long absence there had accumulated volumes of correspondence that his first secretary had demurred to answer. The task of dealing with those formidable piles of documents would take days. At least that was what de Stoeckl told his wife. He sent a message to her that he would be home in time for dinner shortly after eight, adding that he would have to spend both Saturday and Sunday at the embassy getting caught up and also preparing for his Monday morning meeting with Seward.

De Stoeckl's daughters were most unhappy to see their father leave the house so quickly after his return, but they were looking forward to the pleasing prospect of being with him at dinner that evening. As for their mother, she offered no complaint, saying agreeably that she understood. Secretly she was relieved. There was something different about Edouard. He had lost much weight and appeared to be in excellent physical condition, but there was a certain shift in his eyes when they talked. She didn't know quite what to make of it. What she did know was that even after his long absence she felt no physical pull toward him, no desire to touch or fondle him. Even so, she was comforted by her husband's presence and by his company.

When de Stoeckl climbed into his carriage to be driven to the Russian legation he did not go directly there. En route he paid a visit to the northwest corner suite on the third floor of the Willard Hotel. That most elegant establishment grandly catered to the world's elite in government, diplomacy, and business who came to treat with the occupant of the symbolic Washington structure, *the White House*, of which the hotel had a superior view.

Indeed, the visitor to the Willard that day was on business of a sort.

He went to spend an hour with the Honourable Pamela Collins, also by coincidence newly arrived in the capital. His visit was to solicitously ensure that she was comfortably settled in her suite and that her every wish and desire was being accommodated.

De Stoeckl strived pleasurably and mightily and so was able to satisfy both the lady's ultimate desire and his own before proceeding on to the Russian embassy, there to fulfill the obligations of his high office. But he did not leave the sensuous presence of Pamela Collins until careful plans had been made for the timing of his daily visit at approximately six in the evening. He would be obliged to depart the hotel in sufficient time for the short walk back to the legation and then for the ten-minute carriage ride to the family residence, arriving at eight o'clock or shortly thereafter. He was worried that Pamela might not be content in Washington and thus decide to depart for Boston, or London for that matter.

For her part she assured him there was no need to worry. She had friends in Washington with whom she could visit and play whist and enjoy other entertainments. There were all manner of exciting places to go — art galleries, museums, theatres, and so forth. And she could always go and listen to those nincompoops in the Senate.

"How long will you stay in Washington?" de Stoeckl asked. "For ever — or until the day I go to Boston, whichever is the earlier," was her lighthearted reply.

When the Baron finally arrived at the Russian embassy it was close to six in the evening. Notwithstanding the late hour, all the legation staff were waiting to welcome back their minister. Of course the first secretary, Bodisco, who had met de Stoeckl at the train station that afternoon, was there. Bodisco did not want to, indeed, could not afford to, miss his chief's customary briefing of the staff about the goings-on in St. Petersburg. It was de Stoeckl's practice, over the years since he had been promoted minister, to gather the staff and relate the highlights of his trip.

They were all especially attentive when he spoke of his meetings with His Imperial Majesty the Tsar, Prince Gorchakov and, of course, the Grand Duke Constantine. Naturally, he could not reveal all that had transpired. Nor was that necessary because, for the younger members of his staff, just to hear his stories about those near-mythical personages was enough to fairly make them swoon.

There were, of course, no references to a singularly seductive and lovely lady in St. Petersburg by the name of Anna, to a particularly voluptuous and sexually exciting woman by the name of the Honourable Pamela Collins, nor to the Tsar's secret instructions on the disposition of Russian America.

Three-quarters of an hour later, the minister plenipotentiary of the Tsar of all the Russias dismissed his staff and walked alone to his office. There he ruefully observed the table heaped with carefully sorted piles of correspondence and documents. Until his meeting with the distinguished Secretary of State on Monday morning, this mass of material would receive his whole attention except for his periods at home and the time necessary to prepare for the meeting with Seward. And except, of course, for his much-anticipated, discreet, delightful visits to his treasure at the Willard Hotel who could not wait to have him tell her all that was happening in his important, busy life.

In the coming weeks there would be many clandestine coded cables from the Willard Hotel to Uncle in London.

20

March 8, 1867
London

For John A. Macdonald the week ending on Friday, March 8, had been filled with joy one moment and sadness the next, rather like riding a bumpy road with hollows and sharp crests.

Through the Permanent Under-Secretary of the Colonial Office, Sir Frederic Rogers, he had received on Monday, March 4, a copy of a coded cable that Lord Stanley, the Foreign Secretary, had sent to Her Majesty's ambassador in Washington, Sir Frederick Bruce.

The cable advised Bruce that Minister John A. Macdonald, Attorney General of Canada West, currently in London on constitutional business, had been specially entrusted by Her Gracious Majesty and by himself, Lord Stanley, to conduct negotiations with a certain foreign power for the cession to Her Majesty of territorial possessions of that power. Macdonald would be negotiating directly with the appropriate authorities of that power, but it was likely he might need to inform or seek advice from Bruce of developments in the negotiations. Any cables between Bruce and Macdonald, which were to be handled through normal Foreign Office channels, whether in code or decoded, were to be destroyed immediately the receiver had read the contents thereof. The Washington staff were required to monitor the return to Washington of the Russian ambassador and to advise Macdonald immediately of his presence.

On that same day Macdonald had received news that caused him grave concern for the future of the BNA Act: Carnarvon had just resigned from the Cabinet. Disraeli had again presented to the Cabinet his radical scheme of parliamentary reform that would in effect strip the House of Lords of almost all its power. This time the Cabinet had accepted it. Carnarvon, along with Cabinet members Cranborne and Peel, had resigned and then gone into the House of Lords to stand and explain their resignations.

Macdonald had written immediately to Carnarvon expressing regret on his resignation and the hope that he would soon be reappointed. Speaking as a Canadian, he had thanked the Earl of Carnarvon "for the sincere and great heartiness with which you addressed yourself to the object of our mission and for the able manner in which you ensured its success."

Would his friend Harry's disappearance from the scene be disastrous for the BNA bill? Macdonald had the answer on that Monday, March 4, after the bill had sailed through committee of the House with trifling amendments, notwithstanding the objecting voices of anti-colonial members of Parliament Lowe and Roebuck.

On Friday, March 8, the British North America Act had its third and final reading in the House of Commons. It was passed into law subject to the imprimatur of Royal Assent under the hand and seal of Her Imperial Majesty, Queen Victoria. Her commitment having already been given confidentially, John A. knew that his battle had been won for confederation of the colonies of Canada West, Canada East, New Brunswick, and Nova Scotia. What lay ahead was the challenge of extending the new Dominion from sea to sea, bringing in British Columbia and preventing its fall into the hands of the Americans. The pressure now on Macdonald to acquire Russian America was intense.

When he returned late that afternoon to his new marital suite at the Westminster Palace Hotel, a red wax-sealed envelope marked private, confidential and urgent was awaiting him at the front desk. He opened it at once. A decoded message from Bruce read: "The two-headed eagle arrived in its Washington nest today. Will monitor and advise."

John A. Macdonald, elated by the passage of his monumental BNA Act, went up to his suite, embraced his Agnes, burned the cable from Sir Frederick Bruce, then embraced his wife again — and at length.

21

March 11, 1867
Washington

In Edouard de Stoeckl's judgement the offices of the Secretary of State of the United States of America were much too ostentatious. This was his tenth visit during the stormy tenure of William H. Seward. As he sat alone in a high-back leather chair in the anteroom awaiting Seward — who had been called to the White House on an urgent matter but was expected to be back any moment — de Stoeckl reaffirmed his earlier judgement.

If anything the room was a huge wooden box. Its walls and ceiling were made of dark, finely turned, carved, highly polished walnut. Deep rugs covered nearly all of the oak floor. In Seward's office the filled floor-to-ceiling bookcases, the chairs, tables, and the Secretary's cherub-cornered desk — long enough for an eight-person conference — all were of the same rubbed walnut. Behind the Secretary's desk and its matching leather-upholstered chair stood several banners. Apart from the American flag, de Stoeckl had no idea what the others were. Brass abounded: lamps, coatrack, ink and pen stand, picture frames, and fireplace screen, guard, and utensils. And on the mantle a ship's clock and barometer. All that brass set against the rich lustre of the walnut was pleasing to de Stoeckl's eye. In fact he was thinking that the room was not quite so overpowering as he remembered it. Perhaps it was the portraits of Lincoln and Washington, new additions, or so he thought, that softened the room, made it less intimidating. On the other hand it was clear that the Secretary's chamber was designed to exude the power and prestige of the most important official in any presidential Cabinet, the Secretary of State.

Seward burst into the room, mixing his apologies for being late with words welcoming de Stoeckl back to Washington. "Missed seeing you at all the diplomatic parties and the like, Your Excellency. Please sit down. And again I'm sorry about being late but the President, well, you know, he vetoed the Reconstruction Act. Not on my advice he didn't, but he did and the Congress is in open rebellion. I tell you they're mad. The President, well, he sent for me this morning and I can tell you, Mr. Ambassador, when he needs me I just have to be there."

"Yes, of course I quite understand, Mr. Secretary," de Stoeckl said as he sat down at the long desk opposite the chair into which Seward was lowering his lean body.

Seward smiled, saying, "I'm delighted to have this opportunity to talk with you. As you might well imagine, I am being pressed by Senator Cole and his California people to see if I can get some sort of answer out of you on their California Company proposal. My understanding of the situation — and you may correct me if I'm wrong — is that the Senator and some colleagues of his out there want a licence or franchise to trap and trade in furs in Russian American territory."

"That's correct. In the entire territory."

"Now, as I understand it, the charter of the Russian American Company from the Tsar is going to expire some time next year, right?"

The Baron nodded his affirmation.

Seward went on. "The Russian American Company has already underlet to the Hudson's Bay Company all its franchise on the North American mainland between 54 degrees 40 minutes north and Mount St. Elias. What Cole and his people want to do is have their American company get what the Hudson's Bay people have directly from your government, plus the licence for your islands, everything."

Seward had it right. The Baron added, "The California Company is prepared to pay my government five percent of the gross proceeds of their transactions. They say they will aid in civilizing and ameliorating the condition of the Indians by employing missionaries. And they're looking for a charter for the term of twenty-five years."

Seward leaned back in his chair. "Your Excellency, you and I have known each other for what is it now? For about five years, and you've been in Washington how long now?"

"Since 1849. This is my seventeenth year."

"Well, I want to tell you two things." The Secretary was eager to pay compliments in order to reap the positive effects on de Stoeckl — positive for Seward that was. "Of all the ambassadors I deal with, you as the most senior of the diplomatic corps here in Washington and the representative of our good friend the Tsar of Russia — you are really a pleasure to do business with. You are straightforward, direct, and you say things as you see them."

The Baron nodded, smiling. "I try," was his modest response.

"But something else. Your English, and in particular your accent, both have improved by leaps and bounds in the last five years, even from the last time I saw you just before you went to St. Petersburg. When was that, six months ago?"

"Last October. Just before I left Washington you asked me to come here and discuss Senator Cole's proposition, requesting that I further his interests in St. Petersburg — which I did, of course."

"Well, as I say, now you're speaking our language with a bit of an English accent but your heavy Austrian overtones are almost gone. Remarkable."

De Stoeckl stroked his moustache. "My dear Secretary, thank you for the compliment. During my extended absence I had the good fortune to spend a great deal of time with English friends, one in particular, and I tried to learn. What you're telling me is that I have been successful."

Seward went back to business. "Now, you just mentioned the Cole matter and your promise to see what could be done about it in St. Petersburg. And the same with the memorial from the legislative assembly of the Washington Territory."

"Yes, you gave me a copy of their petition to the President. It asked him to obtain rights from my government enabling fishing vessels based in the Territory to enter Russian American ports and harbours for provisioning. Although they were careful not to ask the President to obtain fishing rights, Washington Territory argues that it already has them."

"So, I would be obliged if you might inform me if you were able to further the cause of Senator Cole or the Washington memorialists."

At the forefront of Baron de Stoeckl's mind at that moment was Prince Gorchakov's injunction that "it is essential that the negotiation be managed in such a way that the initiative be taken by the United States, that the Imperial government abstain from any engagement and reserve the right, when the proposition shall be made, to accept or reject it."

The tactical moment had arrived.

"I raised both matters with both the Grand Duke Constantine and Prince Gorchakov. But I regret to inform you that neither proposal was favourably received — no rights or licence to an American company and no privileges for the ships of the Washington Territory."

Seward's narrow face, capped by a thick head of wavy salt-and-pepper hair and bushy eyebrows to match, developed a scowl as he contemplated what de Stoeckl was telling him.

"However," de Stoeckl continued, "I am enjoined to inform you, my dear Secretary, that my government in no way wishes to appear unfriendly or uncooperative. It is simply that in Russian America our resources of administration and control, already at the breaking point, would be incapable of handling or dealing with the presence of a new American trading company or with an onslaught of more fishing vessels."

Still scowling, Seward put the question the Russian ambassador was hoping for. "I understand the concerns of your government. But if your resources are as hard pressed as you describe . . . Let me ask you this. Since you won't lease or license, what about ceding for the right price?"

Baron de Stoeckl resisted the urge to smile. He had done it! Seward had taken the initiative, not he. "Sir, that proposition has been made to us on several occasions during my time in Washington. You should know that, even though the Imperial government has until now refused, I am authorized by the Tsar himself to treat if a proposal to purchase is renewed."

Seward's eyebrows arched and his thin lips opened briefly in surprise. "You're now authorized to negotiate to sell to us?"

"I have direct authorization from the Tsar, who instructed me personally, and I am possessed of certain basic conditions as to the disposition of property rights, citizenship, and that sort of thing."

"Something we can work out, I'm sure." The extremely pleased Seward could scarcely contain himself. "Never mind the price. We'll talk about that later. But first I have to discuss this with the President. If I get approval from him, I'll let you know right away. If we do this, Edouard, I'd like to move quickly. It would have to go to the Cabinet, get the approval of Congress, and so forth. But I like to strike when the iron is hot."

"At this time the iron is white-hot! All that is needed is the master craftsman," de Stoeckl said, waving a hand at Seward, "to take the iron and shape it into an object of diplomatic art." With dexterity de Stoeckl had returned the Secretary's earlier "working" compliment. The Secretary smiled, knowing that he had been matched.

"A final question." Seward had to know. "The British. Are they also going to be given a chance to bid? The United States simply can't have that territory going to them."

De Stoeckl decided to put all his cards on the table — almost all. "I am prepared to tell you that I am not barred from negotiating with the British, should I be directly approached by them. Furthermore, Mr. Secretary, I would hesitate to sit at the bargaining table with you without any negotiating leverage, particularly when it comes to price."

"Have you been approached by the British? I bet they'd like to get Russian America as much as I would."

"Not directly, but I can tell you they, and the Canadians, are interested. They are afraid they will lose British Columbia to you if you get Russian America."

"Do you have instructions concerning price?"

"Explicit instructions. By the way, as to the British, you should know that their ambassador —"

"Sir Frederick Bruce, that pompous ass!" Seward spat the words out.

De Stoeckl paid no outward attention: "— has made a request to meet with me on matters of mutual interest."

"And what do you think that means?"

"I strongly suspect that he knows all about Senator Cole's proposal and the Washington memorialists. He'll know that vis-à-vis the

Russian American Company and the Hudson's Bay Company something's going to have to change. And he certainly knows what you already know, Mr. Secretary."

"What's that?"

"That the Russian American Company is to all intents and purposes bankrupt. So I would not be at all surprised if Sir Frederick is under instructions to open negotiations with me."

"When are you seeing him — if indeed you are prepared to do so?"

"I have no choice. It would be quite undiplomatic for me to refuse to see him particularly . . ." De Stoeckl paused. His eyes looked away from Seward's toward the tall American flag standing behind the Secretary.

Seward waited.

"I will undertake to tell you if he makes a proposal for our territories," de Stoeckl offered.

"And I will undertake to talk with the President immediately. When are you seeing Bruce?"

"Thursday afternoon at three o'clock. He wanted an earlier meeting but I decided to put him off until we had this meeting. I understand he's most anxious to meet."

Seward was anxious too. "Try to put him off until next week. I'll try to put a proposal together so I can take it to Cabinet on Friday. Mr. Ambassador, I simply cannot let the British get their hands on your American territory. I'll be back to you tomorrow."

22

March 12, 1867
London

PRIME MINISTER AND FOREIGN MINISTER STANLEY HAD SUDDENLY switched from a reluctant foot dragger about Macdonald's Russian American cause to a supporter. Carnarvon suspected that Stanley had made the transition during his first audience with Queen Victoria after the Macdonalds had been presented to her.

The Prime Minister called Macdonald to 10 Downing Street, where the two had a comfortable, productive meeting. John A. brought along a map of North America, the best he could find in a superior London bookshop. He spread out the map on the Cabinet room table and gave Lord Stanley a quick briefing and education about British North America, the geographical and political objectives of the Canadians in creating a confederation from sea to sea, and the dangerous possibility that William Seward might take possession of not only the Tsar's territory but all of Britain's colonies and territories in North America.

The Prime Minister stood beside Macdonald as the Canadian folded the map. Stanley was impressed as well as apologetic. "I say, Macdonald, I really didn't realize how serious the situation is for you people. The Americans are ready to gobble you up on the slightest pretext. And those Fenians!"

"They are a major threat. So far as I can tell, Seward and the Johnson administration are encouraging them. The Fenians attack. We counter-attack with the Canadian militia and British regulars, and there you have it. The Americans are looking for an excuse to send in their powerful Grand Union Army to conquer us."

"Exactly."

"Keep in mind, sir, I'm responsible for any military action in

Canada."

Stanley was taken aback. "Isn't that my responsibility? I mean, after all, I'm the Prime Minister and our colonies in North America are just that — colonies."

"Until July the first when the British North America Act comes into effect. Then Canada will have its own prime minister. In the meantime I have been and still am Minister of Militia Affairs."

"Quite so." Lord Stanley acknowledged.

"And, of course, I would keep you informed and seek your cooperation."

"Indeed. I would expect that." The Prime Minister shook his head in amazement. "Yes, I really didn't understand how vulnerable you people are."

"And you can see why it's so important for Canada to have Russian America?"

"Absolutely. It's critical. We must do everything we can to persuade the Tsar to cede it to us instead of the Americans. Thank you, Macdonald, for this review of the situation. It gives me a picture I didn't have before."

"And I thank you for the opportunity, sir."

"Now, let us review the plan of action." He motioned for Macdonald to sit as he did so himself.

"I have instructed the First Lord of the Admiralty to provide his most impressive warship to take you and Mrs. Macdonald — if she wishes to accompany you — to St. Petersburg. I expect him to be in touch with you today, tomorrow at the latest."

"That's wonderful news, Prime Minister. Thank you."

"There is more. Her Majesty was gracious enough to transmit a personal message to the Tsar asking that he receive you. His Imperial Majesty has responded through Prince Gorchakov, saying that you have been granted an audience on Monday the twenty-fifth of this month at ten o'clock in the forenoon. This is the twelfth, so you must be ready to leave immediately. The Foreign Office staff are preparing a formal document setting out in legal terms what amendments to the Treaty of Paris we are prepared to offer."

"D'you think the amendments go far enough?"

"No question. We took your report, and Earl Cowley's, the record of what Gorchakov said to you in Paris. We've conceded every point he raised."

"Then how can the Tsar refuse?"

The Prime Minister became slightly paternalistic. "My dear Minister, dealing with the Russians in matters of diplomacy is like dealing with a labyrinthine mind from another world. Logic as perceived by an Anglo-Saxon intelligence bears little relationship to the way the Slavic brain operates."

It was time to end the discussion. The Prime Minister had other pressing business.

"So there you are, Mr. Macdonald. My government and I are solidly behind you. Whatever you need . . . if there are decisions you need from me on the twenty-fifth, your messages will be handed to me immediately."

"A final question, sir."

"Of course."

"Why did you not send a seasoned senior diplomat to negotiate with the Tsar, someone highly experienced in the art of diplomatic negotiations?"

Stanley gave a knowing smile. "That's exactly what I'm doing, Minister. You have a splendid reputation as a wise leader and negotiator. No one knows all the issues better than you. And you're a minister of the Crown. What better combination could one find? Bon voyage, Mr. Macdonald, and every good wish for success."

John A. Macdonald did not have to wait before the pieces of the trip began to come together. As he went out the door of 10 Downing Street, the Prime Minister's principal private secretary handed him an envelope.

"It's from the First Lord of the Admiralty, sir. I believe this is a request for you to attend upon him at two-thirty this afternoon at the Admiralty."

"Of course." John A. tore open the envelope to confirm the information just given to him. "Please notify the First Lord that I will be honoured to attend upon him and also the First Sea Lord who, according to this note, will also be there."

"Consider it done, sir."

Macdonald's carriage (now hired on a weekly basis with Galt the money-man's approval) waiting outside Number 10 carried him directly to his hotel. There he enjoyed a happy private lunch with Agnes in their suite. John A. couldn't stop talking, so euphoric and energized was he by the positive flow of events.

"Agnes, you'll come with me to St. Petersburg, won't you? Say you will." He pleaded yet another time.

Agnes frowned. "To Russia on a battleship? With all those men? I'd be the only woman on board!" She shook her head negatively. "We'd have to sleep in hammocks and . . ." Her voice trailed off.

Macdonald was about to put forth his argument for the positive aspects when Agnes said, "I'll have to have some time to think about this, John A."

She paused. "All right, I've had enough time." She smiled, reached across the table to take his hand, and whispered, "John A., I wouldn't miss going to St. Petersburg with you to see the Tsar for all the tea in China!"

John A. let out a Scottish whoop, picked up his table napkin and whirled it around his head. Then he stood and marched around the table to lift his beloved to her feet. Their kiss was long and deep and passionate.

Breaking away for a moment, Agnes gasped, "Oh, John A., being on that warship will be such a wonderful experience."

"In the meantime, my darling, we have some unfinished —"

"But well started."

"— yes, well started business before I go to the Admiralty. Would you care to accompany me to my boudoir in order to finish this business?"

"I'd go with you anywhere, John A.," She whispered into his ear as she led him into the bedroom.

John A. Macdonald, plenipotentiary extraordinaire, presented himself at the reception area of the Admiralty at two twenty-five in the afternoon of March 12, 1867. A moderate fog bolstered by a light rain had changed the overlay of London from the broken clouds and partly blue skies of the morning.

At the reception desk of the high-ceilinged, marbled foyer of the Admiralty Building, Macdonald was enveloped in an emotion that rarely visited him. It was fear. The fear of being overawed by two men at the pinnacle of the most powerful navy in the world, men he had yet to meet.

A tall, blond-haired young officer who looked like a boy came down the sweeping, curved staircase. The right shoulder of his dark blue uniform was festooned by the golden loops of an aiglette that signalled his status as an aide to a senior officer. He approached Macdonald. Halting before him at attention, he said in a deep upper-class English voice, "Mr. Macdonald, sir. I am Sub-lieutenant Michael Collingwood, the First Sea Lord's aide."

"Admiral Cairns?"

"Yes, sir. The First Sea Lord Admiral Cairns will receive you in Lord Wolseley's office."

John A. walked up the long staircase with the aide, who allowed that he was indeed related to Admiral Lord Cuthbert Collingwood, the hero, with Lord Horatio Nelson, of the Battle of Trafalgar in 1805 — Britain's greatest-ever naval victory, from which many of the Royal Navy's legends and traditions had developed.

John A. just had time to tell young Collingwood that one of Canada's most thriving industrial ports and towns on the Great Lakes system was named for his illustrious ancestor. Then they were in the secretarial anteroom, where John A. stood waiting while Collingwood knocked on the tall, French-style doors to the First Lord's office, entered by a step, announced the presence of Minister Macdonald of Canada, then stood aside, motioning for John A. to enter.

Macdonald strode into the vast, high-ceilinged room, his eyes focusing first on the man rising behind the expansive, ornate table that served as his desk.

First Lord Wolseley was a short, lean man, probably fifty years of age, with a narrow face, a sharp nose, thin lips, and a mass of straight black hair, a hank of which hung over his broad forehead. Bright blue eyes peered from under puffy lids through gold-rimmed spectacles at this tall, thin, colonial apparition, stovepipe hat still in hand.

As John A. crossed the room toward the desk, he noticed the First

Sea Lord standing in front of the desk and to the right, where he had been sitting in one of the two chairs. Peter Cairns was about the same stature as his political master, probably in his middle sixties. He was heavy of stomach, round of face red with years of exposure to the elements at sea, and broad of forehead. He was completely bald except for grey wisps above protruding large ears. A bulbous nose sat between a pair of chestnut brown eyes that looked as though they fronted for a mind of good humour that was at the same time tough but intelligent.

Admiral Cairns was dressed in his full naval regalia: a high-collared, brass-buttoned, navy blue jacket, its epaulettes embroidered with the golden threads of the symbols that marked his highest of naval ranks. A ceremonial sword hung from the broad gold and black belt that encircled his waist.

By contrast, the First Lord wore the customary conservative civilian dress of the day, the Prince Albert cutaway black frockcoat above tight-fitting grey trousers.

Behind Wolseley were tall, narrow windows along the entire wall. On the right wall, below a huge painting of Lord Nelson, warming flames leaped in a wide, deep fireplace.

After introductions and preliminary greetings were exchanged and tea served, the three men seated themselves comfortably at the table as the First Lord got down to business.

"I must say, Mr. Macdonald, you have the most impressive, should I say most powerful, sponsorship for your Russian venture."

"If you must know, First Lord, I'm more than a little astonished myself," John A. allowed.

"Well, although Admiral Cairns and I are not privy to exactly what your mission to Russia is, we know that it involves diplomatic negotiations at the highest level, and that we of Her Majesty's Royal Navy are charged with the duty of secretly conveying you and your good lady to and from St. Petersburg."

Macdonald replied: "You've summed up the situation exactly, sir. I trust that the presence of Mrs. Macdonald will not be an inconvenience."

"Heavens no," Cairns was quick to respond. "You will have the Admiral's quarters. On *Warrior* the accommodation is spacious — a bedroom, bathroom with a bath, sitting room, dining room. Mrs.

Macdonald will be quite comfortable, I'm sure."

"Excellent." John A. nodded approval.

The Admiral elaborated: "*Warrior* is our top-of-the-line warship, a beauty. Been in service for six years. She has a mix of sails and new coal-fired steam-engine technology and she's screw-driven — her large propeller has driven her along at a record speed of fourteen knots."

Cairns was obviously proud of the vessel. "She's four hundred and twenty feet long and has the graceful hull lines of the clipper sailing ships. There are her two masts — a fore and a main — and in between them are two telescopic funnels." He paused expectantly.

"Those engines must be enormously powerful," was John A.'s appropriate response.

It was the First Lord's turn to praise *Warrior*. "She's our first iron-hulled warship — iron over teak — and she's heavily armoured. For about five eighths the length of her hull, and well down her sides to below the water line, she's covered with four-and-a-half-inch armour."

"What about her guns?"

"She has sixteen ten-inch smooth-bore guns with remarkable range and accuracy," Admiral Cairns replied. "You'll see a demonstration of how good they are while you're at sea. I have the best gunnery officer in the navy on board *Warrior*, a cocky little fellow by the name of Lieutenant Jacky Fisher. I've designated him to be your aide. He'll meet you dockside at Edinburgh. A real charmer is Fisher . . . He loves dancing, sermons, and talking. Mrs. Macdonald will like him."

"It sounds as though you're fairly fond of Fisher yourself."

"That's true. I predict that young Fisher will someday sit in my chair, mark my words."

"You mentioned Edinburgh. What does the navy have there?"

Wolseley said, "It's one of the Royal Navy's facilities on the eastern coast of Scotland. Edinburgh gives us quick access to the North Sea so that we can readily contain any threat coming out of the Baltic — from Germany, Russia, the Scandinavian countries."

"Are they naval threats to Great Britain?"

"Not at this time," Cairns replied. "But it's our duty to be able to respond to any threat to our island. Our security and sovereignty can be threatened only by an attack by sea, so we must be prepared and alert at all times."

"So I must make arrangements to travel to Edinburgh." Macdonald's statement was also a question.

"All the arrangements have been made." The Admiral touched the large white envelope Macdonald had noticed lying on the desk near the naval officer's elbow. "In this are your rail tickets, special diplomatic passports, and a sealed envelope from the Prime Minister's office. It arrived just before you did."

"Yes, I know what that is."

The First Lord smiled at Macdonald. "This will be the trip of a lifetime. St. Petersburg is a near-arctic city, so be prepared for extremely cold weather."

"It can't be much colder than it gets in Ottawa. We'll take warm clothing."

"One final thing, Mr. Macdonald. Her Majesty the Queen suggested to the Prime Minister that he be kind enough to let you travel to Edinburgh in his special railway car."

"And return, as I understand it," the Admiral added.

"I can assure you, Mr. Macdonald, that a more luxurious sleeping car doesn't exist. We wish you and Mrs. Macdonald complete success in St. Petersburg. Bon voyage, Minister."

23

March 12–13, 1867
Washington

IT WAS MID-AFTERNOON ON TUESDAY THE TWELFTH WHEN THE messenger from the State Department delivered the large envelope grandly embossed with the proud American symbol of the great eagle encircled by stars, all in gold. It was addressed to His Excellency, Baron Edouard de Stoeckl, who was waiting and hoping for Secretary Seward's invitation. There it was, for eleven o'clock the next day, Wednesday, at the chambers of the Secretary — should that meet with the convenience of His Excellency — for the purpose of discussing matters of mutual interest.

The words "matters of mutual interest" were the common diplomatic terms for "matters of concern that are at the top of our mutual agendas of which we are both fully aware — or, if not, then we should be."

The Russian minister attempted to discern in the cold, terse words any hint that would signal that the President was agreeable to the Secretary's initiative. However, there was nothing to be discovered. Even so, the message — the acceptance was delivered forthwith — so raised his hopes for the success of his secret mission that he could scarcely concentrate on the matters at hand.

This was also de Stoeckl's state of mind during his rendezvous with Pamela Collins that evening. His incessant running-on about the enormity of the accomplishment — should he bring it off — the showering of honours from the Tsar, and other heady possibilities caused him to lapse. He forgot to draw the ceremonial bath that he and his amour customarily shared in the large gold-footed tub. Usually they eased themselves through those serious moments with sips of champagne, followed by languorous mutual towelling when they emerged from the soothing water. That softly done and with hardening purpose, the powerful Russian would sweep up the petite Pamela and carry her to the bed while showering her with kisses over whatever parts of her body his mouth could reach. At the bedside the nibbling formalities would cease as he placed her in the middle of the bed and then tumbled in beside her.

However, his failure to draw the bath drew no penalty. It was only that he was late in doing so by some ten minutes. That was the exact time by which he was late in arriving home for a happy dinner with his wife and loving family.

It was also almost the exact length of delay in Pamela's writing the next cable to Uncle in London.

The scenario of de Stoeckl's meeting with the Secretary of State the next morning was the same as the last one. The Secretary even had on the same cutaway suit and vest, the same velvet waistcoat, and the same-styled wing-collared shirt. He sported a different four-in-hand tie but the diamond stickpin was the same.

They exchanged the customary formalities and took their seats on opposite sides of the Secretary's desk. Seward began.

"Well, Your Excellency, I did what I said I would do: I spoke with the President. In truth, it's hard to get his attention because he's so fussed about the veto to the Reconstruction Act. Rumours are afoot that there's a groundswell in Congress for starting impeachment proceedings against him. Bad. Very bad." He shook his head negatively. "Baron, I have to tell you that President Johnson is not inclined to the transaction."

De Stoeckl's spirits fell as he heard those words.

"However, nothing is lost because he said he would agree to it if, in my judgment, it is in the interests of the United States to acquire Russian America."

The ambassador's bitter disappointment was momentarily eased. "Pray tell me what is your judgement?"

"In truth, I haven't made up my mind yet. I'd like to do it, but remember I'm only one man in the Cabinet. I really have to put the proposition to my colleagues before I can come to a final decision."

"When do you think you can do that?"

"Today. I've got to do it today because I want their reactions before the next Cabinet meeting, which is on Friday."

De Stoeckl's eagerness showed as he leaned forward. "I have some good contacts in the Senate and the House of Representatives. I can sound them out on the subject."

Seward's reaction was of near-anger. He stood up, saying emphatically, "Absolutely not, Baron! This is *my* deal! Right now the political position of the President and his Administration with the Congress is so bad that if you said one goddam word to anybody on the Hill everybody over there would be howling like a bunch of hyenas — howling *against* the deal."

De Stoeckl was confused. "But doesn't any transaction between us have to be approved by Congress?"

"Of course it does — but at the right moment. In normal times the Administration would seek the approval of Congress for such a treaty before the President signs it. But these are not normal times. On top of that, you told me the British are potential competitors for Russian America. Are you still going to see Bruce tomorrow?"

"Yes, at three o'clock. I really couldn't put him off."

"There you are. If that bastard puts in a bid, I'll really have to act quickly. No, if I decide to go for the deal, I'll have to get Cabinet approval, draft a treaty, then you and I will sign the damn thing. Then and only then we'll announce it to the world and send it to the Senate for ratification. If we get it, the treaty goes on to the House."

The Baron could see the strategy. If that's the way Seward thought it had to be, it suited him. "Very well. You have my pledge of secrecy, Mr. Secretary."

Seward was only partly satisfied. "What about the Englishman? What are you going to tell him?"

"If he raises the subject of acquisition, I certainly will not tell him that we are in negotiations. But you should know that it will be my duty to receive his representations and seek instructions from St. Petersburg."

"Of course." Seward could not quarrel with that reply. "Now, assuming I'm prepared to proceed, how much money are we talking about? I have a figure in mind."

De Stoeckl did not have to ask what the number was. Seward was not a good poker player. The Secretary blurted it out. "The figure is five million dollars in gold."

The Russian ambassador's face showed no reaction. Seward waited for a moment, then added, "We might even go to five and a half, but no more."

The Baron was pleased because his personal objective — notwithstanding Prince Gorchakov's base figure of five million dollars — was six million, five hundred thousand. So Seward's opening quote was clearly within range. But de Stoeckl was not prepared to negotiate the price at that moment. That would come after his meeting with the British ambassador.

"Let us discuss that point when we are further along, Mr. Secretary. As for Sir Frederick Bruce, I propose to be in touch with you after I see him tomorrow afternoon — if his purpose is to make a proposal."

"I will be at the French ambassador's reception at six tomorrow evening — at the Willard Hotel. We could meet there."

De Stoeckl smiled, "How very agreeable. I have been invited as well."

"I knew you had."

24

March 14, 1867
Washington

Sir Frederick Bruce and Baron Edouard de Stoeckl were both distinguished senior representatives of monarchs whose nations were not only incompatible but in all aspects completely different from each other in economic, sociological, and ethnic terms and in the degree of military and naval power that each could use to further its interests around the world.

Despite such differences, de Stoeckl had always found Queen Victoria's ambassador to the United States to be a personable, quite acceptable man, pleasant to speak with, intelligent, and not pompously overbearing the way that so many British dignitaries tended to be.

The two men sat talking and sipping tea, comfortable on settees flanking the roaring fireplace in the Baron's spacious office. Three o'clock in the afternoon was a bit early for Sir Frederick to be having tea, but he graciously accepted de Stoeckl's cordial gesture.

Sucking on his pipe, the portly, pink-faced Englishman, looking as svelte as possible in his dark Prince Albert suit, his wing collar tight around his neck, lost little time in getting to "the matter of mutual interest."

"My dear Baron, it's the Tsar's possessions in North America that I wish to raise with you. Their future is of enormous interest to Her Majesty's government, as you might well imagine." Bruce expected that, at least at the beginning, de Stoeckl would listen but comment rarely. This was a tactic that he himself used quite often in playing the diplomacy game.

Bruce went on. "My government is deeply concerned about the incursions being made by Americans into our colony, British

Columbia, and, as you are, most apprehensive about the activities of the American filibusters in the area." He paused but de Stoeckl said nothing. "My government believes that it is essential to maintain the integrity of British Columbia, particularly since the Canadian colonies in the east are about to receive final approval from Her Majesty's government for the establishment of a confederated form of government in which provision is made for the ultimate inclusion of British Columbia as an integral and essential part of the new nation."

"Which will be called . . . ?"

"Canada. The Dominion of Canada."

"Dominion? That's a peculiar term. I've never heard it used in that context before."

"True. Well, the Canadians have a reputation for doing things a little differently, I must say."

"So, British Columbia, Her Majesty doesn't want to lose it to the Americans. Is that what you mean?"

"Exactly. Now, my government believes that the Russian America Company is — how shall I put it — in dire straits, if not bankrupt. We know that proposals have been put forward to your government to allow a California company to take over the Hudson's Bay Company lease. Of course, we have no news on the status of that application. In addition, we are aware of a memorial of the Washington Territory legislative assembly petitioning the United States to arrange fishing, hunting, and port rights in Russian America territory."

De Stoeckl still made no response.

"My government also believes that you are in negotiations with Seward for the United States to acquire Russian America."

De Stoeckl straightened up, his face full of indignation. "How could you come to such a conclusion? That's ridiculous!"

"How? Very easily, my dear Baron. Through our sources we learned that as soon as you arrived back in Washington on March the eighth — after your well-nursed stay in New York — you made arrangements to see Seward. Your first meeting was three days later, on the eleventh. Then you had another on the thirteenth, yesterday, both at his State Department office."

De Stoeckl's annoyance subsided. "There are many reasons to meet with the Secretary of State."

"Of course. But I know from my excellent intelligence sources that you were negotiating for Russian America." Sir Frederick smiled. "To be sure, you have every right to negotiate with the United States."

"Of course, Sir Frederick. And I have every right to neither confirm nor deny — or disclose the nature of my discussions with Secretary Seward."

"True. But my government instructs me to tell you this. If your negotiations with Seward result in a treaty being signed for the sale of Russian America, the Canadians with the full support of my government will do everything in their power to ensure that the treaty will not be approved by the Senate."

"That sounds very much like a threat."

"Heavens no. It's simply a declaration of intent."

"Intent to fight."

"Using every legitimate weapon we can lay our hands on."

De Stoeckl stood, to relieve the tension. He went to the cigar box and offered one to Bruce, who refused. Lighting a sweet-smelling Havana, he said without looking the Briton in the eye, "I must do what I must do. I have my instructions directly from the Tsar as to what I must accomplish for him in America."

"Understood."

The Russian ambassador sucked contentedly on his cigar as he sat down. "Yes, you do understand. Now, my friend, I am of course obliged to notify Prince Gorchakov of your threat."

"Not a threat. Words of pressure."

"Whatever."

Bruce decided to ask the direct question. Through intelligence information that had been passed to him he already knew the answer. "Has Seward made an offer yet?"

"Not yet, but we have had discussions, fruitful discussions to be sure — as you've already guessed."

"Is there anything you can tell me?"

"All I can say is that Mr. Seward is a highly interested party. If he can get the approval of the Johnson Cabinet —"

"It meets on Friday."

"Quite so. If he can persuade the Cabinet, there will be a firm offer. Of that I am quite confident." De Stoeckl stroked his bushy eyebrows thoughtfully.

Bruce's pipe was alight again. He tamped on its glowing embers as he asked, "Do you know how soon such an offer might come?"

De Stoeckl considered that question for a moment. "Yes. I will venture a guess, but please be good enough not to hold me to it."

"Of course not."

"If Seward is successful tomorrow in his request to the Cabinet for authority to treat, I think he will move expeditiously — a Seward trait."

"No question about that."

"His full proposal will likely be in my hands within the week."

Bruce nodded. "Of course, he'll want to do some negotiating of terms — quite apart from the issue of money."

"As would we. But at this time it is sufficient if he puts forward the main principles of the treaty." De Stoeckl puffed on his cigar with gusts of pleasure. "My tentative plan, only tentative mind you, is to cable Prince Gorchakov and report both your position and that of Seward's, assuming it is forthcoming."

"And if it isn't?"

The Russian diplomat chortled. "More tea, Sir Frederick? No?"

Bruce rose. "I am obliged, Your Excellency. I must now take my leave. Will I see you at the Willard Hotel tonight?"

"But of course."

25

March 14–15, 1867
Washington

The ballroom of the Willard was filled with the sound of French chamber music blended with the loud conversation of some six hundred dignitaries — members of the diplomatic corps, members of both Houses of Congress, judges of the Supreme and lesser courts, admirals, generals, and the host of all, His Excellency the ambassador of France. The presence of such elite personages, together with the tinkling of glasses filled with sparkling champagne and other wines, the glistening crystal in the chandeliers, and the myriad decorations worn by many of the participants, created an aura of pomp and circumstance.

It was de Stoeckl's intent to arrive shortly after six and find Seward as quickly as possible. He would pay his respects to his French host, with whom he intended to plead an early departure because of an urgent commitment at the legation. Then, after words with Seward, he would go straight upstairs to a truly important engagement, his treasured moments with the Honourable Pamela Collins.

The ballroom was crowded when de Stoeckl went through the receiving line to exchange handshakes and formal courtesies with the host ambassador and beg forgiveness for his need to leave in a short time. What could the French diplomat do but kiss him on both cheeks and say "But of course, mon cher Baron!"

That done, and with a glass of excellent champagne in hand, de Stoeckl began his search for Seward. It was only ten past six but, if the Secretary was true to form, he would already be mingling with the other guests because he enjoyed the fawning and deferential treatment he received as the most prestigious senior member of the Cabinet.

Seward's motto for receptions and parties was "Arrive early and leave late for there is much business to be done in between."

When the Baron found him, Seward was engaged in animated discussion with a distinguished gentleman with whom de Stoeckl had done business many times over the years. It was Senator Charles Sumner, the highly respected and influential chairman of the Senate Committee on Foreign Relations.

It would be unthinkable to interrupt the two men. De Stoeckl moved past them and manoeuvred into a position behind Sumner's back, yet far enough away that he could not be perceived as attempting to overhear the conversation. It was no more than a few moments before Seward's eyes shifted slightly and caught sight of de Stoeckl, who signalled with a slight nod of his head that he wished to have words. The Baron then sauntered through groups of people, exchanging salutations and pleasantries but not stopping until he reached the high-mantled fireplace. There he stood and warmed himself by its leaping flames while he waited.

A smiling Seward soon emerged from the crowd to greet him then to caution, "Lots of smiling and laughing, please, as if we were talking about the usual inane nothings."

Following instructions, de Stoeckl quickly gave his report on the Bruce meeting and word he had just received from St. Petersburg about Macdonald. He could see the surprise on Seward's face as the forced smile disappeared and the bushy eyebrows lifted. Then they lowered and the smile returned, but his words did not fit the expession on his face. "Damn those British bastards. The Tsar's actually going to receive Macdonald, negotiate with him?"

Seward sipped his champagne, looking around to satisfy himself that they were not being overheard. Then he looked de Stoeckl in the eye. "I assume you didn't tell him that we were in negotiation."

"I told him you were interested, but that you did not have instructions to negotiate. Nor did I tell him that the Tsar had in fact authorized me to negotiate with you."

Seward looked around. Satisfied no one was within earshot he said, "Now, Baron, I would like you to listen very carefully to what I am going to say. I have canvassed the members of the Cabinet, and their response was positive, so I am prepared to make a recommendation to the meeting of Cabinet tomorrow. But before I do so, I need to have some assurances from you. Therefore let me make a proposal to you, Baron, for your ears only. First you should know that through my impeccable sources I am aware of your liaison with the English lady on the third floor. It's private information that won't be disclosed if you and I reach an understanding here and now."

De Stoeckl, overcoming the impulse to respond, held himself in check, fully focused on the reedy voice of the powerful William Henry Seward.

The Secretary of State was agitated but only his eyes showed it. "Look, Edouard, I'm no diplomat and I can't put things in all your fancy words. What I am saying to you is straight and to the point. We have to do everything we can to make sure the Tsar gives Macdonald the boot. Their meeting is on the twenty-fifth, you say?"

De Stoeckl merely nodded.

Seward looked around again, then spoke intently in a low voice: "Now this is what I want you to do, Mr. Ambassador."

De Stoeckl listened intently as Seward spelled out his proposition. Both men had forgotten about the need to smile and look social. The matter under discussion was far too intense.

"Well, Your Excellency, what do you think?"

De Stoeckl quickly attempted to assess the ramifications of what he had just heard. Seward's proposal meant the Tsar would be paid seven million, two hundred thousand dollars, some two million dollars more than the amount de Stoeckl had been told to obtain. And two hundred thousand more than Macdonald had offered Gorchakov. Furthermore, the Tsar's primary direction was to negotiate with the Americans, not with the British.

The smile returned to de Stoeckl's face as he said, "I am pleased to have your proposal, Mr. Secretary. It is most acceptable."

"Very good. If I get Cabinet approval tomorrow, we're off and running!"

Seward held out his hand. De Stoeckl took it to seal their understanding. Then both men turned away to seek out new faces. The first that de Stoeckl saw, only a few feet away, was that of Sir Frederick

Bruce. Obviously he had been watching them intently.

Edouard de Stoeckl averted his eyes. The last thing he wanted at that moment was an interception by the British ambassador. The first thing he wanted was on the third floor of the Willard. He wanted nothing, not even Queen Victoria's envoy, to stand in his lustful way.

✦

ACROSS THE ATLANTIC, IN LONDON, JOHN A. WAS IN A HEAVY sleep, exhausted. Agnes snuggled close against him after an undisturbed intimate dinner followed by exquisite lovemaking. For both it had been one of their most exhilarating days.

There was a loud, insistent banging at the door of their suite. John A. struggled awake, as did Agnes. "I'll go," he said as he reached for his discarded nightshirt, which he somehow remembered was on the floor.

"All right. I'm coming!" he shouted.

It was Ben, the night porter, at the door with an envelope in his hand.

"Awful sorry, Mr. Macdonald. But this was just delivered. Most urgent it says. Couldn't wait till morning, I thought."

"You were right, Ben. What time is it anyway?"

"Ten past two, sir."

"Thank you, Ben. Well done."

"Thank *you*, sir."

Macdonald shut the door behind him and locked it.

Back in the bedroom, Agnes had lit a candle at her side of the bed. "What is it, John?"

"It's a cable. Most urgent, it says."

"From whom?"

"Don't know yet." He ripped open the envelope and unfolded the paper.

"What is it?"

"It's from Sir Frederick Bruce in Washington."

"Tell me what it says."

"I'll read it out loud — where are my spectacles?"

"Sit down right here and I'll get them for you." Agnes rolled across to John A.'s side of the bed, the right side, reached down to the floor, found the spectacles, then rolled back to him.

"There you are, darling."

"Thank you, my sweet. And I must say I enjoy how you roll across that bed without any clothes on. Gives a young lad ideas!"

He put on the glasses and began to read.

> ***I met this afternoon with Russian ambassador. Expects offer from U.S. Seward going to cabinet tomorrow for authority to treat. Ambassador expects to know within week if U.S. to make offer and what it will be. Advised him will do everything in power to defeat treaty in Senate. Anticipate he will inform Seward of details.***
>
> ***Yours aye. Bruce.***

Macdonald sighed as he slipped off his spectacles.

"Well," said Agnes cheerily, "that doesn't sound too bad, now, does it?"

"No, not really. But I'm afraid nothing's going to stop that conniving bastard Seward."

"Nothing except John A. Macdonald. Remember, Seward doesn't have a Treaty of Paris card to play."

"True." John climbed back into bed. "We're off to St. Petersburg not a minute too soon if Seward gets his authority to treat tomorrow morning."

"Well, at least you are certain now that Seward's on the move — and I'm in your bed."

John A. blew out the candle and slipping off his nightshirt responded with a fervent "Thanks be to God!"

✦

SECRETARY SEWARD'S CARRIAGE ARRIVED AT THE FRONT DOOR OF his imposing stone mansion near half past ten. The Secretary looked in at his sleeping wife, then went straight to his library to set down in his diary the day's events including, and most importantly, his activities during the French ambassador's reception at the Willard.

Like many another politician convinced that he was influencing the course of history and indeed the world, Seward had long since decided that once he was relieved of the burdens of high political office, he would transform his papers and diaries into a series of books that would chronicle the significant events that were encompassed by his career.

After the day's events had been recorded (in particular his dealings with de Stoeckl), Seward directed his mind to the Cabinet and his proposal to acquire Russia's American territories. Would he tell the President about the British bid? He decided against it, reasoning that Andrew Johnson was a pleasant but not politically astute man who was so deeply worried about the growing threats of impeachment that he might express opposition to the project. Seward would inform no one about either his discussion with de Stoeckl or the English offer. No one, that was, except his most trusted assistant and under-secretary of state, his son Frederick.

That being settled in his mind, Seward selected a fresh sheet of paper and with his customary blue pencil wrote out notes for his presentation to the morning Cabinet meeting:

> ***Mr. Seward proposes that Russia cede and convey to U.S. her possessions on the North American continent and the adjacent Aleutian Islands, the line to be drawn through the center of the Bering Straits and include all the islands east of and including Attoo. The dominion to be unencumbered of grants and convey to the Russian American Company and all others therein except individual private titles which shall be confirmed. The white population remaining to be citizens of U.S., the Indians to be on the footing of Indians domiciled in U.S.***
> ***Mr. Seward proposes U.S. pay 7 million dollars gold at Washington.***

At the full Cabinet meeting at the White House the next morning Seward explained that he had earlier advised the President that he would negotiate with de Stoeckl in the range of five million dollars. But from a negotiating standpoint it would be prudent if the Secretary of State in actual fact had authority to go to seven million. Seward uttered not a word about the discussion with de Stoeckl in the ballroom of the

Willard Hotel, although he was aware that at least three of his Cabinet colleagues had observed the two of them in conversation.

After perfunctory discussion President Johnson, who had made no comment, observed that there was a consensus that the proposal as outlined by Secretary Seward should go forward.

Before he left the White House that day Seward made sure that his authority to negotiate was formalized. He fully understood the ramifications of congressional hostility that would likely emerge when the Johnson Administration secretly signed a treaty and then sent it to the Senate for ratification. Secrecy was an element that Seward had absolutely insisted on until the treaty was signed. His authority to negotiate had to be ironclad and immediate. For this purpose Seward had drafted and engrossed a document that certified both the President's foreknowledge and his approval. It was signed by Johnson:

> ***I hereby authorize and direct the Secretary of State to affix the Seal of the United States to a full power to William H. Seward, Secretary of State, to negotiate a convention with the minister plenipotentiary of Russia.***
> ***Dated this day and signed by me and for so doing this shall be his warrant.***
>
> ***Andrew Johnson***
> ***WASHINGTON, MARCH 15, 1867***

From the moment the President handed Seward that signed and sealed warrant, the ambitious Secretary of State had the authority to turn his dream of Manifest Destiny into exhilarating reality. He, William Henry Seward, was now empowered to acquire the vast, rich North American territory of the Tsar of Russia for and on behalf of his beloved United States of America. And, come hell or high water, nobody was going to stand in his way. Nobody — not those goddam Englishmen, not that British colonial, Macdonald, not the Senate — nobody!

26

March 16–17, 1867
London to Edinburgh

THE OVERNIGHT TRIP UP TO EDINBURGH WAS A JOURNEY IN THE most luxurious railway car John A. had ever been privileged to set foot in.

The government had purchased and ornately fitted out the special car for the exclusive use of the Prime Minister of Great Britain. He could, however, designate those ministers of his Cabinet upon whom he might wish to confer the honour of using it — provided, of course, the use related to government business that was of benefit to his party.

But the Prime Minister's car did not have that Northern American luxury that politicians like John A. were delighted to have in whistle-stop election campaigning, the roofed observation platform at the rear of the car.

The long, narrow salon was comfortably furnished with lightweight upholstered chairs and a table that could be used for a conference or whist. From the many windows along each side hung heavy blue drapes split at the middle and tied back during the day with tasselled cords. Double gas-lit brass chandeliers hung from the dark polished walnut that covered the ceiling as well as any wall space not devoted to windows. At the far end of the salon hung a picture of the young Queen Victoria in one of her favourite poses, chosen because Her Majesty used the car from time to time on special occasions. Beyond the salon was the chef's galley, compact and filled with glistening pots and pans. Then followed two narrow, carpeted bedrooms off a shoulder-wide corridor. In each one, along one wall, was a single bed scarcely wide enough for two people and barely long enough for a

Buckingham Palace guardsman. At the window with its tied-back blue drapes were a small oak desk and chair, a workplace for a prime minister. Opposite the bed a door opened into a cramped bathroom with no bathtub but a sink running hot and cold water and a splendid porcelain, wood-seated, throne-like toilet the contents of which could be discharged directly onto the railbed below.

Next to the door into the water closet stood a high, wide oak armoire with a full-length mirror on the inside of each of its two doors. On the wood-panelled ceiling hung a small gas chandelier, and, so the Prime Minister could read himself to sleep, a wall bracket fitted with a light hung over the head of the bed.

Agnes Macdonald chose the bedroom farthest from the galley for herself and John A., the better to avoid the noise and smells of the galley. The second bedroom was assigned to Hewitt, whom John A. wanted to accompany them to Edinburgh. There was a flood of administrative work to be done in setting up working arrangements between confederated government in Canada and Her Majesty's mighty bureaucracy at Westminster. Several hours of dictation and discussion with Hewitt on the train would keep the plans moving along while John A. and Agnes were out of touch on their secret mission to St. Petersburg.

At the last minute a fourth person joined the Macdonald party as it was about to board the train at London's Marylebone Station of the Great Central Railway. It was Lieutenant John Arbuthnot Fisher, John A.'s naval aide.

Jacky Fisher, ever the inventive, aggressive career entrepreneur who loved being at the centre of events, had decided that meeting Minister Macdonald at Edinburgh really wasn't sufficiently good form. The Royal Navy could better perform its courtesies, hospitality functions, and protocols for and toward its special guests if their aide was to take them into his protective custody in London. All Lt. Fisher had to do was convince *Warrior*'s commander and, through a friend, the executive assistant to the First Sea Lord, Admiral Cairns, that this was the right and proper thing to do.

Then, with luck, for at least one night, perhaps two, the footloose and fancy-free Jacky would be in London, cavorting and dancing with his current favourite, Lady Emma Townsend, the gorgeous, long-legged, big-bosomed daughter of Lord Richard Townsend, one of the richest men in the southeast of England!

Putting on his most persuasive personality, Jacky Fisher, by far the best gunnery lieutenant in the Royal Navy, had first targetted *Warrior*'s captain. Within moments of appearing rigidly at attention before Captain Nigel Hamilton, Fisher had persuaded him that the reputation and traditions of the Royal Navy could best be upheld if he escorted their distinguished guests from London to Edinburgh.

That done, and with Captain Hamilton's concurrence, Jacky had immediately fired off an eloquent signal to Admiral Cairns' executive assistant, Commander Tony Flesherton, who had only recently finished a tour as Executive Officer, second-in-command, of *Warrior.* (It would be bad form for a mere lieutenant to send a signal directly to the First Sea Lord.) In a few hours had come the answer the confident Jacky Fisher expected. Permission granted.

At eight-thirty in the evening of March 16, 1867, Lieutenant Jacky Fisher was standing on the Marylebone Station platform of the Flying Scotsman train for Edinburgh. He had already taken command of the Prime Minister's car, issuing instructions to the car's steward and its chef.

Resplendent was Fisher, polished brass buttons gleaming on his tight-fitting naval officer's jacket, the two gold-braided stripes of his rank prominent on the sleeves near the cuffs. His gunner lieutenant's leather gaiters and boots were shining, his peaked cap with its officer's badge sat squarely on his head, and those golden aides' aiglettes hung from his right shoulder and looped under his arm.

Fisher's remarkable eyes searched down the platform looking for the first sign of Macdonald, whom he knew was quite tall and clothed in a heavy black coat with a fur collar, wearing a stovepipe hat, probably grey, and carrying a walking stick. What made Fisher's eyes remarkable were heavily hooded upper lids, which made some people describe them as cobra's eyes. At his full height of five feet seven inches with his large head on his slight but tough, muscular body, the twenty-six-year-old Fisher was a mass of intelligence and energy. He spotted the Macdonalds and Hewitt Bernard as soon as they came through the gate following the porter carrying their several pieces of luggage.

Fisher marched briskly down the platform to halt smartly in front of John A. and Agnes. He threw them an arm-bouncing salute.

"Sir. Lieutenant Jacky Fisher. At your service, sir."

Smiling down on the serious face of the youthful naval officer, Macdonald acknowledged the salute by lifting and slightly tipping his fashionable stovepipe hat, saying, "Thank you, Lieutenant Fisher. This is Mrs. Macdonald and her brother —"

"And your private secretary," Fisher added to demonstrate that he had made a preparatory study of the Canadian minister and his family.

"Yes, Lieutenant Colonel Hewitt Bernard." John A. took care to use his brother-in-law's military rank in order to ensure that Fisher did not overstep the mark.

Hewitt offered his hand to Fisher, who took it firmly and briefly.

"Now, sir," Fisher said, "if you'll just leave everything to me, I'll see that your luggage is stored and secure in the bedroom you've selected, Mrs. Macdonald."

Agnes gave him a charming smile. "You'll make sure the steward handles my dresses carefully, won't you, Jacky?"

John A. and Hewitt maintained the formalities and appropriate distance from this young man. But an attractive young woman only slightly older than Fisher did not want to hold him at arm's length — unless, of course, he overstepped the invisible but unbreachable wall of familiarity that might, as the saying went, breed contempt.

John A. was not pleased with her immediate use of the name Jacky. Nor was Hewitt. But it was not appropriate to counsel her on the point at that moment. Or perhaps at any time.

"Of course, madame, I shall so instruct the steward."

"The small black valise." Agnes pointed to it. "Tell him not to open that one."

"I understand, madame. Now, sir, if you and Mrs. Macdonald and Colonel Bernard would step aboard the Prime Minister's car, just there at the entrance to the salon, you can familiarize yourselves with the comforts it offers while I sort things out in your bedrooms. Which are your bags, Colonel Bernard?"

Hewitt identified them.

"Good. When we're all settled, madame and sirs, I would be pleased to meet with you in the salon to go over some of the details of your itinerary."

John A. pulled his father's huge round gold watch by its chain out of his lower waistcoat pocket, snapped open its engraved lid, checked the timepiece, and said, "It's quarter to nine. I should think nine-thirty would be fine whether or not the train leaves on time at nine."

"It always leave on time, sir."

"And Big Ben never breaks down," Hewitt retorted. "Tell the steward not to open any of my valises." Then he smiled. "Not even the one that is locked."

"I'll keep a special eye on that one, Colonel. God's teeth I will! The chef will serve you tea in the salon while the steward and I take care of things."

The Flying Scotsman gently lurched into motion at the first distant stroke of the massive Big Ben clock secure in its tower above the Houses of Parliament.

At that moment Jacky Fisher, now capless, appeared at the entrance to the corridor to announce to the travellers that their bedrooms were ready for them. "The steward, may I introduce him?" The man behind Fisher had a bright, ruddy, much lined, middle-aged face, a small white moustache, a receding forehead below greying and thinning black hair, and a thick neck half-concealed by the high collar of his brown uniform. The young lieutenant turned, saying, "This is Alfred, your steward. This is his private fiefdom — his and George's, the chef whom you met when you came in."

Macdonald stood, wavering slightly with the motion of the train travelling fast at speeds he had never experienced in Canada. "Alfred, we're ready to inspect our quarters, if you please. But before we do that I have to ask you, Lt. Fisher, how fast are we going?"

Macdonald's naval aide turned to look out the window at the trees and telegraph poles flashing by. "My guess is about fifty miles an hour, sir."

Macdonald swallowed an unuttered oath of astonishment, "Christ!" and said instead, "Alfred, lead on. Fisher, we'll see you here at nine-thirty. By the way, where are you billeted?"

"In the next car, sir. It's the service car for this one. Carries the food, silverware, china . . ."

"Wine and whisky?" John A. tried to sound jocular, but Agnes and her brother knew the question was serious.

"Lots o' that, sir!" Alfred piped up.

"Good!"

"Alfred and George each have a small bedroom back there and there's a spare. I'm in it."

"Not very fancy for the acting gunnery lieutenant of *Warrior*, is it?" Agnes sounded sympathetic.

"Just one of the things I have to do for Queen and country, ma'am. Who knows? If I work hard and always do what's right — what I think is right — maybe someday this poor man's son'll be occupying this beautiful car in his own right."

By nine twenty-five the three travellers had arranged the contents of their luggage, and were ready for the briefing with Jacky Fisher. At least John A. and Hewitt were. Agnes begged off, saying that she had some thank-you notes to write.

Lieutenant Fisher was ready for John A. and Hewitt. He had arranged four chairs around the table with his papers at the chair nearest the galley. From that spot he could quickly nip out to give instructions to Alfred or George.

"So, Lieutenant Fisher," John A. said as they settled into their seats.

"Perhaps, sir, it might be more comfortable if you called me Jacky."

"All right, for the present. But not when we're on board your ship. Now, what do you want to tell us about the itinerary?"

"There's quite a bit, sir. A special engine picks these two cars up at Berwick-on-Tweed and we arrive dockside in Edinburgh at eight tomorrow morning. The trip will take about eleven hours. The Admiral's barge will be there to meet you."

"Which admiral?"

"Piers, sir. Admiral Thomas Piers, commander of the Northern Fleet. His flagship is *Black Prince*, the sister ship of *Warrior*. *Black Prince* was built at Glasgow."

"And *Warrior*?"

"At Blackwall. They both came into service, were commissioned, at the same time. *Black Prince* and the Admiral are at Edinburgh. As a matter of fact it was a toss-up whether the flagship would take you to St. Petersburg."

"But then the Admiral would have had to give up his permanent quarters. Right?" Hewitt observed.

"Right, sir. So by our good fortune *Warrior* has the privilege. I can tell you that the ship's company to a man are excited about this voyage. It will be cold as bloody hell — possibly some ice in transit."

"Will that be dangerous?"

"Could be, sir, you can never tell. This is March, still winter. If we encounter storms we might pick up ice on the superstructure. Have to watch that. The weight of too much accumulation could be dangerous. *Warrior*'s heavy enough as it is with her iron hull."

John A. asked, "The ship's company — why're they excited? Have they, have you, heard rumours about what my mission is?"

"No, sir. Haven't heard a word. But I'm sure there's been some speculation in the wardroom."

Macdonald was not yet familiar with navy jargon. "Wardroom?"

"Sorry, sir. Wardroom is the officers' sitting, drinking, and eating area. Like an army officers' mess."

"I see. What's the speculation?"

"The officers are trying to put two and two together. You're a Canadian minister. From the *Times* and other newspapers we're aware that you and your colleagues have been in London for some time and the government has passed some legislation for a confederation."

"True."

"So we're taking you to St. Petersburg on a secret mission. When *Warrior* is taking you it can only mean one thing."

"Which is?"

"You're going to see the Tsar or the Foreign Minister, someone at that level, to negotiate."

"Negotiate what?"

"We're not sure. Canadians are regarded as British, but they're colonials and not a power. Maybe you're a comfortable go-between between our government and the Tsar on some negotiable issue the two sides can't meet directly on."

"Any other ideas?"

"No, not really."

"Good. Now, you still haven't said why the ship's crew is excited."

Jacky Fisher laughed, his glistening white teeth showing to the gums. "Because the best warship in the Royal Navy's going to be sailing right into the mouths of the two-headed eagle, displaying all her guns, iron hull, and steam engines to the Russians. They'll be quaking in their bloody boots when they see *Warrior*. And that would excite the entire crew from the lower deck right to the top."

"Including Jacky Fisher?" Hewitt asked.

"You can bet your last shilling on that, Colonel."

John A. said, "Tell us about the Admiral's barge, please. It'll be waiting for us dockside, but not the Admiral."

"Correct, sir. Admiral Piers will be waiting to receive you on *Warrior* with Captain Hamilton. When the formalities are over the Admiral will depart for London.

"*Warrior* will up anchor and get under way as soon as you are on board. We will cross the North Sea and enter the Skagerrak between Norway and Denmark. We'll pass by Copenhagen and Stockholm, but we won't put into those ports en route to St. Petersburg because Captain Hamilton has direct orders from the First Sea Lord — *Warrior* has to be standing off St. Petersburg at least twenty-four hours before your scheduled meeting with the Tsar on the twenty-fifth."

"That makes good sense. So we have what . . . tomorrow's the seventeenth, we have seven days' sailing . . ."

"And steaming, sir, as the captain chooses."

"How far is it to St. Petersburg?"

"From Edinburgh, 1327 nautical miles."

"That's roughly two hundred miles a day. If *Warrior* cruises at, say, ten knots an hour she'll be there in plenty of time."

Fisher proudly announced, "She can make fourteen knots. Fastest ships in the navy, she and *Black Prince*."

"What about a backup?" Hewitt asked.

"A what, sir?"

"Will there be a second ship with *Warrior*? In case there are any mechanical problems, engine difficulties, that sort of thing?"

Fisher was momentarily at a loss.

"Is there such a contingency plan?" John A. was concerned. "I would have thought this problem would have been taken into account. There simply can't be any delays, any failure." He was emphatic. "I absolutely *must* be in St. Petersburg on the twenty-fifth."

"I understand, sir, but I don't have any instructions. There's nothing about it here." Fisher's face showed his consternation as he picked up his sheaf of papers, then threw it back on the table.

Macdonald would not show any anger or distress. There was plenty of time to plug the gap in the planning, if indeed there was one. "All right, Jacky, if you're planning to be the First Sea Lord someday how would you go about fixing this situation?"

"I've already worked that out, Mr. Macdonald. As soon as we stop at the next station, Grantham, about two hours from now — Grantham to change engines — I'll send a telegram to Admiral Piers' staff. It will read as follows: 'Minister Macdonald expects contingency plan providing for second ship to accompany *Warrior* so that in case of mechanical difficulties second ship can receive Macdonald party and proceed St. Petersburg in order to arrive March 25 without fail. No information about such contingency plan in briefing material. Probably overlooked. Have assured Minister such plan exists. Please advise earliest. Urgent for Admiral's consideration.' "

"Perfect." John A. was pleased. "That wording will allow the Admiral and his staff to patch in a contingency plan without admitting it did not exist. Good work, Jacky."

"I'll let you see the written message, sir."

"Show it to Colonel Bernard. I'm going to have a rest and do some reading. Then he and I will meet to do some work. There is much to do, too much."

"Yes, sir. One final detail. The Admiralty has tasked *Warrior* to make one-day ceremonial, show-the-flag stops at Stockholm and Copenhagen on the way back. Hope you and Mrs. Macdonald won't mind?"

Hewitt interjected, "I thought you were going to say Oslo, too."

"I was, Colonel. It just slipped my mind." Jacky Fisher grinned. The eyes behind his cobra lids were doing one of the things he liked best — dancing.

✦

BEFORE HIS DEPARTURE FOR RUSSIA, ONE PRESSING PROBLEM Macdonald had to cope with was the consequence of the passage of the British North America Act. There was much to do before the Dominion of Canada became a reality on the first day of July, 1867, and on his shoulders rested the burden of creating the governmental and administrative structure of the new country.

There was no one else to do the job. Galt, Cartier, and all the delegates to the London Conference had scuttled back to North America just as quickly as they could after the BNA Act had received its third and final reading in the House of Commons. All of them to a man had had enough of London and the overbearing attitude of the British bureaucracy toward the colonial ministers.

As Galt had written to his wife on January 14, 1867: "I am more than ever disappointed at the tone of feeling here as to the colonies. I cannot shut my eyes to the fact that they want to get rid of us." Galt had expressed his feeling to John A. many times during their stay in London and had had no argument from Macdonald on that point.

En route to Edinburgh John A. spent several hours closeted with Hewitt in the small second bedroom to allow Agnes the full comfort and freedom of the salon. The two men toiled until two in the morning over the files they had brought with them, and soon the bed, the floor, the desk, and every other flat surface were covered with piles of carefully arranged papers and documents. By the time they reached their destination three of Bernard's notebooks were full of letters and messages dictated by John A. to Her Majesty the Queen; the Prime Minister; the Governor General designate of Canada, Lord Monck; Sir Frederick Bruce in Washington; and the permanent under-secretaries of a score of British ministries with which the government of the Dominion would have to deal.

27

March 17, 1867
Edinburgh

BUNDLES OF COTTON-LIKE WHITE CLOUDS AGAINST A CLEAR backdrop of aqua-blue sky scudded low across the light-green rolling waters of the broad, land-protected roadstead at Edinburgh.

It was one of the many places in which naval legends had their birth as fleets had assembled over several centuries to venture forth against those who might assault the British Isles or who might threaten the many far-flung colonies that flourished under the Union Jack in the empire upon which the sun never set.

In the spotless Admiral's barge, its new steam engine noisily turning a single propeller at the pointed stern, John A. stood on the low deck behind the enclosed engine room, his gloved right hand firmly locked in Agnes's grip. Together they rode the movement of the boat in the almost windless morning's gentle swells as their eyes looked in amazement at the huge black-hulled warship that lay some half-mile ahead.

"That's *Warrior*, ma'am," Jacky Fisher, behind Agnes, said in a loud voice to override the engine's rattling and hissing. "Beautiful, isn't she?"

Agnes could only nod her agreement.

They were approaching *Warrior* from its starboard side, abeam as Jacky explained it. Dark-clothed figures could be seen moving on the ship's decks along its entire length as the crew prepared for the departure that was only a short time away. The lines of the hull were a work of pure art, from the long, pointed, clipper-like bow through to the curved upsweep of the stern. The upper areas of the iron hull, the first of its kind (except for its appropriately named sister ship, *Black Prince*) were dotted with open portholes, their apertures filled with fixed-line modern 10-inch guns, the special charges of *Warrior*'s gunnery lieutenant, Jacky Fisher.

Warrior's pair of telescopic funnels were fully extended, spewing black smoke that sped off in pursuit of the white clouds above. The sails in the masts above the funnels were furled but antlike figures could be seen moving in the rigging as if making ready to break out the sail should the command be given.

Fisher moved behind Macdonald to say, "Those sails, sir, they can move *Warrior* along at eight knots without the engines. If it's not turning the propeller doesn't hold her back when she's running under sail."

John A. turned to shout, "Which is perhaps why there wasn't any mention of a contingency plan in the first place . . ."

"Possibly, sir, but there certainly will be a second ship with us now."

John A. nodded and looked ahead toward this pride of the Royal Navy that would be home for the next two weeks or more.

Would all the effort be worthwhile, would he be successful in his mission? Macdonald wondered if that strange bond between the American Congress and the Tsar could be overcome — a bond that could well be worth more than any sum of money.

He had asked himself these questions many times since his visit with Gorchakov in Paris. John A. knew full well that the task ahead of him was formidable, yes, nearly impossible given the animus that still existed between Russia and Great Britain.

But the point was that, regardless of all the obstacles and the negatives, the Tsar was prepared to receive him and to negotiate. That was the encouraging factor that drove Macdonald. Even so, there was the nagging uncertainty as to what was going on in Washington between de Stoeckl and Seward. Macdonald could only hope that Sir Frederick Bruce had pulled no diplomatic punches when he informed the Russian ambassador that the Canadians would do everything in their power to ensure that the Senate would reject any treaty that de Stoeckl and Seward might produce.

His thoughts were interrupted as the white-gatered and capped crew, operating under the crisp cockney-accented commands of a bos'n's mate, brought the Admiral's barge smoothly up against the base of

Warrior's lowered gangway. Lieutenant Fisher was the first out, carrying Macdonald's small locked valise of secret papers.

Fisher assisted Agnes and John A. out of the rocking barge, then followed them up the steep steps to the main deck. As the distinguished guests stepped onto the freshly scrubbed wooden deck of *Warrior* they were greeted, as Fisher had warned, by the shrill sound of the traditional bos'n's pipes. John A. stopped, as did Agnes by his side. He lifted his tall hat in response to the pipes and to the salutes of the clutch of naval officers in place to greet them, the sun glinting off gold on the peak of the Admiral's cap and off the gold braid on the shoulders of heavy navy-blue greatcoats.

"Welcome aboard *Warrior*, Minister and Mrs. Macdonald. I am Admiral Piers, commander of Her Majesty's Northern Fleet." Piers stepped forward to shake their hands. He was of medium height, a round-faced, stocky man in his early sixties; a false-toothed smile softened his normally stern face. Piers then introduced *Warrior*'s commanding officer, Captain Nigel Hamilton.

Macdonald quickly sized the man with whom Agnes and he would be in close contact for many days to come. The Canadian liked what he saw. Hamilton's eyes were a striking light blue of remarkable clarity. Framed by the fatty lids of a long-at-sea fifty-year-old, those eyes had the hint of a humorous personality, as did the strong, deep-pitched voice that welcomed them. Tall, angular, with a touch of grey in the black hair of his sideburns, he was a most handsome man, so Agnes thought.

"Sir, as the Admiral said, welcome aboard *Warrior*. And Mrs. Macdonald, I do hope that Lieutenant Fisher made your trip up here comfortable." Hamilton said.

Agnes smiled at him. "He was a perfect escort, Captain."

"Jolly good. Minister and Mrs. Macdonald, this is my Executive Officer, my second-in-command, Commander Peter Milsom. If you have any problems and I can't be found —"

"That'll never happen," the Admiral snorted.

"— then Milsom is your man. And of course Lieutenant Fisher will always be at your beck and call, won't you, Lieutenant?"

"Yes, sir, Captain."

If anything, Agnes thought, Milsom was even more dashing than his captain. Pink cheeks, piercing brown eyes under bushy brown eyebrows, strong chin and, when he smiled, pearly even teeth. And beneath that head only slightly higher than hers and under that form-fitting heavy coat she suspected there was a lean, fit, muscular body.

Captain Hamilton motioned. "If you would be good enough to follow me to your cabin. Actually it's the Admiral's quarters."

"When I'm on board *Warrior*, which isn't all that often. Don't say it, Captain Hamilton."

Warrior's captain, obviously a favourite of Piers, responded, "Of course, Admiral. I would never think of saying 'Thanks be to God.' Never!"

Nigel Hamilton escorted the Macdonalds to their cabin at the stern of the ship, where both he and the Admiral himself took them through the compact quarters, in typical navy style magnificently wood-panelled throughout except for the head.

"The head?" Agnes asked.

"The W.C., the bathroom. 'Head' is the navy's term for it."

The Admiral's sitting-room walls were bedecked with portraits of Nelson and Collingwood and scenes of the Battle of Trafalgar, with one all-too-vivid painting depicting the death of Britain's greatest admirals. The bedroom was as large as the sitting room and, like it, had heavy-glassed, rectangular portholes.

Standing at a narrow door near the dining table in the salon were two bare-headed sailors clad in light-blue brass-buttoned cotton jackets. Both were quite short of stature, oval-faced, of stocky build over legs slightly but unmistakably bowed.

"There are your stewards, Petty Officer Bob Joyce on the left and Petty Officer Bob Swift. Both are from Glasgow, as you can see from their mutual six-foot-four statures. Sorry, chaps. Five-foot-four would be more accurate, wouldn't it?"

The more fearless, Bob Joyce, spoke up in his thick Glaswegian burr: "No bloody way, sir, if you'll pardon the expression, ma'am. You had our height right in the first place!" He grinned toothlessly, the two front upper teeth having disappeared long since, probably in a fight in some pub in a foreign port.

"Now that the tour is over, the Admiral will be departing for his flagship shortly."

"And don't let me hear you say 'Thanks be to God!'" Admiral Piers grinned and winked at Agnes.

The Captain, ignoring his Admiral, told the Macdonalds, "As you know, we'll up-anchor in a very short while."

"And so will *Agamemnon*," Admiral Piers said. "Her Captain has been ordered to accompany *Warrior* to St. Petersburg. Actually she was part of the plan but apparently Lieutenant Fisher hadn't been informed."

Macdonald's internal smile did not appear on his face. "Very good, Admiral. I am much relieved. For me to miss my appointment with His Imperial Majesty the Tsar would be catastrophic, to say the least."

"*Agamemnon* will ensure that you won't. But I daresay the Tsar's people, and in particular the head of his navy, his brother the Grand Duke Constantine, will probably have a fit if *Agamemnon* carries you into the harbour of St. Petersburg."

"Why?" Agnes asked.

"Because, ma'am, the superb *Agamemnon*, one of Her Majesty's first steam-powered sailing ships, took a leading part in the highly successful naval bombardment of Sevastapol, a critical turning point in the defeat of the Tsar's forces in the Crimean War."

Captain Hamilton added, "She'll be waiting for us at sea when we depart. She's just up from Portsmouth."

"Well," said Admiral Piers, "it's time for me to be getting back to my ship. I wish both of you, Minister and Madame Macdonald, a safe, comfortable, and successful voyage. I hope that your mission on behalf of Her Majesty and her government will be crowned with the result Her Majesty expects of her servants."

John A. and Agnes knew that the Admiral's oratory would end with a flourish.

"That result is — victory!"

Piers turned to Lieutenant Fisher. "Lieutenant Fisher, dear boy, you will now have the honour to escort me off this splendid ship."

28

March 23, 1867
Western Baltic Sea

The Macdonalds were just finishing lunch in their cabin in the company of the suave Executive Officer, Peter Milsom, and the ever-ebullient Jacky Fisher, who had kept them amused with his raconteur's sharp wit, when the ship began to pitch and roll more than usual.

They had recently cleared Stockholm, where a small packet had delivered mail to both ships and a sealed diplomatic pouch to Minister John A. Macdonald.

Warrior was on schedule and less than a day away from her destination, St. Petersburg, on March 23. She had been moving steadily eastward at an average of just under 10 knots, the captain sometimes using his steam engines to maintain speed if the wind dropped. But the typically strong winds of March had propelled the full-sailed *Warrior* along with only a few brief assists from the ship's pair of huge steam engines located well below the waterline below and behind the after mast.

Captain Hamilton and the Captain of the *Agamemnon*, which had joined *Warrior* off Edinburgh, had agreed on a cruising speed of 10 knots. For *Agamemnon*'s crew's handling comfort she would maintain station two miles behind *Warrior* twenty-four hours a day. But in the likely event of a March storm she would lengthen her station to four miles.

Now, grey-black storm clouds, preceded by powerful gusting winds, could be seen marching down the lowering skies over rolling, whitecapped, mountainous waves. *Agamemnon* dropped back to her storm station while the captains of both warships ordered all sails furled, a command that sent sailors scrambling up the masts in the howling wind.

Just as the last of the sails was stowed on *Warrior* the full force of the storm hit the ships broadside from the port. With the pitching and rolling more intense than Macdonald had ever experienced in his several trips across the Atlantic, he and Agnes sought the safest, most secure shelter possible. They were clutched together on his bunk, both of them holding hard onto the long wooden rail that had been installed on the wall just above the mattress for just that purpose.

Loose articles that they hadn't been able to stow clanged and rattled about on the floor. The sounds of the screaming wind in the ship's rigging were like an orchestra of brass trumpets and violins. The unabated thumping of *Warrior*'s steam engines, now the sole onboard force thrusting her on course through the savage waves, sounded like base drums accompanying the orchestral windsounds of the tempest.

The storm brought with it blinding snow squalls that cut the visibility from the bridge to zero. But of great increasing peril was the spray from the knife-like bow of *Warrior*. The plumes of water she was throwing up froze when they hit the deck, railings, and rigging. Ice was quickly accumulating by the ton, seriously, possibly fatally, affecting the stability of the ship to the point where, like countless other ships in northern arctic waters, she could capsize.

Captain Hamilton had no choice. He ordered the helmsman to bring *Warrior* slowly to port to the heading of 310 degrees straight into the waves. At the same time he instructed his Executive Officer, Commander Milsom, beside him in the bridge, to tell the engine room to slow the engines to half-speed, thereby cutting the ship's bow-on speed into the battering waves to perhaps 1 knot.

To Peter Milsom beside him on the bridge Hamilton barked, "As soon as we're settled into wind give the order to man the axes. I've got to get control of this bloody ice."

"Aye, aye, sir," the Executive Officer responded. "What about *Agamemnon*?"

"The *Aggie*? All I can do, Peter, is hope and pray. She's completely out of touch. We can't see her in this blinding snow, so there's no way to signal her. She may be stopping and turning into wind just as we are. But maybe she's not."

"When last seen she was falling back to her storm position about a quarter-mile to the port of our track."

"Which means if she doesn't stop we could be right in her path." Captain Hamilton, bundled up in his greatcoat with the collar up and buttoned, looked deeply worried. "Cancel my order to cut the engines back. I'll hold that speed until I'm sure *Agamemnon*'s clear. Same with the axes."

"Aye, aye, sir. We're just coming into wind now."

"Good. Keep a sharp lookout for *Agamemnon*. Pass the word to the poor bastard in the crow's-nest."

Milsom took the megaphone off its wall bracket, stepped out the after door of the bridge, and shouted the order at the top of his lungs at the boy midshipman some thirty feet up the mast in the open crow's-nest. "She'll be coming from the port side," Milsom roared. The gloved hand-signal from the freezing figure said he understood.

In the Admiral's cabin John A. could sense *Warrior*'s turning to port. He was no sailor but his sixth sense told him something was wrong.

"Agnes, stay here and keep hanging onto that rail."

"Where are you going?" Her voice revealed her fear.

"To the bridge. There's a passageway from here, so I don't have to go out on the deck. I just have to find out what in Christ's name is going on."

"John, will you please stop taking the Lord's name in vain!"

"Yes, yes," John A. muttered as he rolled out of the bed onto the floor to grab his overcoat. He struggled into it while being thrown around the cabin by the rolling of the ship. He found his tartan wool scarf and mitts in an inside pocket with a wool skullcap that one of the stewards had persuaded him to take when word arrived that a storm was coming.

After a last word of caution from Agnes he bumped along the corridor to the ladder up to the bridge, his wool-mitted hands clutching the side rails.

When he reached the bridge and looked out one of its portholes on the starboard side his eyes flew wide with horror. Christ almighty.

There must be at least a foot of ice on the deck, he thought as alarm clutched at his gut. The snow ripping past the ice-encrusted rigging was so thick Macdonald could barely see *Warrior*'s railings.

He confronted Hamilton. "Captain, what in hell is going on? Are we all right?"

"Only time will tell, Mr. Macdonald. Right now this ship is in serious danger. She could capsize because of the unexpected ice build-up. Or she could be cut in two by *Agamemnon* at any moment."

Macdonald was appalled. "The ice I can see. What's this about *Agamemnon*?"

"Simple. I could not signal to *Aggie* because the snow blinded us first. Her Captain doesn't know I've done a ninety-degree turn to port dead into wind to save us from the ice. That puts us right in his path and I have no way of warning him."

At that instant two of *Warrior*'s guns on her vulnerable port side fired into the dense white blanket of driving snow.

Hamilton staggered to the voice tube marked Gunnery Officer and screamed into it: "Fisher, what in bloody hell are you doing?"

But the Captain figured out what Jacky Fisher was doing as soon as the question was out of his mouth.

Fisher's tinny voice came up the long tube immediately: "I'm telling those bastards on the *Aggie* where we are, sir. If they can't see us they can sure as hell hear us, sir."

"Good thinking, Jacky."

"Sir, I'll give a two-gun salvo every ten seconds." His voice was drowned out by the deafening blast of the second volley. Then: "Not to worry, Captain. They're powder without shot."

Captain Hamilton listened to the distant words. Smiling while looking at Macdonald, he shouted, "They'd bloody well better be!"

The watchkeeper reported. "Dead into wind, Captain, sir." The ship's rolling abated but its pitching nose-up-nose-down action continued. However, less water now swept over the bow.

"All right, Number One. Now man the axes."

"Aye, aye, sir." Milsom again stepped out of *Warrior*'s oval-shaped bridge with the megaphone. His exceptional voice seemed to carry to every part of the ship. "All available ship's company, man your axes.

Cut the ice off *Warrior*. Now!"

All over the slippery main deck and superstructure of *Warrior* men appeared as if out of nowhere. Two-bladed axes flailed away, sharp edges smashing into the thick, rock-hard, frozen surfaces. But enough spume was still spraying up from the ship's sharp bow to settle on the decks and superstructure as *Warrior* continued to be battered head on by the incessant waves.

Macdonald could do nothing but watch and listen. He had moved to the port corner of the bridge, well out of the way of the Captain and his officers and men. Clutching the side of a secured navigation table, he hung on for dear life as Captain Hamilton fought to save his ship.

Milsom shouted, "We're still getting heavy spray, sir!"

"There's nothing for it but to cut our speed."

"We could still be in *Aggie*'s path, Sir."

"I know that." The Captain staggered to the engine room voice pipe. "Engine room, half-speed ahead."

The reply came back instantly: "Half-speed ahead, sir."

In the space of time between Jacky Fisher's ten-second cannonades Macdonald could feel and hear the vibration of the ship's engines and propeller diminish markedly.

The digging of the bow into the waves stopped and with it most of freezing spray.

Suddenly there were panic shouts from the crow's-nest, echoed by some sailors on the port side hacking at the ice. "The *Aggie*. The *Aggie,*" the midshipman was screaming. "She's coming at us on our port bow! Range 200 yards!"

All hands on the bridge except the helmsman rushed to the windows on the port side.

"Christ!" the Captain bellowed. "She's right on top of us!"

"But she's in a turn to starboard." Milsom assessed the situation. "She's in a hard turn. Pray to God she'll miss us!"

"Nothing we can do now except watch, wait, and pray. Thank God Jacky started firing his goddam guns . . ."

Agamemnon, her black hull shrouded in sheaths of ice and snow, looked like a gargantuan battering-ram looming irreversibly toward

Warrior. The forty-five guns on *Aggie*'s port side had been rolled out as soon as her Captain heard the strange cannon fire. The menacing circular gun muzzles of the fast-moving, overtaking warship were now almost bearing broadside at *Warrior*. The *Aggie*'s hard turn was fetching her into the last few degrees before she was running straight downwind in a 180-degree opposite course to the newer battleship.

Silently *Warrior*'s Captain, the men with him on her bridge, together with all her sailors on deck who could see the oncoming ship, watched, helpless, transfixed, speechless, as the *Aggie*, thrust and tossed as she was by the high waves, bore down on their nearly stopped warship. *Agamemnon* kept maintaining the hard turn to starboard, her sharp, deadly bowsprit seeming ready to slice into *Warrior*'s Captain's cabin at the stern where Macdonald had left Agnes. John A. could do nothing but watch in horror as *Agamemnon* bore down.

It was over in a few seconds.

As the *Aggie*'s bow was about to smash into *Warrior* a gigantic wave lifted *Agamemnon*, throwing her bow past and well beyond the stern of Captain Hamilton's struggling vessel. But not before *Aggie*'s thirty-foot-long bowsprit raked the topside of *Warrior*'s railing and deck like a scythe, carrying with it stanchions and some of the rigging that stabilized and secured the tall aft mast.

That blade-like bowsprit also caught two axe-wielding sailors who were too intent on their slippery task to hear their comrades' shouted warnings above the roar of the wind and the waves. Nor, with heads down and backs to the wind, did they ever see the looming bow suddenly appear through the snow-screen, carving a swift path toward *Warrior*. The pair never knew what hit them. *Aggie*'s bowsprit caught both in the middle of their backs just as, in unison, they lifted their axes high above their heads. They were whipped out over *Warrior*'s stern like pins in a bowling alley and flung into the frigid Baltic Sea.

Agamemnon was gone as quickly as she had appeared, swallowed up instantly in the snow, her long hull, guns bristling, passing behind *Warrior* like an icy wraith.

"Number One, get me the identity of the two men we just lost." Hamilton's voice was cold and flat. *Agamemnon*'s threat to *Warrior* was over. *Aggie*'s Captain would now stand her, like *Warrior*, into wind with only sufficient forward speed to keep her steady. Both ships would ride out the storm. Once the weather cleared, the crews of Her Majesty's warships would be able to see each other again and exchange signals. They would then turn eastward once more on course toward St. Petersburg, the city created by Peter the Great, Tsar Alexander the Second's ancestor, the man who began the move of the Russian Empire toward the culture, society, and values of Europe and especially of Britain.

The snow suddenly stopped, and the low clouds moved off smartly to the southeast following the storm that had entangled *Warrior* and *Agamemnon*.

Macdonald was still on the bridge when a relieved Captain Hamilton pointed to starboard. "There she is." *Warrior* was still at half-speed and heading into the wind, which was now coming from the west. He was pointing to *Aggie* some mile and a half to the east, also turning slowly to port and into wind.

"Old Bobbie Fenn's no fool. He saw what we were doing . . ."

"The hard way?" Macdonald asked.

"Bloody right, sir. The hard way. You couldn't come any closer than that."

"But thanks to a certain gunnery lieutenant, disaster was averted. Am I right, Captain?" John A. was sure that Captain Hamilton would recognize Fisher's independent, quick-thinking decision to fire his guns as a warning and as a beacon of sound from which Captain Fenn in *Aggie* could realize the position of *Warrior* and take immediate action to avoid her.

"Absolutely right, sir." Hamilton turned to Milsom. "Number One, I want Fisher up here immediately. We will be turning back on course but only after you and the bos'n's mate are satisfied that we've removed at least a ton of ice off this ship. Signal *Agamemnon* to maintain position until further orders."

"Aye, aye, sir."

Lieutenant Fisher appeared, hat jammed over his ears, greatcoat collar internally fortified with a pink woollen scarf. It had been a gift of the Lady Emma Townsend. She had wound it around his neck with a loving kiss as he shipped out of her flat at five in the morning on the day he began his journey with the Macdonalds.

Captain Hamilton couldn't believe his eyes. "Lieutenant, what the hell are you doing with a goddam pink scarf around your neck? Are you some sort of bloody pervert?"

"No, Captain, sir. It's a souvenir. It was the only thing I could lay my hands on quickly."

Macdonald couldn't help laughing. "Captain, this young man's pink scarf's a trophy. The damn thing probably inspired him to fire those warning cannonades."

"Probably true, Mr. Macdonald." There was an amused twinkle in Hamilton's eyes. He went and sat on his captain's chair with its swivel seat four feet above the deck. Hamilton hadn't been in it since the storm had swiftly rolled in. He was exhausted.

"Lieutenant Fisher, there's something I have decided to do. It's a sort of disciplinary measure because you fired cannons without first getting your captain's consent and approval."

Fisher's young face with its hooded eyes took on a grim look. "Yes, Captain."

"You've completed and passed your promotion examinations. Right?"

"Stood at the top of my class, sir."

"With the best marks by anyone in ten years?"

"No, sir. Twelve years."

"Of course. Now, Lieutenant Fisher, in accordance with the power vested in me as a captain of a ship of war of Her Majesty's Royal Navy I have the privilege of promoting any officer under my command to an acting rank of one above that which he permanently holds."

"Sir?"

Hamilton looked at John A. Macdonald, who smiled and nodded his approval.

"In recognition of your brave and intelligent initiative in firing warning shots to signal *Agamemnon* the whereabouts of *Warrior* — an initiative that I consider to be exceptional — I am promoting you to the rank of Acting Lieutenant-Commander."

Jacky Fisher's jaw dropped. It was one of the few times in his life that he had been caught unawares — with his drawers down as he would later put it in telling the story countless times. The hooded cobra eyes were open wide with astonishment.

There was no smile on Fisher's face. "Thank you, sir."

As Captain Hamilton shook Fisher's hand, the face of the newly promoted young officer finally broke into a broad smile. Then everyone on the bridge stepped up to congratulate him.

Macdonald was the last. He took Jacky Fisher's hand, pumped it as he put his left hand paternally on his shoulder. "Well done, Jacky. Mrs. Macdonald will be delighted, I'm sure, when I tell her how you saved the day. If the *Aggie*'s bow had hit us it would have gone right into our cabin."

"It was nothing, sir."

"I'm going to ask the Captain for permission to have you accompany me as my aide when I go to the Winter Palace to see the Tsar. Would you like to do that?"

"Bloody hell, sir! Would I ever!"

Macdonald gave him a pat on the shoulder, turned, and made his way down the ladder.

"Lieutenant-Commander Fisher!" The Captain's voice was sharp.

"Sir?"

"Go below and tend to the stowing of the guns. My congratulations to your gunners. Then go to the ship's tailor. I want your new rank up straightaway."

Captain Hamilton looked out to the bow of his ship and to the waves rapidly diminishing as the wind dropped. "I think we've got enough ice off. Number One, stop the ice-clearing. Helmsman, turn starboard to zero nine five degrees. Signalman, signal *Aggie* our course and that we're resuming full speed ahead, but without sails. We have to repair the damage *Aggie*'s bowsprit did before we can use that mast again."

Hamilton put his hands on his ship's waist-high circular brass compass housing, looked out and up into the clearing blue sky and said out loud to himself, "*Warrior* will be off St. Petersburg on schedule, come hell or high water! Thanks be to God and Jacky Fisher that we're not this day at the bottom of the Baltic Sea."

29

March 23–26, 1867
Washington

MARCH 23, 1867, MARKED THE END OF A WEEK OF INTERMITTENT secret negotiations between Seward and de Stoeckl. During that time the Russian ambassador made no attempt to be in contact with Sir Frederick Bruce.

Finally, all matters were resolved except de Stoeckl's demand that the United States assume certain obligations of the Russian America Company and another firm that had been granted an exclusive monopoly to supply ice from Russian America to the West Coast of the United States. Seward was adamant. The cession of the territory and dominion over it had to be unencumbered by any reservations, privileges, franchises, grants, or possessions by any associated companies, whether corporate or incorporate, Russian or any other.

To obtain this position Seward offered an additional sum of money to de Stoeckl in a letter dated March 23, 1867:

> ***With reference to the proposed Convention between our respective Governments for the cession by Russia of her American Territory to the United States, I have the honor to acquaint you that I must insist upon that clause in the sixth article of the draft which declares the cession to be free and unencumbered . . . and must regard it as an ultimatum. With the President's approval, however, I will add two hundred thousand dollars to the consideration money on that account.***

On the twenty-fifth Prince Gorchakov sent telegraphed instructions to the effect that the increase in the purchase price and Seward's conditions were acceptable. De Stoeckl received the Gorchakov message early in the morning of the same day. He immediately responded, sending off a coded cable to the Foreign Minister:

> ***Negotiations ended; result, project of treaty as follows. Article 1: Cession of our colonies, frontiers of territory ceded on the east, line of demarkation of our treaty of 1825 with England, on the west exactly the line of demarkation sent to me by Minister of the Navy. Article 2: Property of the Crown ceded to the United States, private property remain with individuals to whom it belongs, Orthodox churches remain sole property of persons of this creed with full liberty to exercise their religion. Article 3: Inhabitants of colonies can return to Russia or remain and enjoy all rights of American citizens. Article 4: Russia will appoint one or two agents to make transfer to United States of ceded territory. Article 5: After exchange of ratification of this treaty all fortifications and military posts will be handed over to troops of United States; Russian troops will retire as soon as possible and practicable. Article 6: the United States shoulders no obligations contracted by our company. Article 7: Ratification to be exchanged at Washington. I send this telegram at request of Seward who told me if I receive answer within six days treaty can be signed and confirmed by Senate next week. A simple authorization by telegraph to sign treaty will be equivalent to full power in due form.***

Late in the afternoon of the twenty-fifth the Russian ambassador sent another cable. It was to the Tsar and was marked private and confidential. It would be in his hands first thing in the morning of the twenty-sixth. De Stoeckl's cable arriving as it did the morning after the Tsar's meeting with Macdonald and before the Tsar's conference with his Council would have a devastating result.

All that de Stoeckl could do now was wait. If he brought this treaty off it would be the most important accomplishment of his diplomatic career. He speculated on the accolades that he would receive from Prince Gorchakov and, of course, from the Tsar himself. Perhaps there would be another decoration. Out of the large sum of money that would be pouring into the Tsar's coffers there might well be a handsome recognition by His Imperial Majesty.

It was impossible to think that the friendly relations between the United States and Russia could be put at risk by the Tsar's agreeing to sell Russian America to Great Britain. The U.S.-Russian ties were too strong for that to happen.

After all, if Queen Victoria had been the subject of an unsuccessful but horrifying assassination attempt, would the American Congress have passed a Resolution of celebration and rejoicing at her survival? Impossible. Unthinkable. But that's exactly what the Congress did when Tsar Alexander the Second survived such an attempt. De Stoeckl had been so proud and pleased when that happened that he had had the Resolution framed and hung in his office.

The Resolution of Congress had been approved May 16, 1866. Addressed to Tsar Alexander the Second, its ornate words spoke eloquently to the close relationship that existed between United States and Russia. In part the Resolution of Congress transmitted under the hand of the President read:

> ***Sire: The Resolution which I have the honor of presenting to your Imperial Majesty is the voice of a people whose millions of lips speak from a single heart.***
>
> ***The many ties which have long bound together the great Empire of the East, and the great Republic of the West, have been multiplied and strengthened by the unwavering fidelity of the imperial government to our own, throughout its recent period of convulsion.***
>
> ***The words of sympathy and friendship then addressed to the government at Washington, by command of your Imperial Majesty, are fixed in the eternal remembrance of a grateful country. As one of the wide family of nations, we yield our willing homage to that act of humanity which is especially referred to in the Resolution of Congress. The peaceful edict of an enlightened sovereign has consummated a triumph over an inherited barbarism which our western republic has only***

> ***reached through long years of bloodshed.***
> ***It is, therefore, with profound emotion that I offer to your Imperial Majesty, to the emancipated subjects, and to all the people of this vast realm, our heartfelt congratulations upon the providential escape from danger, which led to this spontaneous expression of regret for the attempt, and thankfulness for its merciful arrest and failure.***

At this critical time in de Stoeckl's career he kept Pamela Collins reasonably well informed, giving her details of the daily moves and negotiations. But as for Martha, her told her nothing.

His near-daily passionate interludes with Pamela at the Willard fitted comfortably into his work pattern so that at the legation and at home there was neither disturbance or apparent suspicion of his carryings-on. Nevertheless he had been and still remained shocked by Seward's disclosure that he knew about the English lady on the third floor of the Willard Hotel. The Secretary of State had not hesitated to use that blackmail information to force de Stoeckl to comply with his will. No question, Seward would use it again if need be.

How had Seward found out? Did he have a detective or agent following de Stoeckl; had one of the hotel staff tipped him off; or had he heard some rumour? That troublesome question de Stoeckl just might put to the man someday, if the circumstances were right. Whatever the answer, the clandestine affair had been discovered and therefore he was vulnerable. Nonetheless he was determined to continue the liaison with Pamela, believing that, even if everyone else in town knew about the affair, his reclusive wife would never find out because there was no one to tell her. Not that she would leave his roof even if she did find out. After all, there was no longer any physical contact between them.

An acknowledgement of the receipt of de Stoeckl's telegraph of March twenty-fifth came from Prince Gorchakov on the twenty-sixth. The St. Petersburg message contained a commitment that a decision would be made as quickly as possible — whatever that meant.

30

March 24, 1867
Gulf of Finland

As Macdonald wakened on the morning of Sunday the twenty-fourth day of March, it took him a few seconds to figure out where he was. It was the silence that temporarily disoriented him. The cabin was still in darkness even though it was after eight o'clock. The silence — what was it?

It was the absence of the pounding of the ship's engines and the noise of the propeller shaft incessantly turning. Gone, too, the pitching and heaving produced by *Warrior* was stopped, at rest, in calm water.

John A. gently wakened Agnes, whispering, "I think we're anchored off St. Petersburg."

"It's so quiet. I can't believe it," Agnes whispered back.

"Why are we whispering?"

When they had settled that question over many moments of ardent love-making, John A. propped himself up on his elbow to announce, "It's getting light out. Time to get up, my love, have breakfast, go along to the bridge, and see where we are."

"Let's go to the bridge first, then have breakfast."

"I think you'd better get some clothes on before you go gallivanting up to the bridge. You'd cause a riot if you arrived there starkers among those lusty young men!"

Twenty minutes later the bundled-up, warmly dressed Macdonalds climbed up unannounced onto the upper open bridge where the watch-keeping lieutenant and the ship's navigating officer, the only people on the bridge, stood chatting, sipping mugs of steaming coffee.

Morning greetings out of the way, John A. asked as he peered out over and past *Warrior*'s bow, "Where are we, chaps? What's going on?"

"We're anchored, sir. We're off St. Petersburg, still in Gulf of Finland waters," the navigation officer replied. They had talked with Lieutenant Angus Fraser several times during the voyage. He pointed to the horizon ahead. "That's St. Petersburg. The sun will be coming up beyond the city in a few minutes. It's a clear morning so we'll have a spectacular view."

"Have you a map, Angus? Can you show us where we are?" Agnes asked.

"Certainly, ma'am." Fraser led them to the wide navigation table and reached to turn up the covered gas light. Spread out on the table was the chart showing the entrance to St. Petersburg harbour.

"We are standing out here just south of Lesnoy in what's called the Gulf of Finland. Actually it's a long, fairly wide inlet that ends at St. Petersburg, which is here — about ten miles to the east of us.

"Later this afternoon at high tide and while there's still plenty of light, we'll take *Warrior* into the harbour. We'll follow these markers as they're shown on the chart up the narrow channel around this big triangular island."

"What's it called?" Agnes was curious.

"Vasilevsky Island. It divides the Neva River into two forks, here, and creates a big protected basin, the port where we'll anchor."

He rolled up the linen chart with care. Under it on the navigation table was a map of the city of St. Petersburg.

Fraser admitted, "This isn't an Admiralty map. I picked it up at a bookstore in Edinburgh while we were waiting for you to arrive."

"Good thinking," John A. allowed.

"When the sun's up, and if this map's right, we'll be able to see Peter and Paul's cathedral here on the north shore. It's supposed to have a golden spire about four hundred feet high, if you can believe it."

His index finger moved to the southern shore. "Peter the Great's Admiralty buildings are here. And there's the Hermitage. Also the Winter Palace. That's where you'll be going in the morning, sir."

"That's right."

"What a thrill to be going there, to be meeting the Tsar. God, I wish I were going with you, sir."

Macdonald laughed. "Maybe you could take my place," he joked.

"I think Lieutenant — sorry — Lieutenant-Commander Fisher would like to do that. I'm not serious." Angus grinned.

"Well, Jacky will be with me, at least up to the door of the chamber where the Tsar will receive me."

"What about you, Mrs. Macdonald?" Fraser wasn't sure he should have asked the question.

"It's arranged that I will go ashore with my husband. The British ambassador, Sir Andrew Buchanan, and his wife will meet us when we land. I will accompany her to the embassy."

"And I will go on with Sir James to the Winter Palace."

Agnes sighed. "The good Lord knows I'll be glad to put my feet on solid ground."

Macdonald pointed to the map. "What are these three streets? They look awfully wide."

"They appear to radiate out from the middle of the southern bank. The main boulevard is Nevsky Prospect. You'll probably go down it on your way to the embassy and from there to the Winter Palace." Lieutenant Fraser turned to look east out the windows toward St. Petersburg. "There it comes." The first rosy hints of the rising sun were tinting the black horizon, gradually turning the night darkness into a panorama of soft reds, yellows, and pinks. Then the tip of the sun blinked behind a wide sweep of low but large buildings, snow-covered roofs, and tall towers that formed the skyline of what was reputedly one of the architecturally beautiful cities in the modern world, Peter the Great's masterful creation, St. Petersburg.

To the northeast the new rays of the sun transformed the golden spire of St. Peter and St. Paul Cathedral into a glittering gold-red flame reaching up into the frigid heavens above this near-arctic metropolis.

These few unforgettable moments of light, colour, and vista were forever etched in the memories of those aboard *Warrior* who were fortunate enough to be able to watch St. Petersburg emerge from its blanket of night.

Minister Macdonald and Agnes returned to their cabin to be served a full breakfast. John A. then went to the desk where he sat, unlocked his valise, and, as instructed by Lord Stanley, for the first time opened the sealed envelope.

In it were Stanley's letter to Macdonald on the Prime Minister's official 10 Downing Street letterhead. The operative paragraphs, so far as John A. was concerned, read:

> ***You are authorized to hand to the Tsar our document of agreement rescinding or altering certain provisions of the Treaty of Paris only if you have an unconditional verbal acceptance of both the money and Treaty proposals. Under no circumstances should His Imperial Majesty or his staff be allowed possession of the document unless his aforesaid acceptance is pledged to you.***
>
> ***I reiterate that it is imperative that so far as possible there should be absolutely no paper record of this initiative unless, of course, you are successful.***

Pinned to the letter was a small, plain piece of paper with a note in Stanley's own hand, the formal letter being inked by a private secretary but signed by the Prime Minister.

The note cautioned:

> ***The Tsar is known to be a conniving duplicitous bastard. Pleasant, courteous, kindly but not known to be trustworthy.***
>
> ***Prenez garde!***
>
> ***Stanley***

As *Warrior* entered the calm, protected harbour basin of St. Petersburg shortly after three o'clock that afternoon the best gunners in the Royal Navy, the lads of Lieutenant-Commander Jacky Fisher, stood by their splendid, gleaming guns waiting for his command. To a man they were as proud as peacocks of their banty Jacky and his promotion at sea, and only twenty-five at that. Crickey!

With the command from the bridge to drop anchor and the first sound of the massive anchor chain fast-moving along the upper deck, Jacky Fisher shouted at the top of his lungs: "Commence firing twenty-one-gun salute in sequence. FIRE!"

The heavy iron hull of *Warrior* shook from stem to stern as one ten-incher after the other was fired at precise ten-second intervals.

In his office chambers on the upper floor of the Winter Palace, His Imperial Majesty Alexander the Second heard the boom of the first gun and the rattle of his windows. He lifted his eyes away from the decree he was about to sign and said to the portly elderly man across the desk who was looking out the windows over his pince-nez: "Well, Mikhail, the conquering British have arrived and, we assume, their peasant colonial emissary has a message for us that we cannot refuse." The sarcasm in the Tsar's tone matched the twist in his smile.

Prince Gorchakov replied, "Sire, after the tongue-lashing I gave Macdonald in Paris, he may well be bringing an offer you would find difficult, nay, impossible to reject."

Out in the Gulf of Finland just over the horizon from St. Petersburg, *Agamemnon*'s Captain, Robert Fenn, was forward on the main deck looking at his damaged bowsprit. His keen ears caught the distant rolling thunder of *Warrior*'s saluting guns. To his Executive Officer with whom he had been discussing the necessary repairs he said, "Sounds as though they're dropping anchor in the harbour and all's well."

"Can we set course for home now, sir? Our task is finished, isn't it?"

"Not on your bloody life, Number One. You can never tell what those goddam Russians are going to do next."

"Yes, sir."

Fenn's voice lowered. "I am now required to give you this order. If from this moment *Warrior* fires three volleys five seconds apart that means she's in trouble."

"And we go in after her."

"With all our ninety-one guns blazing! Not a word to anyone. I don't want the crew to get the wind up."

"Aye, aye, sir. Mum's the word."

31

March 25, 1867
St. Petersburg

The British ambassador, Sir Andrew Buchanan, and his wife arrived at dockside at nine o'clock as the Macdonald party was being assisted out of *Warrior*'s Admiral's barge. The ambassador's sleigh-mounted enclosed carriage, a small Union Jack flying on its roof, was drawn by two magnificent, blanketed white horses, their nostrils steaming in the bitter-cold morning air. The spacious carriage readily accommodated all five warmly dressed, fur-rug-covered subjects of Her Imperial Majesty, a version of whose royal arms was on the outside of both doors of the coach.

The screeching of metal runners on hard-packed snow startled John A.'s aide. Fisher had never ridden in a sleigh before.

"Just like home, Kingston and Ottawa. You'll get used to the squeal," Agnes assured him.

His Excellency, Sir Andrew, provided a tour guide's patter while the carriage was pulled jerkingly down the busy Nevsky Prospect. The diplomat knew every building, every monument, every park in St. Petersburg.

When the carriage went through the curved, gold-tipped iron gates of the British embassy, Sir Andrew gave an unexpected piece of news to John A.

"I'm sorry, Minister Macdonald, but I do not have the privilege of accompanying you to the presence of the Tsar this morning."

Macdonald was shocked. "Why? My information is that you're on good terms with the Tsar and his brother, Constantine, and even with Prince Gorchakov. I was counting on your being there. I need your support!"

"My dear Minister, nothing would please me more than to accompany you. You'll be just fine. As you've been informed, the Tsar speaks English very well and Gorchakov —"

"We had to deal with him in French in Paris."

"Don't worry. The old codger understands English and speaks it. He was putting you and Earl Cowley on in Paris."

"I still don't understand. Is it the Tsar or Gorchakov who has excluded you?"

Sir Andrew smiled ruefully. "No. It was a chap called Stanley, who happens to be my direct superior at the Foreign Office."

"I think I know why."

"I'm told that you're on a secret mission that no one should know about unless it is absolutely essential to the mission's success. I'm not absolutely essential."

"What about Fisher?" Macdonald nodded at his aide sitting opposite next to the ladies, his large ears and mind taking in every word.

"Same injunction. He can escort you to the palace, to the door of the Tsar's conference chamber, but he can't go in with you."

"Lord Stanley again?"

The ambassador tapped the left side of his chest. "I have his message in my pocket if you wish to see it."

The plans had been executed in clockwork form. "Not a bloody hitch," Lieutenant-Commander Fisher had proudly announced as John A. Macdonald and he, guided by Oleg, the Tsar's wizened principal secretary, walked across the deep Persian rug toward the entrance to the Tsar's conference chamber.

Then they were at the doorway and under the massive portrait of Peter the Great hanging to the right of it.

Jacky Fisher handed the locked valise to Macdonald, looking up at him and saying simply, "Good luck, sir."

Oleg motioned to Fisher to sit in one of the overstuffed velvet chairs clustered beneath the portrait. Then the Tsar's man knocked three times on the tall door covered with exquisitely carved, life-size figures. Somewhere outside the Winter Palace the bells of a clock began to stroke the hour of ten. At that moment the permission to enter the chamber came in the form of one word:

"Enter!"

Macdonald thought, If that's the Tsar's voice we will indeed be speaking English. No bothersome translator. A good start.

The old secretary pulled the door open and stood aside to allow the visitor to enter.

Macdonald's focus was totally on the person of the Tsar striding toward him alongside the long conference table, his hand extended in welcome.

Alexander the Second was of medium height, slight of frame, narrow shouldered in his dark cutaway morning suit. His long, angular face was made even longer by a closely trimmed black beard which, with his moustache, covered a good portion of his face. His rounded, high forehead was capped by greying hair which his barber had long since persuaded him to part in the middle. Below bushy eyebrows, behind circular gold-rimmed spectacles, glinted brown eyes that had an uneasy shift.

John A. took the Tsar's offered hand, and, as instructed by Buchanan, made a short bow from the waist while tipping his head forward.

"Welcome to our capital city, Minister Macdonald, and to our Winter Palace," the Tsar said, his English accent uncoloured by his native tongue.

"It is an honour to be in your presence, Your Majesty, and to be able to speak with you directly about a matter of such importance."

"It's a pleasure." The Tsar turned and gestured toward the portly, greying figure standing at the end of the conference table. "You have met our distinguished Foreign Minister, Prince Gorchakov."

"Of course. In Paris."

"Indeed. Now, Minister, if you would be good enough to take the chair on the far side of the table to the left of ours, just there. As usual Prince Gorchakov is at our right hand."

Locked valise in his left hand, John A. made his way to the place the Tsar had designated. Then he reached across the table to shake Gorchakov's hand.

"I am pleased to see you again, Your Highness," he said courteously.

"And I to see you, Minister," Gorchakov replied in English.

John A. laughed as he waited for the Tsar to be seated, then sat himself. "Prince, your newfound ability in English is astonishing."

Gorchakov looked over his pince-nez at the Canadian. "I thought you would be surprised."

"And no liquid refreshment for toasts today."

"I'm afraid His Majesty frowns on such celebratory practices when there is serious business to be done."

"That is correct," the Tsar confirmed. "Now, Minister, you have come a very long way aboard one of Her Majesty's most modern and powerful warships to bring us information and, as we are advised, to treat with us with regard to our valuable, resource-rich territories in North America."

"I have indeed come a very long way, and I am indeed authorized to negotiate with you for your cession to Great Britain of all of your North American lands on behalf of the newly forming Dominion of Canada."

Tsar Alexander nodded his understanding. "And we are prepared to hear your representations and give serious consideration to them."

"Good. May I deal with the monetary —"

Gorchakov interrupted. "By your leave, Your Majesty — Minister, I want to confirm to you that His Majesty's officials are in the mature stages of discussions on the same topic with the President of the United States and his Administration."

"You mean Secretary of State Seward."

"Exactly. But, like these talks with you, those discussions are secret and privileged. Nothing is public."

"Understood." Macdonald did well understand Gorchakov's message that time was running out. "I take it that no final agreement has been reached with the Americans."

The Foreign Minister looked to his Tsar for guidance. There was a barely discernable approving nod.

"No. No final agreement. But to be perfectly honest, Minister, we are very close."

Macdonald leaned forward over the table, his hands clutched together beneath to conceal their trembling under the pressure of negotiating with one of Europe's most powerful monarchs.

"If I may deal with the monetary aspect, Your Majesty?"

Once more the slight approving nod.

"Her Majesty's government has authorized me to propose nine million American dollars in gold."

"Again it's dollars instead of British pounds," Gorchakov noted.

"As it was in Paris, Minister," Macdonald confirmed.

"True. But the amount is greater than in Paris."

"A great incentive to cede to Britain."

The Tsar interjected: "Any incentive you are able to offer must not only be greater than your Paris proposal; it must also be substantially more than what our friends the Americans are offering."

John A. was frustrated. "But I don't know what your American friends are offering."

Clenching his hands together on top of the conference table, Gorchakov was firm. "You won't know, you won't find out unless and until we have signed a treaty agreement with the United States."

"Then Prince, on that basis I may never know what they've offered because if I can persuade His Majesty to cede Russian America to Canada you will not sign an agreement with the Americans. You'll sign it with us."

The Canadian leaned back in the heavy, cushioned chair. "Assume, Your Majesty, that our sum of money exceeds what Seward's offering. That's an assumption I have to make, Sire."

Neither Russian gave any sign of confirmation. Macdonald went on. "If that's valid, then the next matter is the Treaty of Paris. The Americans can't propose any counterweight to a British proposal to waive certain Black Sea provisions of the Treaty of Paris."

The Tsar reacted. "Oh, really? What about a free-trade agreement with the Americans? What about a mutual defence pact, defence against the British, for example? Come now, Mr. Macdonald, there can be countless counterweights — to use your word."

"Perhaps so, Your Majesty. But nothing so simple, so immediate, so readily a restoration of your nation's pride as the removal of those provisions of the Treaty of Paris that, as I am advised by Prince Gorchakov, were so personally humiliating for you."

"Did our Foreign Minister tell you that the Treaty was personally humiliating?"

"So I did, Your Majesty. The Black Sea neutralization conditions . . ."

"Are just that, humiliating!" The Tsar clenched his teeth and his fists.

Macdonald touched the still-locked valise that he had placed on the chair next to him. "I have here, Your Majesty, a document in both your language and Her Majesty's, signed by her and by the Prime Minister, that rescinds and makes null and void Articles Eleven, Thirteen, and Thirty-three of the Treaty of Paris."

There was no response from Tsar Alexander. His gimlet eyes now unwaveringly held Macdonald's.

"This agreement will restore your right to maintain a Black Sea fleet once again and to re-establish forts and military-maritime arsenals on your sovereign Black Sea coasts. It will permit you to fortify your Aland Islands."

"The conditions?" Gorchakov asked.

"That His Majesty will offer, in writing, to cede his North American territories to Great Britain for the sum of nine million dollars in gold."

"May we see this document, this proposal you say is signed by Her Majesty and the Prime Minister?" The Tsar's voice was subdued.

"Of course, Your Majesty. I can show it to you, but I cannot deliver it to you unless and until I have your collateral offer in writing over your signature."

"Agreed."

John A. took the key from his waistcoat, unlocked the valise, extracted the broken-seal envelope and handed over the one-page document. At the bottom were the clear signatures of Victoria, Regina, and Lord Stanley, the Earl of Derby, Her Majesty's Prime Minister.

The Tsar took the document. His eyes moved over it carefully. Then he passed it to Gorchakov, who also studied it. When he was finished he handed it back to Macdonald.

John A. announced, "I have another document."

"Yes?"

"It is also signed by Her Majesty and the Prime Minister."

"Its purpose?"

"Your Majesty, it gives me or Sir Andrew Buchanan full power to execute the proposed Treaty of Amendment to the Treaty of Paris and the cession of your territories in North America. Do you wish to see it?"

"No, it is not necessary at this moment," Tsar Alexander said. He turned to Gorchakov. "Mikhail, we wish to have private words with you. Would you be so kind as to excuse us for a few moments, Mr. Macdonald?"

John A. rose as the Tsar and his Foreign Minister left the conference chamber. Alone, he paced the large room, hands behind his back as he thought about the consequences of a yes and the results of a rejection. Or a delay, which would be difficult indeed because the Captain of *Warrior* was under instructions to clear St. Petersburg at first light the following day.

Within perhaps ten minutes the Tsar reappeared. But to John A.'s surprise Gorchakov was not with him.

When they had resumed their seats the Tsar said, "We have given the proposal our serious consideration. We have heard the counsel of Prince Gorchakov and, in the last few minutes, of our brother, the Grand Duke Constantine."

John A. Macdonald was on tenterhooks as the Tsar continued.

"We have decided that, subject to the advice of our Advisory Council, which we have just summoned to convene tomorrow morning at nine o'clock, we have decided to look with favour on Her Majesty's proposal."

Macdonald's face beamed with pleasure. "Your Majesty, I am most grateful for your concurrence. You can't imagine what possession of your North American lands will mean to Canada."

His Majesty nodded. "And you cannot imagine how much our coffers will benefit from Britain's gold. As to the removal of the onerous Treaty of Paris provisions, need we say anything?"

"No, absolutely nothing, Sire. But . . . *Warrior* must depart at first light tomorrow and I must be aboard her."

"That's before the meeting of our Advisory Council at nine."

"Exactly. I must not delay my return. Just before I left London I was invited to be Canada's first prime minister, so I must get back as soon as possible. With your approval I will leave Her Majesty's treaty proposal with the ambassador, Sir Andrew Buchanan."

The Tsar smiled. "Our congratulations, Mr. Macdonald. An onerous task and a high honour."

"Thank you, Your Majesty. Sir Andrew will deliver the treaty to Prince Gorchakov for signature by Your Majesty. The ambassador, as I told you, is empowered to execute the document in my absence."

"That procedure will be followed immediately following our Advisory Council meeting if . . ." The Tsar smiled again as he spoke the words.

"If the council looks favourably upon the matter." John A. finished the sentence.

The Tsar rose, signalling the conclusion of the audience. He looked Macdonald in the eye. "We hope it will be favourable. But Minister Macdonald, you should know that the bitterness we feel toward the British since our defeat remains intense, whereas our feelings for our friends the Americans are strong and warm."

The Canadian also stood up without speaking, taken aback by the Tsar's words of warning.

His Imperial Majesty shook John A. Macdonald's hand. "God speed, Mr. Minister, and our best wishes for the success of your new Canada."

32

March 29–30, 1867
London and Washington

At ten o'clock of the morning of March 29, having dispensed with instructions to her private secretary concerning various household matters, Queen Victoria went to her desk to deal with the documents that the Prime Minister had sent for review. If it pleased Her Majesty she might honour the Prime Minister by putting Her Hand and Royal Seal to those bills which had been passed by the House of Lords and by the House of Commons, thereby giving those bills Royal Assent. Then and only then would they become the law of Her Imperial Majesty's lands and territories.

On this day the first bill placed before her by the ever-present Sir Philip Moore was the British North America Act.

"Ah, Sir Philip, this is a most special bill. We are absolutely delighted to see it."

"The briefing note does not indicate any problems, Ma'am."

"Just let us read it for a moment . . . Now then, it appears to be in good order. Do you realize, Sir Philip, that with the stroke of our pen we will be creating a new nation within the framework of our great empire?"

"Upon which the sun never sets, Your Majesty," the secretary replied.

"Quite so, Sir Philip. Quite so."

With that, Queen Victoria, not yet obliged to wear reading spectacles, picked her favourite quill pen out of its holder to dip the point into the inkwell. Then with a sweep of her hand she wrote Victoria, Regina, in the place designated for her signature.

"There. You see, Sir Philip, a new nation now exists under the

British North America Act. Although we are not particularly pleased with its name — the Dominion of Canada. May it flourish and grow and may our other North American colonies be embraced within it."

"Which are those, Your Majesty?"

"Newfoundland, Prince Edward Island, and westerly the area known as the Northwest Territories. And, then, on the Pacific Coast, our thriving colony of British Columbia, that is so vitally important to the concept of a Canada."

She touched the document gently, then stood and went to the enormous globe near the tall windows of the high-ceilinged, large, yet comfortable room in which Victoria customarily received her ministers and conducted the daily affairs of government.

That splendid globe had been a gift from, of all people, that enormous bear of a man, Prince Otto von Bismarck of Germany. The Queen often went to it when discussing or, if alone, thinking about the innumerable places upon it where the Union Jack was flying. She turned the globe until the continent of North America was before her, bright in the sunlight streaming through the Palace windows on that crisp March day.

"It is our concern, Sir Philip — perhaps it is a fear — that if British Columbia here" — she pointed — "becomes part of the United States, the next domino to fall will be the vast Northwest Territories, which have been the fiefdom for so long of the Hudson's Bay Company. We pray that Macdonald will be successful in his negotiations."

"Ma'am?"

"Ah, Sir Philip, you have not been privy to Minister Macdonald's activities and there's no need for you to be."

"Of course, the Canadian minister."

Victoria went to her desk, tucking the skirt of her black dress under her as she sat. She reached for a sheet of her personal stationery and with that favourite quill pen wrote in her elegant hand:

Dear Minister Macdonald

Pray know that on this day we have given our Royal Assent to your most treasured bill, the British North America Act.

Pray we also do for your success in your negotiations in St. Petersburg.

Victoria, Regina
March 29, 1867

"Sir Philip, please be good enough to put this in an envelope and have it delivered to the residence of Minister John A. Macdonald so he'll have it when he returns from St. Petersburg. He stays at the Westminster Palace Hotel, I believe. I fully expect Macdonald will be the first Prime Minister of this newly born Dominion of Canada."

✦

DE STOECKL'S CODED TELEGRAM HAD GONE TO GORCHAKOV ON THE twenty-fifth. He had asked for a response within six days to the message requesting approval of the treaty with the United States. By Friday the twenty-ninth, de Stoeckl was in a state of frustration and worry. As consolation, he had a two-hour session during the early afternoon in the third-floor suite at the Willard Hotel, where among other things and, as usual, he discussed all his business with the Honourable Pamela Collins.

Returning to the embassy, he suffered through a late-afternoon meeting with a merchant banker from Murmansk who had finished his business in America and was about to return to Russia. Afterward, de Stoeckl's carriage took him to his home.

At seven-thirty Madame de Stoeckl and the Baron left for dinner at the nearby residence of his American banker, George Riggs, and his lady. Riggs, the owner of Riggs Bank, was de Stoeckl's financial adviser and was on a retainer to the Russian government for counsel in general financial matters, including the ambassador's dealings with Seward, about which the banker was fully informed.

The Riggses and their guests were just leaving the table after a delicious meal of Texas steak and Beaujolais red wine when Bodisco arrived at the front door urgently asking to see his minister. When de Stoeckl saw Bodisco standing in the foyer, an envelope in his hand and a smile on his face, he knew that the St. Petersburg reply had arrived — and that it was positive.

As he read the dispatch his pleasure was muted — but only temporarily — when he saw that there were two stipulations. The Secretary of State had wanted to have the purchase price paid some ten months after the signing of the treaty. The Tsar required the time to be substantially reduced. Also, if possible, the payment should be made in London instead of New York. De Stoeckl could see no problem in getting Seward to agree to those minor adjustments.

De Stoeckl was overjoyed but gave no outward sign of his feelings except to pronounce, "Ah, this is good news indeed." Smiling at Bodisco, he instructed, "If you'd be good enough to wait in the carriage for just a few minutes, I would like you to take Madame de Stoeckl home. I'm going to see Secretary Seward immediately. It's only a few minutes from here, so I'll walk. I'll fetch Madame and pay my respects to our hosts."

De Stoeckl found the banker and his wife in the parlour, where coffee was being served and Riggs was already sucking on his after-dinner cigar.

"Everything all right?" he asked solicitously.

"More than all right, George. I have the telegram from St. Petersburg that I've been waiting for."

Riggs looked furtively across the room toward the two women who were engaged in animated conversation. He didn't know how much de Stoeckl's wife knew about the negotiations with Seward, but his own wife knew nothing and he wanted to keep it that way. In a whisper he said as he seized de Stoeckl's hand, "Congratulations, Edouard. That's excellent news. I hope the Tsar appreciates what you've done. There isn't anyone else who could have worked out the deal with Seward."

"George, I want you to know how very appreciative I am of your advice and counsel. I hope someday to be able to repay you for everything you've done for me and, of course, for my country."

"Just get the money. Then I'll be paid well enough." Riggs laughed. "What's the next step?"

"I have to let Seward know. Then it's a matter of writing a final draft of the treaty and signing it as soon as possible. Seward's at home this evening. He took the precaution of letting me know where he was going to be so that I could find him immediately if any word came. So I'm going there immediately, if you don't mind, George. I hate to cut this most pleasant evening short."

"Don't worry. You go and see Seward — that's the most important thing right now."

Fifteen minutes later de Stoeckl was shown into the parlour of William Seward's home where he found the Secretary of State playing whist with his wife, his son Frederick, and Frederick's wife.

The Sewards all greeted the ambassador warmly and with much courtesy.

"Well, Edouard, what's the news?" the Secretary of State asked. "You've had word from St. Petersburg, I assume." He saw de Stoeckl's eyes move questioningly to the two women. "Don't worry. I've already told the ladies what's going on. There are few secrets in this house."

De Stoeckl smiled. "Good. Well, the news is this. His Imperial Majesty has graciously consented to approve the treaty except for two items."

The smile that had begun on Seward's face abruptly disappeared. "What do you mean, except for two? What are they?"

After the slight changes as to the timing and place of payment of the purchase price were explained, Seward responded. "If that's what the Tsar wants, de Stoeckl, my friend, we have a deal. Excellent!"

Congratulations were happily exchanged, and then they discussed the matter of preparing the document.

"Tomorrow, if you like, I will come to the State Department, and we can enter upon the treaty," de Stoeckl ventured.

"Why wait until tomorrow?" Seward replied. "Let's make the treaty tonight."

De Stoeckl was caught off guard. He knew that Seward liked to do things immediately. But on a Friday night?

"I want to get this signed, sealed, and delivered before the British get any further into a deal. Right?"

"But the Department is closed. You have no clerks. And my secretaries are scattered about the town."

"Never mind that. You'll find me and my team waiting for you at the Department, open and ready for business whenever you get there."

The preparation of the treaty document was one thing — a near final draft had already been worked up. But the matter of handling Charles Sumner, the Chairman of the Foreign Relations Committee of the Senate, was quite another.

If Seward hoped to get the treaty approved by the Senate — not one member of which knew that the negotiations were going on — everything possible would have to be done to get Chairman Sumner on their side. The first thing, of course, was to fully inform him.

By rights Senator Sumner ought to have been told about the treaty negotiations as they were developing, yet he had been kept in the dark. That meant he might very well react negatively when first informed of the situation because his pride would have suffered a blow. Therefore the need to soothe Sumner's feelings while soliciting his support was paramount.

Seward knew what to do. Before he left for the State Department he wrote a brief letter for delivery to Sumner at home, inviting him to come to the Seward house on a matter of urgent state business. De Stoeckl and Frederick would wait for Sumner to arrive. After offering gracious apologies from and for Seward, the two men would diplomatically brief the Senator on the secret negotiations and than cautiously broach the delicate matter of obtaining his support for the treaty.

When Sumner returned home and found the note, he hurried over to the Seward residence on Lafayette Square, wondering what manner of "urgent state business" the Secretary had in mind.

The Senator was stunned and vexed after listening to de Stoeckl and the younger Seward, but he gave no outward hint of his feelings. The absence of any response frustrated de Stoeckl, who had expected a strong reaction to the news he had just given Sumner. Finally, after the situation had been fully explained and explored, Sumner courteously bade de Stoeckl and Frederick Seward good evening and left, merely giving an evasive reply to de Stoeckl's plaintive request, "You will not fail us?"

Concerned by the Senator's noncommittal stance, the Russian minister and Frederick went immediately to the State Department. With the Secretary in his office was Assistant Secretary William Hunter, the recognized authority on diplomatic procedures who had served the State Department since the days of John Quincy Adams. Also present was the State Department's Chief Clerk, Robert Chew.

The Secretary's opinion about Sumner's reaction — or lack of it — was optimistic. "At least he knows. I'll work on him tomorrow."

Toiling at top speed on the already existing draft of the treaty, the group produced the final document — twenty-seven pages in all. It was ready for signature shortly before four o'clock in the morning. Weary, but with as much dignity as they could muster at that hour, and as befitted the occasion, William H. Seward, the Secretary of State of the United States of America, and Edouard de Stoeckl, the Russian Minister to Washington, thereupon signed the treaty and caused the appropriate seals of each party to be affixed.

The document was approved that morning, Saturday the thirtieth day of March, 1867, by the President of the United States. It was forthwith submitted by the Administration to the Senate for its advice and consent on the morning of the same day it was signed, with a covering note from President Johnson to the president of the Senate:

> ***I transmit to the Senate, for its consideration with a view to ratification, a treaty between the United States and His Majesty, the Emperor of all the Russias, upon the subject of a cession of territory by the latter to the former; which treaty was this day signed in this city by the plenipotentiaries of the parties.***

33

March 30, 1867
Washington

THE TREATY INSTANTLY BECAME PUBLIC KNOWLEDGE. THE Washington-based news correspondents converged on the Senate building on Capitol Hill like a flock of starving crows. By noon on Saturday, March 30, word of the delivery of the Russian-American treaty to the Senate was conveyed to Sir Frederick Bruce at his residence. It was given by a senior member of his staff who, by coincidence, had been delivering a packet of information on the British colony of Hong Kong to the offices of a senator who just had to have it by Saturday. To reach the senator's offices the staff member, one Grant Dunn, had to push his way through the crowd of noisy, excited journalists blocking the wide marble-floored hallway outside the chambers of the president of the Senate.

Curiosity prompted Dunn to ask what was going on. The enthusiastic journalist to whom he put the question shouted, "The President's just sent over a secret goddamned treaty with the Russians! The sneaky sonofabitch has just agreed to buy all the Russians' territory way up almost to the North Pole — and for seven million, two hundred thousand dollars. This is big news!"

Big news, indeed. The British embassy staff had not, of course, had any knowledge of Sir Frederick's instructions on Russian America or his dealings with de Stoeckl. They all knew that their ambassador had gone to the Russian embassy on March 14. Therefore, Dunn reasoned, Sir Frederick had to be up to something with the Russians. Would he want to know about this news? The senior staff member correctly reasoned that Bruce would indeed want to know.

Immediately Dunn had delivered the packet, he rushed to his

waiting carriage, hurriedly instructing the driver to take him to the ambassador's home. Bruce, still in his dressing gown, received Dunn in the entrance hall.

When Sir Frederick heard the news he was aghast. "Grant, this can't be true!"

"Sorry, sir. I can only tell you what I heard and what I saw with my own eyes."

Now Bruce was furious. "De Stoeckl, that bloody whore! God, what a disaster! Whatever am I going to tell Macdonald?" He paced the hall, shaking his head. "I knew that de Stoeckl and Seward were up to something. But I didn't really believe things had gone as far as this."

"Wait here," he ordered Dunn. "I want to write a message for London. You can telegraph it for me."

Sir Frederick went to his library and quickly scratched out the bad news on the first piece of paper he could put his hands on.

TO ***Hon. John A. Macdonald***
Aboard HMS Warrior
via British embassies
Stockholm and Copenhagen

Subject to confirmation, my staff reports that at ten this morning Seward delivered to the Senate for its approval an executed Treaty between the United States and Russia for the purchase of all of the Tsar's territories and interests in North America for the sum of seven million two hundred thousand dollars.

In my considered opinion now that the Treaty has been executed and delivered, the cession to the United States is still reversible if the Senate fails to ratify the Treaty. As instructed I will pursue this option.

Frederick Bruce, Bart.
Washington
March 30, 1867

Copy to Hon. Alexander Galt
Westminster Palace Hotel
London, England
and to
Under Secretary
Foreign Office
London, England

34

March 31, 1867
Copenhagen

Agnes and John A. had just finished breakfast when Lieutenant-Commander Jacky Fisher appeared at their cabin door with a message from the Captain inviting them to the bridge to witness the docking at the Danish naval base at Copenhagen. It being a pleasant, sunny day, they decided to accept the offer. They stood close by as Hamilton skilfully completed the tricky manoeuvre of bringing his huge warship gently to the dock and securing her. That done and having waved to the dignitaries waiting on the pier, the Macdonalds returned to their cabin to prepare for the day's ceremonial events.

Copenhagen was now the only planned stop for *Warrior* en route from St. Petersburg to Edinburgh. Hamilton needed to take on food and water and give the crew some shore leave.

Agamemnon had rendezvoused with *Warrior* as she departed St. Petersburg. But to the disappointment of her crew, *Aggie*, by orders delivered to her as she approached Copenhagen, bypassed that delightful city and pressed on toward Portsmouth.

Macdonald was anxious to send a secure telegram to Lord Stanley, and the British embassy at Copenhagen was the ideal place to do so. Before breakfast he had given Jacky Fisher a sealed envelope with instructions to deliver it to the embassy as soon as *Warrior* docked. Its contents were to be seen only by the person responsible for its transmission. Therefore John A. was surprised to find Fisher waiting in their cabin and not off to the embassy. He had an envelope in his hand.

"I have this for you, sir. It's a cable from Sir Frederick Bruce in

Washington. I thought you might want to read it before I leave for the embassy."

Macdonald took the envelope, unfolded it, and began to read its short message. His face turned ashen with shock. He muttered in disbelief, "My God, what went wrong!"

John A. collapsed in a chair. "Agnes, we've been defeated. We've lost." He handed her the cable, saying, "Unbelievable. Stanley warned me about that two-faced conniving fraud who calls himself the Tsar!"

His wife's hand flew to her mouth in astonishment as she read the stunning words. "Oh, John, how could this have happened?"

"God knows. Jacky, give me that cable for Bruce. I want to tear it up and write a new one."

"Yes, sir."

"Now be kind enough to come back in ten minutes."

Fisher left without a word.

John A. immediately went to the desk and began writing. Finished his rapid scribbling, he turned to Agnes. "You should hear this before I send it. Tell me if I'm doing the right thing."

He read the new message to Bruce in Washington:

> ***"The Eagle in St. Petersburg had promised his lands to me but something went drastically wrong after I departed. I know not what. Am bitterly disappointed. But must be realistic. My judgement now is that it would be unacceptable and inappropriate for Great Britain to lobby or otherwise attempt to defeat the Treaty in the Senate. I therefore direct that, contrary to my earlier advice, you take no steps in this regard, subject to your receiving orders from Whitehall to the contrary. Will be at sea and out of touch for the next few days. Will contact you as soon as am in London. Macdonald."***

Agnes had returned to her comfortable stuffed chair and picked up her needlepoint to calm herself. She stopped her fingers while she thought about her reaction. "Really, John, you haven't much choice. The animosity toward Britain for lobbying would be intense. It would make certain the Senate approved."

"That's true."

Fisher returned and Macdonald handed the message to him. "Jacky, make absolutely sure the embassy people encode it before they send it off."

When Fisher had gone Macdonald sat heavily on the edge of the bed, his forehead in his hands. He shook his head slowly. "Agnes, what could have gone wrong? The Tsar agreed . . . !"

She was back at her needlepoint. "Subject to his Council's approval."

"Yes, but there was no visible hurdle."

Agnes was pragmatic as always. "Whatever happened, it's over with. Done. The world knows Seward has Russian America."

"And the world knows nothing of my effort . . . or my failure."

Agnes looked up and smiled. "Come now, John. The world will never know. Everything was secret."

Macdonald took his hands from his face. Straightening up, he managed a wan smile. "Of course. You're right. No one knows or will ever know. But I just don't like to be beaten . . . or tricked."

"Of course not. But remember, there's Canada . . ."

"Yes, there's Canada to be united, Canada to be built, and British Columbia to be saved from the clutches of Seward."

35

April 1–9, 1867
Washington

THE TREATY CEDING THE TSAR'S AMERICAN POSSESSIONS TO THE United States was ratified by the Senate on the ninth day of April, 1867, notwithstanding nationwide negative editorial comment that dubbed the purchase as Seward's Folly. The approval came after a monumental dissertation in support of the treaty made on the Senate floor by Charles Sumner, the Chairman of the Committee on Foreign Relations. During that long, eloquent, and moving speech, Sumner, for the first official time, referred to the territory as "Alaska."

Ratification by the Senate was by a vote of 73 to 2. However, it would be a year later, on July 27, 1868, before the treaty was ratified by the House of Representatives and approval given for payment of the money to complete the transaction.

Ratification was immediately followed by an investigation by the House of Representatives into questions of bribery and corruption relating to the purchase of Alaska. The question was whether any members of the Senate or the House of Representatives had received from the Russian Minister consideration or payment for their votes, either directly or indirectly. Nothing conclusive came of the hearings, and the storm of controversy and suspicion gradually subsided.

The Tsar's gratitude for his loyal minister's significant accomplishment was expressed in a note written by Alexander: "For all that he has done he deserves a special 'spasibo' (thank you) on my part." That spasibo was a reward to de Stoeckl of only 25,000 silver rubles, some $19,000.00.

De Stoeckl, hurt by the Tsar's lack of generosity, told a sympathetic

Pamela Collins during their final rendezvous at the Willard, "I think that he might have been more generous, considering that I obtained more than the maximum that had been fixed for me and that in order to take charge of this affair I lost a post in Europe, and God knows if I shall have another chance. But still, this is something and brings me nearer to the time when I shall be able to enjoy a modest independence, the summit of my wishes."

De Stoeckl was exhausted by the treaty's aftermath and controversy. Furthermore he was without the stimulating presence of his paramour. The Honourable Pamela Collins suddenly became bored with Washington — and with him, although she spared him that information.

On the morning of April 1, 1867, All Fools' Day, the second day after the treaty had been delivered to the Senate, she packed her huge trunk and assorted cases and went to Boston for a short visit with her sister before returning to England.

Before she left the Willard, Pamela sat down to write her final cable to Uncle:

Rt. Hon. Lord Richard Heath
Chancellor of the Exchequer
Government of the United Kingdom
11 Downing Street
London, England

Dearest Uncle

This is my last cable to you and unlike the others it is not in my basic code. I depart Washington this day for Boston to visit with Elizabeth and her husband for one week. I will book passage for Liverpool by the first ship available after that.

My chance meeting with Edouard de Stoeckl was indeed fortunate, although in the end all our efforts failed to prevent the cession of Russian America to the United States.

I should like to think that my frequent cables to you, especially from Washington, enabled you and the appropriate members of the Cabinet to know exactly what Edouard's dealings with Secretary Seward were on a day-to-day basis and

that they were of assistance in planning the tactics of our government's attempt to buy Russian America and knock the Americans for six!

Now that the match is over, it is time for me to come home. My divorce from that wretched adulterer Charles is near finished and I should be ready now to return to our lovely London society and, with luck, find a new husband.

Yours affectionately,
Pamela

To be on the safe side, the Honourable Pamela Collins did not send that uncoded cable from the Willard Hotel. Instead she filed it directly with the Western Union telegraph office at the railway station when she arrived in New York en route to Boston. Edouard de Stoeckl never knew that his every movement and all his negotiations with Seward had been the almost immediate knowledge of Her Majesty's government in London.

36

July 1, 1867
Ottawa

IT WAS THE FIRST DAY OF JULY, 1867, THE DAY THAT HER Majesty Queen Victoria and Her Majesty's Loyal Parliament at Westminster had decreed was the date for the Confederation of the British colonies in eastern North America to come into being. According to the provisions of the British North America Act on which Macdonald, Cartier, Galt, Tilley, Tupper, and all of the honourable representatives of Canada West, Canada East, Nova Scotia, and New Brunswick had laboured so hard and diligently, it was confirmed that the new British State in America would henceforth be known as the Dominion of Canada.

As its first Prime Minister (as designated by the Queen's Vice-Regal representative, Lord Monck) Macdonald was a natural choice. John A. had accepted without hesitation Monck's offer of the premiership. As soon as the Prime Minister-designate and Agnes had returned to Ottawa at the beginning of May, Macdonald had set about the difficult task of choosing a Cabinet. Actually it was an interim Cabinet, in place only until the first general election, which Prime Minister Macdonald would be obliged to call within a few weeks.

On Confederation Day in Ottawa, the capital city of the new Dominion, the stone walls of the massive, impressive, recently completed Parliament buildings were bathed in the bright sunlight of yet another clear blue sky. A perfect summer's day for the promised military parades and ceremonies.

John A. stood with a host of people in the ornate Privy Council chamber of the East Block of the Parliament buildings. With him were other designated members-to-be of the Privy Council as well as judges of Her Majesty's courts of law and several military officers resplendent in their colourful uniforms and medals.

Precisely at eleven His Excellency the Governor General, Lord Monck, entered the chamber. As was typical of him, he was not in an official uniform. Rather, he wore plain clothes and was attended only by his private secretary, Godley.

Standing on a small platform in front of those to be sworn in, Monck began the ceremonies. Godley faced Monck and read out Her Majesty's new commission appointing him her representative in the Dominion of Canada. Then the oaths of office, administered by several senior judges in their full judicial regalia, were solemnly sworn by Monck, Macdonald, Cartier, Galt, and the other Privy Councillors. Thus the new government of Canada was formally established in accordance with British traditions and law.

Monck then seated himself in the throne-like chair of state facing his Privy Councillors and others attending the ceremony. What he did next was without any warning or notice. Nor had he had prior consultation with the Prime Minister-designate.

Settling into the chair of state, Monck took the sheet of paper that Godley handed to him. Adjusting his spectacles, he read from it to the assembled men and women, among them Agnes Macdonald and the spouses of other newly sworn officials.

Monck began his little speech.

"Her Imperial Majesty, Queen Victoria, has commanded me to extend to the people of the Dominion of Canada her congratulations and her warm best wishes on this the occasion of Confederation."

Polite applause followed.

"Her Majesty has also charged me to announce that she has been pleased to create a special honours list by which Her Majesty is able to give recognition to certain of her loyal Canadian subjects whose unflagging efforts have led to this moment of Confederation."

Macdonald and Cartier, standing shoulder to shoulder, passed quizzical looks between them as Lord Monck went on.

"Her Majesty has been pleased to appoint the following gentlemen to be Commanders of the Order of the Bath and I will ask each of them to step forward so that I might place around their necks the beautiful decoration of Commander. They are the Honourable George Cartier, Alexander Galt, Charles Tupper, Samuel Tilley, William McDougall, and William Howland."

Was there to be nothing for John A. Macdonald? The question was on everyone's lips as they watched the solemn investiture of the worthy Commanders.

That done, Lord Monck spoke without reference to notes. "Her Majesty has commanded me that she is desirous of paying special tribute to Canada's new Prime Minister. Queen Victoria wishes to honour John Alexander Macdonald not only for his exceptional leadership in the bringing together of the Confederation but as well for his achievement in a personal mission that Prime Minister Macdonald recently carried out at considerable risk and with extraordinary skill.

"For these reasons Her Imperial Majesty, Queen Victoria, has been pleased to appoint John Alexander Macdonald a Knight Commander of the Order of the Bath with all the rights, honours, and privileges here and elsewhere thereto appertaining."

The room was filled with thunderous applause and shouts of surprise.

But Sir John A. Macdonald was not happy about being given an honour that ranked above his cherished colleagues. He knew it would cause him political discomfort in the future.

As for the newly minted Lady Macdonald, there was no prouder or more pleased woman to be found in the length and breadth of Queen Victoria's Dominion of Canada.

37

March 4, 1869
Paris

EDOUARD DE STOECKL HAD DESPERATELY WANTED A CHANGE. He had pleaded with Prince Gorchakov for a new posting. "Let me have the opportunity to breathe for a time an atmosphere purer than that of Washington." Gorchakov had given him four months' leave of absence. De Stoeckl and his family departed Washington in October 1868, stopping in London and Paris on their way to St. Petersburg.

In 1869 he resigned from the Russian diplomatic service and retired to Paris.

Edouard de Stoeckl had comfortably ensconced himself, Martha, and their daughters in a large, fashionable flat he had purchased in an elegant, modern, stone residence within walking distance of the ever-beautiful Champs Elysées.

On the morning of March 4, 1869, while enjoying a breakfast of delicious warm croissants, strawberries, and black coffee he read, as was his custom, his day-old copy of the newspaper he considered to be the very best in all of Europe, the London *Times*. His attention was riveted by the brief story on the second page. William Henry Seward was no longer the Secretary of State and no longer in office in the United States of America.

De Stoeckl finished the newspaper and the breakfast, and then went to his desk to write a letter to his old friend with whom he had conducted so much valuable business on behalf of the miserly Tsar, Alexander the Second.

In his peculiar vertical handwriting, de Stoeckl wrote:

My Dear William,

Now that you are relieved of the burdensome office of Secretary of State it is appropriate for me to write a note to express my undying gratitude to you for your exceedingly kind generosity.

The promise you gave me at the Willard Hotel to compensate me for my services to your country in making certain that Macdonald's British/Canadian bid for Russian America would fail was a promise that you might or might not have kept. I was not sure that you would.

You can therefore understand my great joy when my bankers here in Paris advised me on my arrival that a deposit had been made to my account in the amount agreed upon, two hundred thousand American dollars.

This generous sum, together with a small token from the Tsar and funds I had been able to accumulate during my period in Washington, today provides my family and me with an exceedingly agreeable lifestyle in this, the most cultured and civilized city in the world.

I think it is appropriate that you should now know the contents of the personal and confidential cable I sent to the Tsar late in the afternoon of March 25, 1867. It was that cable which destroyed the Tsar's readiness to cede his North American territories to Great Britain and Canada. He received my message just moments before he was to meet with his Advisory Council on the morning of March 26. As I have heard, he reacted violently and negatively.

The message I sent was this:

"I beg to inform Your Imperial Majesty that I have information from an unimpeachable authority at the highest level in Washington that the British ambassador here, Sir Frederick Bruce, has attended upon, among others, the Secretary of State, the Honourable William Seward, to threaten to do all in Britain's power to ensure that the Senate refuses approval of a treaty if it was signed with the United States. Also, Bruce made serious

personal allegations to Seward about the personage of Your Imperial Majesty, saying that you are untrustworthy, dishonest; that you are one of the most dissolute monarchs in the history of Europe; and that the President of the United States would be a fool to do business with you. Bruce made other defamatory statements about Your Imperial Majesty that are of such a personal nature that I dare not set them down on paper."

William, I wish you a long, happy, and productive retirement, just as mine has been, is and will, I trust, continue to be.

I am, sir, your humble and obedient servant

Edouard de Stoeckl

This letter in its heavily sealed envelope marked private and confidential was forwarded by the State Department to the home of the Honourable William Henry Seward in Rochester, New York, where he had taken up residence once again.

Seward arrived home late one evening to find de Stoeckl's letter waiting for him. After reading it he shook his head in silent amazement. Smiling, he lifted a corner of the white sheets of the letter paper to the yellow flame of the reading lamp.

As the pages curled and the words were consumed, forever disappearing in the fire, Seward was well pleased with his own masterful contribution to the Manifest Destiny of the United States of America.